MORAY DALTON

THE BODY IN THE ROAD

KATHERINE DALTON RENOIR ('Moray Dalton') was born in Hammersmith, London in 1881, the only child of a Canadian father and English mother.

The author wrote two well-received early novels, *Olive in Italy* (1909), and *The Sword of Love* (1920). However, her career in crime fiction did not begin until 1924, after which Moray Dalton published twenty-nine mysteries, the last in 1951. The majority of these feature her recurring sleuths, Scotland Yard inspector Hugh Collier and private inquiry agent Hermann Glide.

Moray Dalton married Louis Jean Renoir in 1921, and the couple had a son a year later. The author lived on the south coast of England for the majority of her life following the marriage. She died in Worthing, West Sussex, in 1963.

MORAY DALTON MYSTERIES

Available from Dean Street Press

One by One They Disappeared

The Night of Fear

The Body in the Road

Death in the Cup

The Strange Case of Harriet Hall

MORAY DALTON

THE BODY IN THE ROAD

With an introduction by Curtis Evans

DEAN STREET PRESS

Published by Dean Street Press 2019

First published in 1931 by Sampson Low

Cover by DSP

ISBN 978 1 912574 91 9

www.deanstreetpress.co.uk

LOST GOLD FROM A GOLDEN AGE

The Detective Fiction of Moray Dalton (Katherine Mary Deville Dalton Renoir, 1881-1963)

"GOLD" COMES in many forms. For literal-minded people gold may be merely a precious metal, physically stripped from the earth. For fans of Golden Age detective fiction, however, gold can be artfully spun out of the human brain, in the form not of bricks but books. While the father of Katherine Mary Deville Dalton Renoir may have derived the Dalton family fortune from nuggets of metallic ore, the riches which she herself produced were made from far humbler, though arguably ultimately mightier, materials: paper and ink. As the mystery writer Moray Dalton, Katherine Dalton Renoir published twenty-nine crime novels between 1924 and 1951, the majority of which feature her recurring sleuths, Scotland Yard inspector Hugh Collier and private inquiry agent Hermann Glide. Although the Moray Dalton mysteries are finely polished examples of criminally scintillating Golden Age art, the books unjustifiably fell into neglect for decades. For most fans of vintage mystery they long remained, like the fabled Lost Dutchman's mine, tantalizingly elusive treasure. Happily the crime fiction of Moray Dalton has been unearthed for modern readers by those industrious miners of vintage mystery at Dean Street Press.

Born in Hammersmith, London on May 6, 1881, Katherine was the only child of Joseph Dixon Dalton and Laura Back Dalton. Like the parents of that admittedly more famous mistress of mystery, Agatha Christie, Katherine's parents hailed from different nations, separated by the Atlantic Ocean. While both authors had British mothers, Christie's father was American and Dalton's father Canadian.

Laura Back Dalton, who at the time of her marriage in 1879 was twenty-six years old, about fifteen years younger than her husband, was the daughter of Alfred and Catherine Mary Back. In her early childhood years Laura Back resided at Valley

House, a lovely regency villa built around 1825 in Stratford St. Mary, Suffolk, in the heart of so-called "Constable Country" (so named for the fact that the great Suffolk landscape artist John Constable painted many of his works in and around Stratford). Alfred Back was a wealthy miller who with his brother Octavius, a corn merchant, owned and operated a steam-powered six-story mill right across the River Stour from Valley House. In 1820 John Constable, himself the son of a miller, executed a painting of fishers on the River Stour which partly included the earlier, more modest incarnation (complete with water wheel) of the Back family's mill. (This piece Constable later repainted under the title *The Young Waltonians*, one of his best known works.) After Alfred Back's death in 1860, his widow moved with her daughters to Brondesbury Villas in Maida Vale, London, where Laura in the 1870s met Joseph Dixon Dalton, an eligible Canadian-born bachelor and retired gold miner of about forty years of age who lived in nearby Kew.

Joseph Dixon Dalton was born around 1838 in London, Ontario, Canada, to Henry and Mary (Dixon) Dalton, Wesleyan Methodists from northern England who had migrated to Canada a few years previously. In 1834, not long before Joseph's birth, Henry Dalton started a soap and candle factory in London, Ontario, which after his death two decades later was continued, under the appellation Dalton Brothers, by Joseph and his siblings Joshua and Thomas. (No relation to the notorious "Dalton Gang" of American outlaws is presumed.) Joseph's sister Hannah wed John Carling, a politician who came from a prominent family of Canadian brewers and was later knighted for his varied public services, making him Sir John and his wife Lady Hannah. Just how Joseph left the family soap and candle business to prospect for gold is currently unclear, but sometime in the 1870s, after fabulous gold rushes at Cariboo and Cassiar, British Columbia and the Black Hills of South Dakota, among other locales, Joseph left Canada and carried his riches with him to London, England, where for a time he enjoyed life as a gentleman of leisure in one of the great metropolises of the world.

Although Joshua and Laura Dalton's first married years were spent with their daughter Katherine in Hammersmith at a villa named Kenmore Lodge, by 1891 the family had moved to 9 Orchard Place in Southampton, where young Katherine received a private education from Jeanne Delport, a governess from Paris. Two decades later, Katherine, now 30 years old, resided with her parents at Perth Villa in the village of Merriott, Somerset, today about an eighty miles' drive west of Southampton. By this time Katherine had published, under the masculine-sounding pseudonym of Moray Dalton (probably a gender-bending play on "Mary Dalton") a well-received first novel, *Olive in Italy* (1909), a study of a winsome orphaned Englishwoman attempting to make her own living as an artist's model in Italy that possibly had been influenced by E.M. Forster's novels *Where Angels Fear to Tread* (1905) and *A Room with a View* (1908), both of which are partly set in an idealized Italy of pure gold sunlight and passionate love. Yet despite her accomplishment, Katherine's name had no occupation listed next it in the census two years later.

During the Great War the Daltons, parents and child, resided at 14 East Ham Road in Littlehampton, a seaside resort town located 19 miles west of Brighton. Like many other bookish and patriotic British women of her day, Katherine produced an effusion of memorial war poetry, including "To Some Who Have Fallen," "Edith Cavell," "Rupert Brooke," "To Italy" and "Mort Homme." These short works appeared in the *Spectator* and were reprinted during and after the war in George Herbert Clarke's *Treasury of War Poetry* anthologies. "To Italy," which Katherine had composed as a tribute to the beleaguered British ally after its calamitous defeat, at the hands of the forces of Germany and Austria-Hungary, at the Battle of Caporetto in 1917, even popped up in the United States in the "poet's corner" of the *United Mine Workers Journal*, perhaps on account of the poem's pro-Italy sentiment, doubtlessly agreeable to Italian miner immigrants in America.

Katherine also published short stories in various periodicals, including *The Cornhill Magazine*, which was then edited by Leonard Huxley, son of the eminent zoologist Thomas Henry

Huxley and father of famed writer Aldous Huxley. Leonard Huxley obligingly read over--and in his words "plied my scalpel upon"--Katherine's second novel, *The Sword of Love*, a romantic adventure saga set in the Florentine Republic at the time of Lorenzo the Magnificent and the infamous Pazzi Conspiracy, which was published in 1920. Katherine writes with obvious affection for *il bel paese* in her first two novels and her poem "To Italy," which concludes with the ringing lines

> Greece was enslaved, and Carthage is but dust,
> But thou art living, maugre [i.e., in spite of] all thy scars,
> To bear fresh wounds of rapine and of lust,
> Immortal victim of unnumbered wars.
> Nor shalt thou cease until we cease to be
> Whose hearts are thine, beloved Italy.

The author maintained her affection for "beloved Italy" in her later Moray Dalton mysteries, which include sympathetically-rendered Italian settings and characters.

Around this time Katherine in her own life evidently discovered romance, however short-lived. At Brighton in the spring of 1921, the author, now nearly 40 years old, wed a presumed Frenchman, Louis Jean Renoir, by whom the next year she bore her only child, a son, Louis Anthony Laurence Dalton Renoir. (Katherine's father seems to have missed these important developments in his daughter's life, apparently having died in 1918, possibly in the flu pandemic.) Sparse evidence as to the actual existence of this man, Louis Jean Renoir, in Katherine's life suggests that the marriage may not have been a successful one. In the 1939 census Katherine was listed as living with her mother Laura at 71 Wallace Avenue in Worthing, Sussex, another coastal town not far from Brighton, where she had married Louis Jean eighteen years earlier; yet he is not in evidence, even though he is stated to be Katherine's husband in her mother's will, which was probated in Worthing in 1945. Perhaps not unrelatedly, empathy with what people in her day considered unorthodox sexual unions characterizes the crime fiction which Katherine would write.

Whatever happened to Louis Jean Renoir, marriage and motherhood did not slow down "Moray Dalton." Indeed, much to the contrary, in 1924, only a couple of years after the birth of her son, Katherine published, at the age of 42 (the same age at which P.D. James published her debut mystery novel, *Cover Her Face*), *The Kingsclere Mystery*, the first of her 29 crime novels. (Possibly the title was derived from the village of Kingsclere, located some 30 miles north of Southampton.) The heady scent of Renaissance romance which perfumes *The Sword of Love* is found as well in the first four Moray Dalton mysteries (aside from *The Kingsclere Mystery*, these are *The Shadow on the Wall*, *The Black Wings* and *The Stretton Darknesse Mystery*), which although set in the present-day world have, like much of the mystery fiction of John Dickson Carr, the elevated emotional temperature of the highly-colored age of the cavaliers. However in 1929 and 1930, with the publication of, respectively, *One by One They Disappeared*, the first of the Inspector Hugh Collier mysteries and *The Body in the Road*, the debut Hermann Glide tale, the Moray Dalton novels begin to become more typical of British crime fiction at that time, ultimately bearing considerable similarity to the work of Agatha Christie and Dorothy L. Sayers, as well as other prolific women mystery authors who would achieve popularity in the 1930s, such as Margery Allingham, Lucy Beatrice Malleson (best known as "Anthony Gilbert") and Edith Caroline Rivett, who wrote under the pen names E.C.R. Lorac and Carol Carnac.

For much of the decade of the 1930s Katherine shared the same publisher, Sampson Low, with Edith Rivett, who published her first detective novel in 1931, although Rivett moved on, with both of her pseudonyms, to that rather more prominent purveyor of mysteries, the Collins Crime Club. Consequently the Lorac and Carnac novels are better known today than those of Moray Dalton. Additionally, only three early Moray Dalton titles (*One by One They Disappeared*, *The Body in the Road* and *The Night of Fear*) were picked up in the United States, another factor which mitigated against the Dalton mysteries achieving long-term renown. It is also possible that the independently wealthy author, who left an estate valued, in modern estimation, at nearly a million American dollars at her death at the age of 81 in 1963, felt less of an imperative to "push" her writing than the typical "starving author."

Whatever forces compelled Katherine Dalton Renoir to write fiction, between 1929 and 1951 the author as Moray Dalton published fifteen Inspector Hugh Collier mysteries and ten other crime novels (several of these with Hermann Glide). Some of the non-series novels daringly straddle genres. *The Black Death*, for example, somewhat bizarrely yet altogether compellingly merges the murder mystery with post-apocalyptic science fiction, whereas *Death at the Villa*, set in Italy during the Second World War, is a gripping wartime adventure thriller with crime and death. Taken together, the imaginative and ingenious Moray Dalton crime fiction, wherein death is not so much a game as a dark and compelling human drama, is one of the more significant bodies of work by a Golden Age mystery writer—though the author has, until now, been most regrettably overlooked by publishers, for decades remaining accessible almost solely to connoisseurs with deep pockets.

Even noted mystery genre authorities Jacques Barzun and Wendell Hertig Taylor managed to read only five books by Moray Dalton, all of which the pair thereupon listed in their massive critical compendium, *A Catalogue of Crime* (1972; revised and expanded 1989). Yet Barzun and Taylor were warm admirers of the author's writing, avowing for example, of the twelfth Hugh Collier mystery, *The Condamine Case* (under the impression that the author was a man): "[T]his is the author's 17th book, and [it is] remarkably fresh and unstereotyped [actually it was Dalton's 25th book, making it even more remarkable—C.E.]. . . . [H]ere is a neglected man, for his earlier work shows him to be a conscientious workman, with a flair for the unusual, and capable of clever touches."

Today in 2019, nine decades since the debut of the conscientious and clever Moray Dalton's Inspector Hugh Collier detective series, it is a great personal pleasure to announce that this criminally neglected woman is neglected no longer and to welcome her books back into light. Vintage crime fiction fans have a golden treat in store with the classic mysteries of Moray Dalton.

TRUTH COMES GLIDING

Moray Dalton's *The Body in the Road* (1930), *The Night of Fear* (1931) and *Death in the Cup* (1932)

IN 1928 AGATHA CHRISTIE, still disheartened and demoralized by a rapid succession of psychic hammer blows--the recent death of her beloved mother, ongoing marital discord with her estranged husband Archie and her brief though highly publicized and embarrassing "disappearance" of two years earlier--published *The Mystery of the Blue Train*, her fifth Hercule Poirot detective novel and one the Queen of Crime remembered ever after with pronounced distaste. "Really, how that wretched book ever came to be written, I don't know!" she exclaimed with exasperation of *The Blue Train* in her posthumously published Autobiography, composed between 1950 and 1965. "I had no joy in writing, no élan," she recalled of those dismal days, adding bluntly:

> I had worked out the plot—a conventional plot, partly adapted from one of my other stories. I knew, as one might say, where I was going, but I could not see the scene in my mind's eye, and the people would not come alive. I was driven desperately on by the desire, indeed the necessity, to write another book and make some money.
>
> That was the moment when I changed from an amateur to a professional. I assumed the burden of a profession, which is to write even when you don't want to, don't much like what you are writing, and aren't writing particularly well. I have always hated *The Mystery of the Blue Train*, but I got it written, and sent off to the publishers. It sold just as well as my last book had done.

Not only did the book sell well, but contemporary critical notices of the latest Hercule Poirot murder opus were good and modern mystery readers, obviously not burdened with Christie's emotional baggage, continue to give the novel good marks today. Moreover, whatever one's feelings about the quality of *The Mystery of the Blue Train*, there assuredly is found between its covers at least one notable character (aside from Poirot himself): a certain mysterious individual named Mr. Goby. Early in the novel this enigmatic private inquiry agent is consulted by American millionaire Rufus Van Aldin. (An inordinate number of American millionaires in Golden Age British mysteries seem to have come of Dutch extraction by way of New York, formerly New Netherland.) The demanding tycoon desires to collect dirt on his son-in-law, Derek Kettering, on behalf of his daughter, Ruth, who is planning, with her father's encouragement, to slap her errant husband with a divorce suit. In Chapter Five Mr. Goby is introduced to readers as "a small, elderly man, shabbily dressed, with eyes that looked carefully all around the room, and never at the person he was addressing." After concluding his succinct interview with Mr. Goby, who during the entire time successively gazes at the radiator, the left hand drawer of the desk, the cornice and the fender, but never at his client, a gratified Mr. Van Aldin confidently pronounces to his secretary: "That's a very useful man. . . . In his own line [the sale of information] he's a specialist. Give him twenty-four hours and he would lay the private life of the Archbishop of Canterbury bare for you." Despite his mild appearance, Mr. Goby, one imagines, could have gone toe-to-toe with Dashiell Hammett's private dick The Continental Op, who in novel form debuted the next year in *Red Harvest* (1929).

Despite her later dismissal of the worth of *The Blue Train*, Christie from some corner of her clever mind must have recollected Mr. Goby with gratification, for many years later she revived him in three additional Hercule Poirot mysteries: *After the Funeral* (1953), *Third Girl* (1966) and *Elephants Can Remember* (1972), the latter work the very last Poirot tale that she wrote. Elderly Mr. Goby ultimately enjoyed nearly as great longevity as the brilliant Belgian sleuth himself. Another crime writer upon whom Mr. Goby may have made an impression was Moray Dalton, whose sixth mystery novel, *The Body in the Road* (published in the UK and US in 1930, two years after *The Mystery of the Blue Train*), introduces a Mr. Glide, a Mr. Hermann Glide, who rather resembles Christie's own Mr. Goby. However, Mr. Glide in contrast with Mr. Goby is far from a minor character, being, rather, the man who actually solves the puzzling murders in *The Body in the Road* and two successor novels, *The Night of Fear* (1931) and *Death in the Cup* (1932).

In *The Body in the Road* Mr. Glide is first mentioned nearly four-fifths of the way into the novel. This is after Lord David Chant--formerly an investigator at Scotland Yard but now moodily ensconced at Spinacres, a rural estate in southern England, having against all odds inherited the family title--travels to London to meet with his former superior. Lord David is seeking advice on how to help the legally imperiled young woman whom he holds most dear: Linda Merle, a former piano accompanist in the town of Jessop's Bridge near Spinacres, who shockingly has been charged with the murder of her friend Violet Hunter, the beautiful, blonde and ingenuous violinist whom Linda Merle accompanied at the Tudor Café. Declaring that nothing can be done through official channels to help Lord David and his lady love, David's onetime Chief advises him to seek the aid of Hermann Glide. "I've heard of him," responds Lord David doubtfully of the private inquiry agent. "A bit of a mountebank, isn't he?" To which his Chief judiciously responds: "He is none too scrupulous about the means he employs to attain his ends, though I fancy he is clever enough to keep within the law. . . . we keep in touch with him here. We don't approve of him—but we find him useful."

Ushered into Mr. Glide's office by his loyal secretary, Miss Briggs, Lord David finds seated before him at a shabby desk a "little man, noticeably frail in appearance, with wistful brown eyes in a small puckered face," who rather reminds him of a "monkey on a barrel organ." Although, in contrast with Mr. Goby, Mr. Glide apparently can look his clients evenly in the face, he prefers to devote his surface attention to a lump of modeling wax, which during interviews he molds into "fantastic shapes" with his "long slender supple fingers." Yet Mr. Glide is paying close attention indeed to what Lord David has to tell him, and it is he who engineers a far happier outcome to the case than readers might well have expected when Glide was first consulted by the master of Spinacres, for things then looked very dark indeed for David and Linda. Just how Mr. Glide accomplishes this feat makes an ingenious finish to a most gripping tale of murder, which though primarily a detective novel shares some affinity with the Golden Age thrillers of Edgar Wallace and Agatha Christie. (Over the course of the novel we observe two characters, both women, reading Edgar Wallace novels.)

A year after the publication of *The Body in the Road*, the perspicacious Mr. Glide reappeared, this time about forty percent of the way into the story, to solve another strange killing in *The Night of Fear*, Moray Dalton's bravura turn on a classic country house Christmas mystery. Family and friends and assorted servants were gathered at Laverne Peveril, home of George Tunbridge and his wife, when bloody murder struck, during what was meant to be a jolly holiday game of hide-and-seek. Evidence points to George's old public school friend Hugh Darrow, but this view is challenged by Inspector Collier, who made his first appearance a couple of years earlier in *One by One They Disappeared* (1929) and within a few years would supersede Hermann Glide as Moray Dalton's primary series sleuth.

The conscientious Scotland Yard inspector happens to be on the scene visiting his friend Sergeant Lane and at Lane's invitation he unofficially participates in the early stages of the investigation. He later briefly takes over the investigation after Lane is sidelined. However, at the behest of George's string-pulling cousin, Sir Eustace Tunbridge, Collier is pulled off the case and replaced by a disliked rival from the Yard, who proceeds to arrest Darrow. At Collier's suggestion, visiting American Ruth Clare, who loves Hugh dearly, turns to Hermann Glide for help—a most fortunate decision, as it transpires.

In 1932 Hermann Glide again arrives to save the day, this time in *Death in the Cup*, an absorbing account of murder in the poisoned bosom of a genteel, if alarmingly dysfunctional, family in Dennyford, a smugly insular provincial town in southern England that a visiting character ironically describes as a "peaceful little place . . . so typically English, almost Jane Austen still in the twentieth century, where the most exciting thing that could happen would be the lowering of somebody's golf handicap. . . ." Mr. Glide appears halfway through the novel, in service of Geoffrey Raynham (lately retired from the East), the concerned uncle of young Lucy Rivers, who is in love with Byronically handsome Mark Armour, the chief suspect of the local police in a most dreadful murder case. An offstage Inspector Collier acts as Glide's and Raynham's go-between.

As the title suggests, both the initial slaying (that of the unhappy Armour family's domineering and blindly unfeeling eldest sister, Bertha) and the one which follows it appear to have been accomplished by means of a poison classically favored by murderers in need: arsenic. Students of English true crime will recollect, as no doubt the author herself did, the unsolved poisonings at Birdhurst Rise, a Victorian villa in Croydon, south London. There between April 1928 and March 1929 a man, his sister-in-law and mother-in-law died most mysteriously, all of them in all likelihood from the ingestion of fatal amounts of arsenic. In contrast with the Croydon poisoning case, however, the killer in *Death in the Cup* is finally collared, with credit going once again to the wit and wiles of wizened Mr. Glide. Surely even Agatha Christie's Mr. Goby could not have put in a more impressive performance than Mr. Glide in these three superb Moray Dalton detective novels.

Curtis Evans

Chapter I
A DUET AND A TRIO

"Lady Pianist Wanted to Accompany Violinist, 11 to 1 and 4 to 6. Apply Manageress, Tudor Café, Jessop's Bridge."

Linda Merle had never been to Jessop's Bridge, but she had seen pictures of that ancient market town, with its Abbey church and Guildhall and quaint old houses clustering on the slope of a hill above the winding river. She preferred the country to the noisy suburb where she had been earning her living by playing in the orchestra of a cinema, and it was time she made a change. So she answered the advertisement, enclosing references and her photograph, and was duly engaged.

The café proved to be a teashop in the High Street. It was under new management and the floor above had been turned into one large room which could be used for dancing. A space was left in the middle; there were little tables around it, and at the end, partly screened by artificial palms, there was a platform for the orchestra.

The violinist was a local girl. She was introduced to Linda as Miss Hunter and presently informed her that her name was Violet. Her playing was mediocre and obviously she did not trouble to practise, but she was charming to look at, tall and willowy, with a mass of red-brown hair, big grey eyes, and a pathetic droop at the corners of her red mouth. Like a Burne-Jones drawing, thought Linda, admiringly. She loved beauty, and Violet's gentle yielding manner and her evident helplessness appealed to her stronger nature. When, on the third Sunday, they met by arrangement to go for a walk together, the foundations of their friendship had been laid. They wandered along the towing-path and then, sitting on a bench, Violet talked about herself and Linda listened.

"I hope you won't find it dull here," said Violet. "I do, but then Annie is so particular. She's awfully good to me, but she fusses like a hen with one chick, and I must say I get fed up."

"Is she your elder sister?"

"Annie Coleman? Oh, no. Mother and I went to lodge with her and her mother when I was quite small. Mother was an invalid and couldn't do much for me, and Annie practically brought me up. When mother died there was only a hundred pounds in the bank, but Annie said I must stay on, and that I'd be able to earn before it was spent. She wanted me to take up dressmaking, but I'd had some violin lessons and I applied for the job at the café and got it. I was very pleased, but Annie wasn't. She'd like to keep me in cotton wool. I do get sick of it. A girl is only young once."

"You'll marry," said Linda.

Violet's lovely eyes filled with tears. "I was engaged once. Annie didn't approve at first, but after a while she came round and was quite nice to him. He was the veterinary surgeon here and everyone liked him. I think perhaps he overworked himself. He wasn't really strong. He used to have bad turns, and in the end he died quite suddenly. He had given me a most beautiful ring that had been in his family a long time. Really valuable. I wear it always on a chain round my neck. The stones are opals. They say opals are unlucky."

"How awful!" said Linda, sympathetically.

"Yes. He was getting on so splendidly and was so happy over our engagement. Everyone was so sorry. Lord Haringdon sent a beautiful wreath. Poor Tom had saved the life of his favourite horse only a few weeks before. I shall never really get over it." She looked at her wrist watch. "Heavens! It's past four. We must simply tear. I don't want to upset Annie."

It was half past four when they arrived. Miss Coleman's was the last house in a terrace of four standing back from and above the road. She had evidently been watching for them, for she opened the front door as they came up the path and gazed at them unsmilingly as they approached. She was a stout, middle-aged woman with blunt irregular features and a dark and greasy complexion. She greeted Linda with a flabby handshake and led the way directly to the dining-room, where an ample tea had been laid ready.

"I'm sorry we're late," said Violet.

"Yes, it is a pity. I had the kettle boiling and the hot cakes ready at four. I thought, as your friend was living in a bed-sitting-room and doing for herself, some decent food would be a nice change."

"Very kind," said Linda, smiling, "but I take care of myself."

"All very well if you're strong, but a girl like Violet would soon be ill if she didn't have home comforts," pursued Miss Coleman, with the air of one developing a familiar theme.

"Would she?" Linda was polite but unconvinced. Miss Coleman's dogmatic manner roused a spirit of opposition in her. "I find it very convenient being near the café," she said. "It's a long way from here."

"The walk does her good, but if the work is too much for her she can give it up. There's no real need for her to earn. This isn't shop jam. Try some on your bread and butter."

"Thank you."

Miss Coleman refilled the cups. Evidently she was casting about for a fresh topic. "Are you one of a large family, Miss Merle?"

"No. I was the only one and my parents are gone. I've a cousin in New Zealand. That's all."

"How sad for you!"

"Not at all," said Linda, flippantly. "Rather a blessed state. I can do what I choose."

"Oh, of course, if you look at it like that. Another slice of cake?"

Violet had pushed back her chair. "You've finished, haven't you, Linda? Come into the front room and we'll have some music."

"All right." Linda was rising when Miss Coleman interposed:

"Remember it's Sunday, please, Violet. I won't have anything but sacred music in my house on a Sunday."

"Annie is very trying at times," Violet said when the girls were alone together in the dreary little front sitting-room, where the fire had only just been lit. "The fact is she's jealous of any friend I make. I'm awfully sorry, Linda dear. I could see you didn't enjoy your tea a bit. It was unfortunate we were late. That upset her. She'd taken a lot of trouble, making cakes and putting out the best china. I hope you'll get on better the next time you come. She's all right when she gets used to people. She got quite fond of poor Tom—Mr. Lovell, you know—my *fiancé*."

"Oh, I didn't mind a bit," said Linda, but inwardly she was resolving that her first visit should also be her last.

"Her bark is worse than her bite," said Violet, "but I don't think we'd better try over that fox-trot after what she said. She's not musical, but I'm afraid she'd know it's not a hymn tune."

Linda laughed. "All right. I ought to be getting back to my diggings, anyway. I wish you shared them with me. There's a bedroom to let on my floor. We'd have such fun."

"It would be jolly!" said the other, wistfully.

"Come for a walk with me next Sunday," said Linda. "We'll take my thermos and some grub and go a good way. I want to explore the country about here. It looked lovely coming through in the train."

"It is. Annie used to be fond of country walks, but since she's got so stout her feet have given way."

Violet went to the gate with her new friend. "Goodbye, dear." Annie Coleman, meanwhile, was washing up the tea things and nursing her grievance. Keeping her waiting about and wasting the gas. Selfish and inconsiderate! She had made Violet walk much too far! The poor child was quite white when she came in. And then she had the nerve to say that it was a long way from the café! "And if I hadn't stopped it she'd have been playing jazz on my piano!" she thought, angrily, as she replaced the best cups, which had been got out to impress the unwelcome guest, in the cupboard.

When she returned to the dining-room she found Violet sitting by the fire, reading an Edgar Wallace. "She's gone, has she?"

"Rather! You didn't expect her to stay longer than she could help, did you?"

"Did she think I ought to drop a curtsy to her?"

Violet was silent, but Annie could not let the matter rest.

"I thought she was just the new pianist at the Tudor Café. Of course if she's a princess in disguise—"

"Don't be a fool, Annie. No one cares to be insulted. I'll never ask any friend of mine here again. That's all."

"Friend!" Annie's voice was trembling. "You've known her three weeks. You've known me twenty years."

"What's that got to do with it?"

"Everything, I should have thought. She can laugh and talk. Oh, I dare say she's amusing, and I'm not! But do you suppose she'd put herself out to nurse you if you were ill or make any sacrifice for your sake? Do you suppose she really cares two straws what becomes of you or that she'd mind if you died tomorrow? While I—I worship the ground you tread on, and you know it."

Violet reddened. "I wish you wouldn't talk like that, Annie. It's so—so soppy! I know you're fond of me and you've always been good to me, but I don't see why I shouldn't have other friends nearer my own age. Now do stop it and let me read! I hate rows, especially when they're all about nothing."

"You may call it nothing! I don't think that Miss Merle is a nice girl. I don't like her manner. You mark my words, she'll do you no good!"

At supper Violet brought her book to the table. It was her habit to read at meals when relations were strained. The older woman's eyes were red. When she spoke her voice was subdued.

"Have another helping of the apple charlotte, dearie. I made it specially for you. Do now."

"All right. It's jolly good."

Annie's anxious face relaxed. She was forgiven. If only the manageress at the Tudor Café would get rid of the new pianist, she thought, she might be happy again as she had been through those years when she had her darling girl all to herself!

The tearoom of the Tudor Café was upstairs, a large room extending over the hat shop next door, where a space was kept clear when the café orchestra was playing for customers who wanted to dance. The innovation was only fairly popular. There were seldom more than three couples of rather awkward and self-conscious girls gyrating at one time. The place had changed hands just before Linda came, and was advertised in the local papers as being under entirely new management. "It's a good thing Annie has not been in lately," said Violet. "Old Miss Potter would never have allowed the waitresses to use lipsticks. We shall lose the church people, the ladies who dropped in for a cup of coffee after the morning service at the Abbey."

The waitresses had dresses of delphinium-blue linen and white muslin caps and aprons.

"And I would like you to wear blue velvet of the same shade," the manageress told Linda, "both of you. And, by the way, this room upstairs is being let three nights a week for dances. Will you two supply the music? The hours would be from eight until twelve. It would mean thirty shillings a week more for each. Yes or no? I'm giving you the first offer, but there are several in the town who would jump at it."

"We'll do it," said Linda, briskly. The manageress nodded and turned away. It was one o'clock and they were in the tiny ladies' room putting on their hats before the mirror.

"I'd like the extra money," said Violet, slowly, "but how can I get back so late? Annie never would let me have a latch-key. You don't know how strict she is."

Linda shrugged her shoulders. She had not seen Miss Coleman since she went to her house, and she told herself that she would not care if she never saw her again.

"You're not a child. Tell her you mean to go your own way. You're twenty-three, a year older than I am. Of course it's too far to go back so late at night. I see that. But you needn't be there."

Violet was silent. Number Six, Linden Road, had been her home ever since she could remember. Annie—of course, there were times when she felt she could not stand Annie's petty tyrannies and exactions a day longer. On the other hand, she was well fed, warmed, cherished as she never would be elsewhere for the price she paid for mere board and lodging.

"I don't know where else I could go," she murmured.

"You can share my digs if you like!" said Linda.

Violet brightened. "I should love that! What fun! But—I don't know—Annie would be fearfully upset! You see, since her old mother died she's only had me. Of course if poor Tom had lived I should have left her when I married, but as it is I'm sure she expects me to be with her always."

"Do you want to?"

The pretty weak face clouded over. "No. Only—I hate rows and fuss—"

"Well, you can come in with me. We might get other evening engagements, and on Sundays, when the weather gets warmer, take sandwiches and go for long tramps. You'll have to make up your mind one way or the other. I don't see why you should sacrifice yourself entirely for Miss Coleman," argued Linda. "After all she's no relation. Perhaps she won't mind so much. No one's indispensable. I shouldn't care to be alone in that house myself, but she can easily get another boarder."

"Yes—but Annie doesn't like strangers."

Chapter II
LINDA'S LEGACY

One rainy morning some weeks later Miss Coleman came in to the upper room at the Tudor Café and seated herself at a table by the window that overlooked the steep High Street. It was a market day and a stream of cars was being held up while a drover and his dog tried to induce a flock of frightened sheep to turn down one of the narrow alleys to the square. The café was crowded with the wives and daughters of farmers come in to the town to do their shopping. Annie knew some of them by sight but none to speak to. She had never been sociably inclined, and during her mother's lifetime she had been very much tied. She was wearing a coat and skirt of an unbecoming shade of brown and a hard felt hat was perched precariously on rolls of mouse-coloured hair that no power on earth could have induced her to have removed. She carried a string bag filled with groceries and a wet umbrella which she placed on the chair next to hers. She gave her order and a waitress brought her a cup of hot milk and a bun. The orchestra was playing a one step and two couples occupied the space set apart for dancing before the platform. Annie heard some one at an adjoining table criticising the tempo.

"The pianist is good but the girl with the fiddle can't play for nuts. She's ripping to look at though. Hair like burnt sherry, what?"

The speaker was, of course, a man. Another man replied.

"Is she—approachable?"

"Probably. This place used to be awfully prim, but it's altered—"

Annie glanced at her watch. It was nearly time for the interval. She wrote a few words in pencil on the back of her shopping list and beckoned to a passing waitress.

"Will you give this to Miss Hunter?"

The two men at the table behind hers had got up and gone out. Annie sat stolidly munching her bun. She had avoided looking toward the platform and she did not turn her head when the music stopped. Violet had read the pencilled message.

"Bother!" she said.

Linda glanced up from the music she was sorting. "Does she want to speak to you?"

"Yes. As if writing every day wasn't enough!"

"Go to her. Don't have a row here for heaven's sake—"

Violet left the platform and crossed the room to the window. She was uncomfortably conscious of the curious stares of the customers. It was an unwritten rule at the café that the violinist and pianist were not to leave the platform until the programme was concluded and she knew that she might get into trouble, but fortunately the manageress was downstairs.

"Hallo, Annie—"

"Well, Violet." Miss Coleman's broad face expressed complete disapproval of her surroundings. "You're looking thin and tired. Late hours and rubbishing food. A little more of it and you'll crock up, and then you'll come to me to be nursed, I suppose."

"I'm perfectly well."

"Well, you'd better come back anyway. Don't be silly, dearie. A joke's a joke, but this one has lasted long enough. Come tomorrow. I've kept your bed aired. I'll make one of the cherry cakes you like and we'll have a chicken for Sunday dinner—"

Violet had seated herself in the chair facing Annie's.

"No, Annie. I don't want to hurt your feelings and I'm not saying that you didn't make me comfortable, but I really must be nearer the café. I got simply worn out going to and fro. I'm sorry you miss me so much. You should try to get somebody else."

"I don't want anybody else."

Violet sighed impatiently. "You want to put me in the wrong and make me feel I've treated you badly. You won't listen to reason." Miss Coleman was fitting on her fabric gloves. The wicker chair creaked ominously as she leaned forward. In that place, surrounded by a forest of little tables, each with its vase of flowers, she looked more uncouth than usual. Violet fancied that the knot of waitresses lounging near the service hatch were laughing at her. It seemed to her that the ten minutes which normally passed so quickly when she sat behind the screen with Linda would never end. She was too young and too self-centred to realise what her careless refusal meant to the lonely woman whose whole life had been devoted to her, but she knew Annie well enough to be made vaguely uneasy by her silence.

"I don't want to be unkind. I'd come to see you more often if you did not keep on about my coming back to live."

"I don't blame you. It's that girl, it's her influence—"

Time was up. Linda, seated at the piano, struck a warning chord. Violet was not intentionally cruel, but she was not good at hiding her feelings, and her relief was evident. She rose with a wounding alacrity. "I must go. Good-bye, Annie, and do try to be sensible about this. I'm just as fond of you now as I ever was."

The obvious retort that that was not saying much rose to the older woman's lips, but she refrained from making it. What was the use? She sat through another one step and then mechanically collected her string bag and her other parcels and her baggy old umbrella and went out.

She was punished, she thought bitterly, for her over-confidence. She had been so sure that Violet would never leave her. The interlude with the young veterinary surgeon had been disquieting but it was soon over, and then it had seemed almost a blessing in disguise, like getting over measles. But that affair, with its tragic ending, had left Violet restless and dissatisfied. She had become so irritable and depressed that Annie had been frightened and when she refused to take up dressmaking had herself suggested that she should apply for the post of violinist at the Tudor Café. The work had sufficed to give her an interest and had been well enough until the place changed hands and the new pianist came to put ideas in her head.

"It's all her doing," thought Annie bitterly. She hated Linda for the influence she had gained over Violet and for having all that she lacked. She hated her for being young and slim, efficient at her job, and able to say amusing things.

"But Vi'll come home in the end," she told herself as she opened her front door with her latch-key. And then, standing there in the dark little passage between the umbrella stand and the sitting-room door, she shed a few tears.

Linda had no idea of the strength of the feeling she had aroused. She had never taken seriously Annie Coleman's jealous devotion to the girl she had brought up from her childhood. To her Annie was merely a tiresome exacting person whose whims prevented Violet from developing her personality and becoming self-reliant. As she came to know Violet better she even began to wonder if her intervention had not come too late.

"Annie," Violet said, "was fussy, but she could not be always after me. Sometimes I did things without telling her."

"That's the worst of those dreadfully narrow people!" tried Linda. "It ends in one keeping quiet about perfectly harmless things!"

Violet said nothing to that, but she smiled, and there was something a little furtive and enigmatic about that smile which was vaguely disquieting to the younger girl.

Occasionally, too, Violet would go out alone without saying where she was going. Linda never questioned her about these expeditions but she would have preferred her to be more open about them. She had no secrets of her own.

It was early in April that a letter came for her that was destined to change the course of several lives. It was from a firm of lawyers in London and it informed her that a second cousin who had died in New Zealand had left her a legacy of five hundred pounds. It was Linda's habit to get the breakfast for herself and Violet and take it on a tray into the latter's bedroom. She had soon realised that though they might share the lodgings and the rent the work must be done by her if it was done at all. Violet was lazy. It was difficult to induce her even to practise her violin, and she was only dressed in the morning just in time to get to the café at eleven, leaving her bed unmade and her room in the utmost confusion if Linda did not run in to put things straight. She was sitting up, sipping her tea, her lovely eyes still clouded with sleep, while Linda read her letter aloud.

"What will you do? Chuck your job at the café?"

"I don't know," said Linda thoughtfully. "I'm sick of playing dance music. Violet—do you remember that empty cottage we passed last Sunday week when we did that long walk through the Haringdon woods?"

"Yes. What about it?"

"We wanted tea so badly and there wasn't a tea place for miles. If I could buy it and furnish it I believe we could do quite well out of teas for motorists. There was a strip of garden by the roadside and quite a large piece at the back. Can you make cakes, Vi?"

"No."

"Neither can I," said Linda cheerfully, "but I could soon pick it up. You needn't, but you'd have to help with the washing up, my child, if you came in with me."

"Do you want me to, Linda?"

"Yes, if you think you'd like it. It would be better for you than these late hours. You ought to go to bed earlier than you do the nights we're off duty." She hesitated, loth to break the rule she had made herself and ask for information that had not been volunteered. "You went to the pictures yesterday evening, didn't you, with a friend?"

"Yes."

"Who is he?" Linda tried to speak casually.

"Nobody you know, dear."

"Oh, all right. Better get up, hadn't you?" She picked up the breakfast tray and her letter.

"She'll go wrong if I leave her," she was thinking anxiously. "She's too pretty. Some rotter will get hold of her. I'm responsible now in a way. I asked her to join me here." And then, with a flash of insight. "I suppose the Coleman woman felt like this about her."

She went to the house agents in the High Street that afternoon. The cottage she had seen was on their list and proved to be unexpectedly cheap, four hundred pounds for a quick sale.

"There must be some drawback," said Linda.

The clerk was hunting for a photograph of the place under a pile of papers and he did not look at her as he answered.

"Well, it's isolated, of course. Over two miles from the nearest hamlet and nearly four to Laxworthy, which is the station. Only the very slow trains stop there. And it's primitive, naturally. No modern conveniences."

"What about the water supply?"

"There is a well at the back which has never been known to fail. Good water. It's been analysed."

"Can you let me have the key? I'd like to go over it, but I can't until Sunday."

He had abandoned the search for the photograph and was giving her his undivided attention. Linda was not startlingly beautiful but she had a complexion of cream and roses that atoned for the irregularity of her profile, and a pair of lucid grey eyes that inspired confidence. The young man hesitated.

"You're not thinking of it for yourself, madam?"

She was a little surprised but she answered frankly. "For myself and a friend. A lot of motors go that way instead of by the main road to London. We thought there would be an opening for providing teas."

He seemed about to speak when an older man who had been hovering in the background came forward. "I will attend to madam. You can get on with that correspondence—"

Linda was given the key on condition that she return it on the Monday.

"There's a snag somewhere," she told Violet when describing her interview. "The young one was going to tell me something but the other one stopped him. On the other hand, he may be trying to hang on to the place for some friend of his own."

"If there's anything wrong we ought to be able to spot it," said Violet. She seemed to be more attracted by the enterprise now that she had had time to think it over, but then, as Linda was beginning to find out, she usually agreed with the person she was with.

They got up very early on Sunday morning and caught the only possible train to Laxworthy and walked the four miles through a densely wooded and sparsely populated valley to their goal.

The cottage was of brick and timbered, with a roof of old lichened tiles and a quaint twisted chimney stack overgrown with ivy, and the tiny deep-set windows had leaded panes.

"It's lovely!" said Linda enthusiastically, "the real thing after the sham Tudor of the café. We ought to be happy here, Vi!" The garden was overgrown with weeds. "Grass and crazy pavements," said Linda, "and little tables with big green umbrellas. I shall only have a hundred for the furnishing. We shall have to be careful. We can do the painting and whitewashing ourselves."

"Not me!" said Violet.

Linda laughed. She was too happy and excited to feel critical of her friend. But you do want to live here with me, Violet?"

"Of course, darling. I think it will be ripping—"

They went over the rooms and found them small and dark but apparently weather proof.

"We must have an oil cooking stove," said Linda eagerly. "I don't mind sleeping on the floor at first. We can make ourselves comfortable by degrees. The main thing is to be ready to catch the passing motorist. Tables, chairs, crockery. There's a car passing now."

"We haven't discovered the drawback," said Violet.

But Linda had fallen in love with the place. "There isn't one! Don't be a wet blanket!"

She went over the cottage again, looking for traces of damp, while Violet, who was slightly bored by her ardour, leaned over the front gate. It might be fun bringing out teas into the garden to their customers, but suppose they had a wet summer? And, in any case, there would be a lot of drudgery behind the scenes. Violet disliked drudgery of any kind, and now that the novelty had worn off she was not sure that she cared much for the picnic existence she shared with Linda. This tea business was going to mean hard work.

"Oh, bother!" she sighed, but only to herself. To Linda she said, "How thrilling!" and Linda, like a child with a new toy, was too absorbed to notice how perfunctory were her comments.

In the weeks that followed Linda was up to her eyes in work. There had been papers to be signed and witnessed, and then came the buying of distempers for the walls and matting for the floors, the choosing of cretonnes for curtains and the making. Linda had given a week's notice and left the café, but Violet was to remain with the new pianist secured by the management until the cottage was fit for habitation.

This arrangement meant that the two girls scarcely saw each other except on Sundays when they spent the day together at the cottage. Linda never knew how Violet dreaded those Sundays. She hated the long walk from the station, the sticky jobs that were assigned her. "Violet, will you stain the floor of the smaller bedroom this week?"

"Violet, you might give the butt another coat of green." She hated sitting on packing cases to eat a scanty lunch of bread and butter and apples; and when Linda, tired and dishevelled, but with shining eyes, waved her paint brush and cried, "We're getting on. Isn't this fun?" she sometimes felt that she hated her too. She had almost forgotten the time, not so many months ago, when she had depended on the stronger nature to help her to escape from the stuffy tyranny of Annie Coleman. Violet was not introspective. She seldom thought, but she followed her instincts, and her instinct now was to find a new deliverer.

There was a large bland personage who came in to the Tudor Café occasionally for a cup of tea on his way to and fro between London and Bournemouth, where he often spent his week-ends. He drove himself in a high-powered and obviously very expensive car and was lavish with tips to the waitresses, who were flattered by his arrival. His whole attention, however, was given to the slender bright-haired girl standing on the platform with her fiddle tucked under her chin, and after his fifth visit he was waiting for her in the street when she came out of the café at six o'clock at the end of the afternoon programme.

"I wanted to tell you how much I enjoyed your playing," he lied. He knew a good deal about music, and she had played more carelessly than usual, but when a girl was as pretty as that what she did or left undone did not matter.

"My name's Smith. Look here, I want to talk business. Will you come for a little run in my car?"

"No, thanks," she said, but she smiled and he saw that she was not offended. He became more urgent.

"No kidding. It's just that I don't like to see a girl like you wasted. I've got influence, see? I can pull strings, but I shouldn't have to in your case. There aren't many girls with your appearance. Straight."

He spoke with the utmost earnestness in the tone he would have used in giving a new acquaintance whom he wished to conciliate a tip for tomorrow's race. Violet peeped up at his coarse red face through her long lashes. Her heart beat a trifle faster than usual. Could he really do something for her? His car, huge and glittering, waited for him by the curb, with a foreign-looking chauffeur in the driver's seat.

"Come along," he said persuasively.

But Violet was much better able to take care of herself that either Annie Coleman or Linda realised. "I don't know you well enough," she said, "but if you really want to talk to me there's a cinema just opposite."

"That'll do," said Mr. Smith. "Wait a bit." He plunged back into the café and re-emerged with a huge box of chocolates tied with pink satin ribbon. Violet rewarded him with another of her dazzling smiles. He beamed in answer. "Got a sweet tooth?" he said paternally. "I thought you might have."

Presently they were sitting side by side in the stuffy darkness of the Picturedrome. The film was *Ben Hur* and the place was crowded.

"You don't want to look at this stuff," said Mr. Smith, in a tone of authority. "Listen to me—"

And Violet listened, while the racing chariots thundered on and on, roaring an accompaniment to what he had to say. "No, I can't get you concert engagements. Take it from me that music's a wash-out. I'm talking business now not being polite. You play well enough for a tea shop in a town like this. You'd never get a job in one of the big centres. You don't practise, do you? I thought not. Quite right. Why the hell should you? If you were a horse-faced young woman with pink eyelids—but you're not, see? You're not engaged to be married?"

"No."

"I'm glad of that. You'd be throwing yourself away here. No choice for a girl like you. Let yourself be seen, see? Give yourself a chance to make good."

"How do you mean?" asked Violet. She was favourably impressed if also made slightly nervous by the fact that he was not trying to make love to her. He had not even taken her hand.

"I'm telling ye, aren't I? I want to help you. I've taken a fancy to you, see? You listen—"

CHAPTER III
SPINACRES

THE OLD Aberdeen dog lying by the fire wagged his tail approvingly as Lady Agatha Chant left the piano and came to warm her big bony hands at the blaze. They both disliked the vast, pale, chilly drawing-room with its air of mustiness and its disconcerting mirrors multiplying reflections of shaggy little dogs and gaunt and formidable looking old ladies in black lace and diamonds.

"She's going tomorrow, Mac," said Lady Agatha reassuringly, "and then we shall all sit in the library again after dinner as usual." She paused and stifled a sigh. "Until David marries. And then I shall probably go to Italy and live in *pensions* in Florence and Rome. And you—I don't know, Mac, but I'm afraid, I'm very much afraid that the future Lady Haringdon does not care for dogs."

The clock on the mantelpiece ticked on, the ashes fell in the grate. Lady Agatha picked up a book and laid it down again. She wished David had chosen some one she could be fond of. Diana Culver was beautiful but as hard as nails. A modern type. But David had always been mad about her. They had been engaged for a few weeks when he was twenty-one and she nineteen, but the girl was ambitious and there were five lives then between David and the title. She had thrown him over and married old Culver, of Culver's custard powders. That was in the summer of 1914. Then had come the War. David had joined up at once and had got a commission after serving for a year in the ranks. He was three times wounded. Lady Agatha had seen him in the hospital, but he was not asked down to Spinacres. His father had quarrelled with his family at the time of his marriage to an actress in a touring Shakespearean company, and had died unreconciled. Only Agatha had stuck to him through thick and thin, braving the cold displeasure of her elder brothers, Paul and Ambrose, each time that she went on to stay with the prodigal and his wife and their little son in their shabby house in Balham. During David's childhood she had never missed sending him a present at Christmas and on his birthday, and while he was in France she had supplied him with parcels, had written him long letters, and had treasured his brief replies. But after the Armistice she had lost sight of him completely.

One of Paul's boys was killed at Ypres and one at Gallipoli. Paul himself died in 1919 and his only surviving son was killed in a motor smash six months later. His uncle Ambrose succeeded to the title and what was left of the estates when the Revenue had had its share. He was a bachelor and was then in bad health. When he died it became necessary to find David. The family lawyers advertised for him and a few days later he presented himself at their London office. He said nothing about what he had been doing since he was demobilised, but, after all, that was his affair. His identity was never in question. He had the necessary papers, and the junior partner, who saw him, for Mr. Pettigrew was abroad, was struck by his likeness to the family. The bold blue eyes, the long chin and mobile sensitive lips could be seen in most of the Chant portraits hanging on the walls of the dining-room and library at Spinacres.

Lady Agatha had received him with open arms, and his affection for her was apparently undiminished.

"You'll stay on and run the house for me—" he said.

"Until you marry—" she answered, wondering as she spoke if there was anyone in the neighbourhood who would do for him. It should be some one with money, for he would be very poor. Ambrose had sold several farms and Spinacres was not kept up. Lady Agatha told herself that she ought to be glad that Mrs. Culver, after a chance meeting in London with the new Lord Haringdon, had invited herself down. A rich young widow with whom he had always been in love. What more could he ask for? "But he's thirteen years older than when she threw him over for the custard powder," thought Lady Agatha. "He's not a boy now to be taken in by a pretty face."

And, in fact, there were signs that Diana was finding the going unexpectedly heavy. This was her last evening. She was motoring on to friends in Wiltshire the next day. She had come down to dinner in a marvellous rose and silver frock, far too elaborate for the occasion. After dinner, at her suggestion, she and her host had gone for a stroll in the park. Would David take the opportunity to ask her to marry him? He had not been himself since she came. He was moody, restless, uneasy.

"I suppose he still cares for her even if he sees what she is," thought his aunt with a sigh. She glanced at the clock. Past eleven. The Aberdeen pricked up his ears with a whimper of eagerness and trotted across the drawing-room to meet his master. Lord Haringdon was alone and he did not appear particularly elated.

"Time you were in bed, Aunt Agatha."

"Yes. I'm just going." She hesitated. "You haven't—you're not—"

He sat down and lit a cigarette. "No."

"Where is she?"

"Diana? She went upstairs some time ago. She found it rather damp in the garden."

Had he asked Mrs. Culver to marry him and been refused? Somehow his aunt thought not. "I don't think she cares much for the country," she ventured.

"No." He smoked his cigarette to the end and then stood up and stretched himself. "You know she's leaving Spinacres tomorrow? I may go for a couple of days' tramp across country. I need more exercise than I've been getting lately."

Lady Agatha was always down to breakfast at half past eight and at nine was at her desk in the morning-room, dealing with her correspondence before she interviewed the cook. Diana Culver seldom left her room before midday, but on this day of her visit she made an effort and appeared just as her hostess was preparing to go round to the stables.

"Where's David?" Diana had the directness of a savage or a spoilt child. She never pretended to find her host's aunt anything but a bore.

"I'm so sorry, dear," said the elder woman sweetly. "He's gone off somewhere and I don't think he will be back until lunch time. He did not expect you to come down so early. It is early for you, isn't it?"

"It doesn't matter," said Diana, but she looked sulky. "I shall be seeing him in Town. I just wanted to say—it doesn't matter. No, I won't come round to the stables. I'm not keen on horses. I like cars. Lady Agatha—"

"Yes?"

"What has David been doing all these years since he was demobbed?"

"Why not ask him?"

"I have. He won't say."

"Really?" said Lady Agatha vaguely. "How tiresome of him. I must be going. Robin will be waiting for his sugar."

The luncheon gong had sounded and the two ladies were at table when David came in. He explained that a bullock at the Grange Farm had shown symptoms which Hobden had feared might be those of foot and mouth disease and they had got the veterinary surgeon over from Jessop's Bridge.

"He says it's all right. It's been a worry."

"I hope he's capable," said Lady Agatha anxiously. "He's a new man. Poor young Lovell was so splendid. Ambrose thought a lot of him. He saved Robin's life, and he was very good with dogs too."

"What became of him?"

"He died. I don't think he was ill long. I know it was a shock to Ambrose. He sent a wreath, and I'm not sure that he didn't go to the funeral."

There was a silence. Diana looked sulky still though she had brightened up when David entered. She was accustomed to receiving a good deal more attention than she was getting from either the aunt or the nephew. She glanced at her host's lean brown face. He was eating his lunch with a hearty appetite.

Why had he not made love to her last night? She knew she had been looking her best. Most men would have been only too glad of the chance. Certainly he had kissed her, but only once. Was he afraid that she was not in earnest, that she would let him down again? But it was all so different now. Surely he must see that. A boy and girl, both penniless. He laid down his knife and fork and turned to her.

"I must say I'm awfully glad about that bullock," he told her.

"Are you?" she said coldly.

Lady Agatha laughed. "You are boring poor Mrs. Culver with your raptures, David."

"Not at all," said Diana, "but he'll get stodgy if he's not careful, won't he, Lady Agatha? I think I ought to start now—"

David went down the steps with her to the waiting car, a racing model which Diana drove herself.

"Come and see me in Town, David"—and there was more urgency in her tone than she herself realised. He attracted her far more now than he had ever done in the days when he had been hers to command. "Ring me up. We'll dine and dance somewhere."

"Thanks very much," he said coolly. "I'm afraid I'm rather tied here just now. Good-bye—"

Half an hour later he looked into the morning-room where Lady Agatha, relieved to be rid of her uncongenial guest, was enjoying a novel, and announced that he was going for a walk.

"I may not be back for a few days. I shall just mooch round," he said vaguely. It was obvious that he did not want to be questioned, and his aunt who, in spite of her blunt manners, was not lacking in tact when dealing with those whom she wanted to please, showed no curiosity, whatever she may have felt.

"Very well, dear. I hope you'll have decent weather. That French Abbé who knows says we are to have a wet summer. Are you taking Mac?"

"He'd never forgive me if I didn't," said Mac's master. He came farther into the room. "Take care of yourself, Aunt Agatha—"

"Of course," she said placidly. "I always do. Don't be gone too long—"

Chapter IV
DAVID WONDERS

To David the hilly and thickly wooded country about Jessop's Bridge was all fresh ground though he knew most of the landmarks by name from hearing his father's reminiscences of his boyhood at Spinacres. He was in no hurry and he spent most of that afternoon on the crest of Arding Gap beyond Saxons looking at the view. On a clear day three counties are visible from the copse of wind-blown firs that crowns the hill. To be raised to a height from which one can look down on the activities of one's fellow men is soothing to a troubled mind, and after David had smoked a pipe or two, sitting on the turf cropped by generations of conies, with Mac dozing at his feet, the tension of his nerves relaxed.

Diana, in his house and ready and willing to marry him, had appealed to one side, not the best side, of his nature. He had no illusions concerning her, he saw her as she was, beautiful to look at, shallow, selfish, vain, but—perhaps—with a man who could master her, not such a bad wife after all. And there was her money—there was no denying that the Culver money bags would be useful! Money talks. He had loved her once, but he knew well enough that he would not be considering the possibility of their marriage now if she had not been a rich woman. "Just as she, my dear Mac, wouldn't be thinking of me if two uncles and three cousins were still standing between me and Spinacres. Her ladyship—Yes, Di would like that."

He knocked the ashes out of his pipe presently and pursued his way, and before long, after skirting a chalk pit and following a track that descended the hill through dense woods he found himself on a road again. Clouds had come up from the south-west while he was under cover of the trees and it had begun to rain heavily. He put on his coat and trudged on.

A quarter of a mile farther on where the road made a sudden turn he came upon a man and a girl standing talking together. He was passing when the girl called to him.

"Would you help? There's been an accident—"

"I'll do what I can," said David. He looked at the pair keenly. It was a lonely road and it would soon be dark. "What sort of accident?"

"A dog run over by a beastly motorist who left the poor thing in the track of anything else that might come along. My friend and I found him. I did what I could, and he was so good and licked my hand. But he was too heavy for us to lift. I told Vi—that's my friend—to go back to the main road and hold up the next car that passed, and I came this way. There's a house here. That's the park wall. But this—this gentleman says it would be no use going there."

The person to whom she alluded cleared his throat nervously, deprecating her youthful indignation. He was a meagre little man with weak eyes and a straggling moustache, and he was obviously ill at ease.

"I'm sorry, miss, but it reely would be no use at all. Worse than useless I should say. I—I'm employed there. It's not the sort of place—what I mean is—I'm not supposed to talk—" he flapped his bony little hands, a gesture eloquent of complete helplessness—"I have no choice. And I'm late as it is—"

"All right," said David, "I'll carry on." He looked curiously after the shambling figure as it hurried away, and then turned to the girl. "Now," he said, "I'll come with you. What sort of dog is it?"

"An Airedale, I think. I managed to pull it to the side of the road. I was so afraid that something would come along and run over it again in the dusk."

They passed the park entrance, high gates of wrought iron between carved stone gate posts. An avenue of holm oaks led away from it. The house itself was not visible from the road.

"Quick!" said the girl. "I can't bear to think of the poor beast lying there alone—"

"Is it much farther?"

"No. It was here. But—how extraordinary! It's gone!"

"Perhaps it wasn't so badly hurt as you thought," suggested David.

"It was! It couldn't have moved of itself!" she cried. "Both its forepaws were injured. Of course Violet may have found some motorist to take it away—"

"Your friend? But wouldn't she have waited to tell you?"

"I don't know," she said uncertainly. "It's queer—"

"I don't see any marks of a car," David said half to himself. "The ground's soft after all this rain. You're sure this is the place?"

"Certain. Look!" She pointed to a darker patch on the wet road, and, as she did so, Mac, who had been sniffing about uneasily, trotted up to investigate, threw up his head, and gave vent to a prolonged and melancholy howl. "He knows—" said the girl.

"If he bled as much as that he would leave tracks," said David. "There's a smear if you look closely from the spot where you found him to the grass by the roadside—"

"Yes. This is where I left him. I remember noticing that silver birch in the wood."

"Your friend went one way and you the other?"

"Yes. I walked as fast as I could until I came to the park gates. I tried to open them but they were fastened with a padlock and chain. There's smoke coming out of the chimney of the lodge but I could not make anyone hear. Then I went on until I met that little man and tried to get him interested, but he seemed to be frightened. Of course it may have been his people from the big house in there who ran over the dog in their car! I never thought of that!" she cried.

David agreed. "It might. I suppose he came in and out by that little door in the park wall over there. You met him where I found you about half a mile farther up the road?"

"Yes."

"Wait a moment"—David crossed the strip of grass by the roadside to the door in the wall. It was a heavy door, with a lock but no latch. He glanced up at the iron spikes on the top of the wall and noted that they were imbedded in cement that was obviously much newer than that which held the bricks together. Poachers were a nuisance, but the spikes seemed excessive. He stood for a moment perfectly still gazing up at them before he returned to the girl, Mac following closely at his heels.

"You must not worry," he said reassuringly. She had been flushed and a trifle breathless when he saw her first, but now, in the gathering dusk, her face looked white. "I'd like to get my bearings." He asked her to hold his electric torch while he unfolded his ordnance map. "Can you show me where we are?"

"Yes"—she traced the road with her forefinger. "This road crosses the main road about half a mile this way. Vi went back to the crossroads. I've got a cottage a couple of hundred yards farther along. We'd been spending the day there and were on our way home. We were going to catch the seven-forty at Laxworthy. We shall never do it now. But I expect some one's motoring her back to Jessop's Bridge."

He did not manifest any interest in her friend's movements. He was still studying the map. "Then this place on the left is Black Ridge."

"I still don't understand," she murmured. "She must have got some one to come and pick the poor thing up, but—"

"Would she leave you like that?"

"She might. We—we had had a row and we hadn't really made it up."

"Well, you can't stop here," he said decidedly. "It will be dark soon."

"Yes, but she may be waiting at the crossroads. I shall have to go back and see—"

"I'll go if you like," he offered.

"Thanks awfully, but I should hate to be left here alone. There are too many trees. It's eerie somehow."

"We'll both go."

They walked on together, the Aberdeen following his master. "She's not here," said the girl as they reached the cross-roads. There was still light enough to see. There was no house in sight and they had left the woods behind as they came to higher ground.

"Some one has given her a lift. Vi's like that. She gets things. She's so pretty."

"What will you do?" asked David.

"Go on to the station."

"A longish tramp and a lonely road," he said. "Let me see if I can hold up a car for you. There's one coming now"—he stepped forward and shouted but the motor swept by them without slackening speed. "Damn!" he said.

"Never mind! I can walk."

"I'll come with you."

"I hate bothering you! It's clean out of your way."

"That's all right." He hesitated for an instant. "My name's Haringdon!"

"Mine is Merle, Linda Merle."

An hour and a half later he was standing on the platform at Laxworthy while she stood at the door of her third-class compartment and tried to thank him.

"You've been so very kind, Mr. Haringdon—"

"I hope you'll find your friend has reached home safely. Good-bye—"

The train was moving. She leant out waving her handkerchief, and he waved back. A jolly girl, he thought. He liked her straightforward, unaffected manner. She had told him all about the cottage she had bought and her hopes for the future. She had pluck evidently and initiative. And, incidentally, she had done him a good turn by diverting his thoughts into another channel. The beautiful Mrs. Culver would have been surprised at the rapidity with which her victim was recovering his balance.

"The fact is," he told himself, "I need more exercise for my brain than I've been getting at Spinacres. I've half a mind to chuck everything and go back to my job. Aunt Agatha would have a fit, I suppose—"

There was an inn near the station and he put up there for the night and went on the following morning. He reached Winchester about one o'clock, had lunch at Ye God Begotte, and rang up Spinacres. A servant answered, and then, after an interval, he heard his aunt's voice faintly over the wire.

"I rather wish you'd come back, dear. Mr. Pettigrew came—the senior partner—he happened to be in the neighbourhood. He's had an offer for Alderslea copse and he wants to know if you'll sell."

"All right. Ask him to dinner tonight, Aunt Agatha—"

"Oh, he's staying here, dear. He always does. He's an old friend of the family—"

David had not yet met Mr. Pettigrew. He had been abroad recuperating after an attack of influenza when he called on the lawyers to establish his identity and the necessary business had been undertaken by another member of the firm. He found him sitting with his aunt before the fire which was lit every evening all the year round in the library.

"This is David, James," said Lady Agatha. There was pride in her voice. She had not cared very much for her other nephews, but this one had always been dear.

The old gentleman adjusted his glasses. "Dear me! Good evening, Lord Haringdon. You are the image of your poor father, if I may say so. We were boys together, you know."

David smiled. "I'm afraid I don't—unless—were you called Fatty in those days?"

Mr. Pettigrew chuckled. "I was. I had a tendency to plumpness—though you wouldn't think it to look at me now."

They went in to dinner. Afterwards Lady Agatha left the two men sitting over their wine.

"Your aunt is a wonderful manager," said Pettigrew, "and she tells me that you are trying to get the hang of things, but I'm afraid you'll find it hard to make ends meet. The death duties. Crushing."

"I shall have to be careful," David agreed. "The cigars are in that box." He lit a cigarette himself.

"I have had an excellent offer for the Alderslea copse," said Pettigrew. "It is no use to you since your uncle Ambrose sold the land between it and the Haringdon wood. It's just a strip of undergrowth on the crest of the hill above Black Ridge, too far from the road to be any use for building."

"What does the prospective buyer want it for?" inquired David.

"I gathered that it overlooks his place and he wants to insure privacy."

"I see. A retiring disposition. Who is he? I don't know my neighbours yet."

"His name is Saigon. He is a stranger about here. He bought Black Ridge last year. It had been empty a long time and I believe he got it cheap."

"I passed his gates yesterday," said David. "He's got some pretty useful spikes set along the top of his park wall. Saigon. It does not sound English. I didn't know I owned any land in that direction."

"Well, I suppose I had better close with his offer," said the lawyer. "You are never likely to get a better one."

David's eyes narrowed. He was recalling his adventure of the night before. He had not been able to account for the disappearance of the dog. Perhaps the other girl would be able to explain it, but meanwhile it had left an unpleasant impression on his mind.

"I'll write at once," said Pettigrew.

"No," he said. "I'd like a few days to think it over."

"Very good," said Pettigrew rather stiffly. He fancied the young man was anxious to show that he was the master. "I suppose if I had advised him to take his time he would have told me to clinch the bargain," he thought. He had several clients of that type.

Perhaps David read his thoughts, for he smiled as their eyes met, and David's smile was particularly attractive.

"I expect you're quite right, sir, and it's a bit of luck for me, but I have reasons. I'll tell you all about it another time if you care to hear. If Mr. Saigon writes or rings you up, you might say the matter is receiving your best attention or that you have it in hand. Something polite and noncommittal. I don't want the chap to think I don't want to sell. What is he like?"

"I have no idea. He wrote to us. I have not seen him."

"Is he popular in the district?"

"I really could not say. Lady Agatha might be able to tell you."

David rose briskly. "I'll ask her."

Lady Agatha had gone back to the library fire. There was some fancy work on her lap and she was reading the latest Edgar Wallace. She laid the book down as the two men entered.

"How is Penelope's web getting on?" inquired Pettigrew. "Your aunt has had that piece of embroidery on the stocks this last seven years to my knowledge."

"Ten, you mean," she replied without shame. "I started it after the Armistice when I gave up making socks for the mine-sweepers."

"And how many socks did you knit?"

"Three. Not three pairs. One pair and one of the second."

David grinned. He knew what his aunt's war record had been. Her O.B.E. had been well earned. "When you two have done ragging," he said, "I want to hear about the modest violet at Black Ridge. What is Saigon, who is he, Aunt Agatha?"

"My dear," she replied, "people talk. You know how they talk in the country. I don't suppose there is anything in it."

"What do they say?"

"Well, some say that he does research work, and of course they always make a great fuss about secrecy, don't they? And some say he's a nerve specialist and that he's turned the old place into a sort of asylum, very private and very expensive, where the patients undergo a new and very unpleasant kind of treatment."

"You haven't called?"

"Good heavens, no!"

"I see." The parlour maid was bringing in the coffee. David changed the subject.

CHAPTER V
MISSING!

SOON AFTER eleven the following morning one of the waitresses at the Tudor Café whispered to another. "That's the new Lord Haringdon, him over there by the window. I've just served him with a small coffee. Isn't he good-looking!"

Her friend did not admire the type and said so. "Too thin and brown. Not what I call smart. I mean, I do like ties and socks to match. But"—she relented—"he has got nice eyes."

David, unconscious of the interest he had aroused, was gazing thoughtfully at the elderly pianist who was plodding her way through a fox trot. Presently he beckoned to his waitress. "Where's the violinist?"

"She's not here this morning, sir."

"She lodges with Miss Merle, doesn't she?"

"Yes."

"Can you give me the address?"

The girl hesitated. "I'll ask the manageress."

"Do," he said easily.

She left him and, after an interval, the manageress approached. As she came up, threading her way among the tables and chairs, he realised that he was beginning to enjoy himself. Life, lately, had been too easy. It had presented no problems.

He rose, with his disarming smile. "Sorry to bother you—"

The manageress was forty-five. She was heavily made up and wore a harassed expression. "It does not matter, though, as it happens, I am rather busy. Do you come from Miss Hunter?"

"No."

"She hasn't been here this week!" said the manageress bitterly. "Our pianist does her best, but really—oh, here is Miss Merle—"

Linda was coming towards them. The manageress moved away, signing to them to follow, and took them both into her private room, a small space partitioned off at the head of the stairs.

"Now, Miss Merle—"

Linda looked troubled. "I haven't heard a word, Mrs. Dutton. I'm awfully sorry. But this is the gentleman I told you about." She turned to David. "I'm frightfully worried about Vi. She wasn't at our digs when I got back Sunday night, and she hasn't been near since! I thought she might have gone to another friend whom she used to live with so I didn't bother so much the first night, but yesterday Mrs. Dutton sent round to ask why she had not come to play at the café, and she sent to Miss Coleman's place too. Vi wasn't there. She seems to have simply vanished off the face of the earth."

Mrs. Dutton sniffed. "Most inconsiderate. I've rung up an agency, Miss Merle, and they are supplying us. You may tell your friend, if she does come back, that her place here is filled. And now you really must excuse me—"

"What do you think?" Linda appealed to the young man. They had left the café together and were standing on the pavement outside.

"I don't know enough about it to think anything," he said. "Shall we thresh it out a bit? There's no room here. We're blocking the traffic. Will you come into the Precincts?"

It was very quiet in the Precincts not a hundred yards away from the bustle of the High Street. A few old men drowsed in the sunshine on the benches set along the broad flagged path that led to the great west front of the Abbey. Rooks cawed in the elms overhead, and from the Deanery garden came the intermittent whirring of a lawn mower. David led the way to an unoccupied seat.

"It's very good of you," began Linda. She glanced up at his grave face apprehensively. "You don't think anything can have happened to her? I mean—anything dreadful?"

"I haven't formed any theory," he said. "She left you on Sunday night and went back to the main road with the idea of stopping a car and asking for help. Was it her idea or yours?"

Linda thought a moment. "Mine, I think. I—perhaps I was more upset about the dog than she was. She isn't specially fond of animals, you see, and I am. And we'd had a row and hadn't really made it up. We should have done before long, but we were still being very polite. I said 'Do go back to the crossroads, Vi, and hold up the first car that comes along!' and she said 'Very well' and went."

"You had quarrelled. Isn't it just possible that she is keeping you in the dark as to her movements intentionally?"

"I suppose so," said Linda doubtfully. "But would she go off anywhere without taking her clothes?"

"Hardly. Where is her home?"

"She has none. Her parents are dead. She used to live with a Miss Coleman here."

"Miss Coleman? The café people sent round to her. It might be a good plan to go round and see her yourself," he suggested.

"I'd rather not. She does not like me. You see Vi had always lived with her. She went to lodge with her, she and her mother, when she was quite a small child, and Miss Coleman rather resented her leaving to share digs with me. She was very fond of Vi, in her way, and fussed over her a good deal too much. I think people ought to be allowed to make their own mistakes, don't you?"

"We do," he said grimly, "whether we're allowed or not."

I suppose so, she sighed. "You think I ought not to have persuaded Vi to come to me?"

"I don't say that. Why shouldn't she?"

"Well, I realise now that she's the sort of person that needs a good deal of looking after. Annie Coleman was right there. I did my best, but of course I've no authority over her. As a matter of fact, she's two years older than I am. She's twenty-three. But she seems much younger."

David thought a moment. "What do you mean exactly by her being a person who needs looking after?"

"Well, she's so wonderful to look at. I don't say"—again she hesitated, this time evidently out of loyalty to her friend—"I don't say in any other way. I mean she's not specially clever or—or anything."

"Have you got a photo of her?"

"Yes. I have one at home. Would that help?"

"Well, if she does not turn up within a few days you may have to hand it over to the police, but I'd wait a bit longer if I were you. Let me see. Today's Tuesday. Will you meet me here about this time Saturday morning? I may have found out something by then."

"It is most kind of you, but—"

"I'm at a loose end," he assured her. "I used to lead a very busy life. I worked hard. And then I had what everyone thought was a stroke of luck. I thought so myself. Now—I'm not so sure. Will you give me your address in case I want to see you before Saturday?"

"I've got the top rooms in one of those old houses overlooking the river. Nine, Rosemary Passage."

He produced a notebook and tore out a leaf after scribbling on it. "Here's my telephone number. Write, if you have any news, to Lord Haringdon, Spinacres—"

She turned her head quickly to look at him. "Are you Lord Haringdon? I've been calling you Mr. Haringdon—"

"It's all right," he said. "Now, we've got to take this thing seriously, Miss Merle. It may be a joke some one is playing on you—rather a poor one—but we don't know, and until we do we've got to be rather careful. In fact—"

"Yes?"

"You go most days to your cottage you told me—"

"Yes. I want to be ready by the beginning of June, and there's still heaps to do."

"I want you to promise me not to go there again this week."

"Oh! Why!"

"Never mind why. Promise!" he insisted.

She yielded. "All right. I've got to sew the rings on all the curtains. I can do that at home—"

He was a little late for lunch. Lady Agatha had not kept house for her brothers without learning something of masculine psychology, and she waited until he had satisfied a hearty appetite before asking any questions.

"You went off so early, dear. Mr. Pettigrew was disappointed not to see you again."

"Was he?" The servants had left the room. David passed the box of cigarettes to his aunt. She took one and lit it at his.

"Am I to be told?" she inquired.

"Soon," he promised, "if you're good. Aunt Agatha, will you do something for me?"

"Anything in reason, my dear."

"I want you to pay a call this afternoon on Mrs. Saigon."

"Good gracious! So far as I know there's no such person! And if there were I don't wish to meet her. David! You're joking, aren't you?"

"Never more serious in my life."

"Then you must explain."

"When you return from Black Ridge. I want you to go with an open mind. Frankly, I don't think you'll get past the lodge gates."

"Then what is the use?"

"There's an off chance that you'll be admitted."

"Really, David, you are too tiresome. I don't want to be mixed up with that sort of people."

David was disappointed. He had a vivid recollection of his aunt's visits to the shabby house in Balham where his boyhood had been spent. She had come usually when his mother was away on a tour and he and his father were living a picnic existence, at the mercy of casual charwomen. Aunt Agatha, in those days, had been such a sport!

"I expect you're right," he said quietly. "It doesn't matter." He glanced at his wrist watch and pushed back his chair. "I must hop it. Don't wait tea for me."

An enemy had once said of Lady Agatha Chant that she had a face like a horse. There was an element of truth in the gibe. As a girl she had been considered exceedingly plain; but though she had no lovers she had—and kept—some very faithful friends. That equine countenance, sensitive, humorous, with the clever mobile mouth and the shrewd blue eyes, was attractive in its fashion, and the straight-cut silvery-white hair made a becoming frame.

"Don't go yet!" she said quickly. "You took me by surprise. I don't understand in the least, but if you really wish it I will do what you ask."

He shook his head. "No. I was wrong. I ought to be ashamed of myself for thinking of dragging you into what may prove a very queer business."

"That settles it!" she said firmly. "I'm coming in. Ring the bell. I'll order the car for three o'clock."

Chapter VI

Lady Agatha Pays a Call

The lodge keeper came running to unlock the gate as the chauffeur sounded his horn. Lady Agatha, who had been sitting very erect, clutching her card case and preparing to parley, felt a measure of relief as he stepped back to allow the car to pass. He was a horrible looking man, she thought, and why was he so hot and bothered? But it was in his favour that he had not even inquired her name. She was not used to pushing her way in where she was not wanted and would have greatly disliked the process. The car traversed half a mile of park land. Once through the thick belt of trees that screened the house from the road, Lady Agatha saw it plainly, a big Georgian building of red brick with the arched gateway of the stables on the left surmounted by a clock tower. There seemed to be nobody about, though the net was up on the tennis court. Perhaps the players had been driven indoors by the rain that had come pattering down a few minutes earlier. It had ceased now but the clouds still threatened. Lady Agatha got out of the car at the foot of the steps.

"You'll wait for me here, Bell."

"Yes, m'lady."

As Lady Agatha went slowly up the steps, the door was opened by a fattish man with a round pale face and a creased waistcoat.

"Will you step this way, madam? The doctor is engaged just now. We did not expect you quite so early. But he will be with you immediately."

Lady Agatha opened her mouth to speak and thought better of it. Evidently she was being mistaken for some one else. An electric bell rang sharply in a room on the left as she trod on the mat, and she realised that she must have touched a hidden switch. She had noticed a similar device in some shops but it was surely unusual in a private house. She followed the butler across a large chilly hall in the pseudo classic style, with Corinthian columns in stuccoed brick and a floor of black and white tiles, and was shown into a small waiting-room, furnished with divans against the walls and a table strewn with magazines. The only window was too high up to afford any view.

"Doctor Saigon will come," said the manservant again and went away, closing the door after him.

Lady Agatha sat down to wait for the doctor, and, as she waited, she wondered if his butler drank. "His hands can't be shaking like that all the time," she thought, "he'd never be able to wait at table."

How quiet the house was. Not a sound anywhere. And how slowly the minutes passed. Suppose the woman for whom she had been mistaken arrived before she had an opportunity to explain? It might be rather awkward. She decided that she would go into the hall and tell the butler that she could not stay much longer. But when she tried to open the door it resisted all her efforts. For an instant she knew fear, the instinctive unreasoning terror of any living thing that finds itself caught in a trap. Then common sense came to her aid. The door had stuck. That was all. And in any case she was safe enough. She was not friendless or obscure. David knew where she had gone, and Bell was outside with the car. He would corroborate her if necessary. Five minutes more dragged by and then the door opened quite easily and the doctor came in.

"My dear lady—"

Looking up she saw a face so ravaged by some emotion at which she was unable to guess that she forgot the speech she had prepared.

"You are ill!" she exclaimed.

"I? Not at all." He controlled himself with an effort that brought the blood to his sallow cheeks, and actually contrived to smile. "You must not imagine things, Miss Walsh. That won't do." His voice, with its slightly foreign intonations, had assumed the factitious heartiness of the physician bent on reassuring his patient. "How is it that you are alone? Your niece was to bring you."

"That door sticks," she said. "You should have it attended to. I tried to get out just now and couldn't."

"Too bad," he said mechanically. His heavy-lidded dark eyes were dull with fatigue. "The housekeeper will show you your room."

She could not sail much longer under false colours. "Doctor Saigon—"

It was apparent that he was thinking of something else for he started slightly when she spoke. Perhaps, she thought, he was engaged in some form of research work and had been working in his laboratory when the servant fetched him.

"I'm rather a nuisance," she said, trying to speak lightly. "You were frightfully busy, weren't you?"

"Not at all. No." She saw that, however innocently, she had said the wrong thing. He was glaring at her now suspiciously. "You are not the lady I saw in Town." His face had hardened and his voice was harsh.

Lady Agatha drew herself up. When she chose she could be the great lady. "I was about to explain. I fancy your servants mistook me for some one you are expecting. I am Lady Agatha Chant of Spinacres. We are neighbours. I came to call on Mrs. Saigon."

"Oh"—his veiled gaze had grown piercing, it challenged her, but she met it without flinching. "My wife is not here. She does not care for the country." He went to the door and held it open for her.

"What a pity!" she said. "Well, I must apologise for taking up your time. I hope you like Black Ridge. I used to be brought here when I was a small child, fifty years ago. The Charltons had it then."

They were crossing the hall while she spoke. The doctor opened the front door. He made little or no attempt to conceal his anxiety to get rid of her.

"You take resident patients?"

"A few. Yes. For special treatment. Quiet is essential. That is why we do not encourage visitors. But thank you for coming, Lady Agatha. I will tell my wife."

He came down the steps with her to the car.

"Are they all mental cases?" she asked.

"Professional etiquette does not allow me to discuss the nature of my patients' ailments with outsiders, Lady Agatha."

She laughed. "How crushing! But you are right, of course. Good-bye, Doctor Saigon." She did not offer him her hand.

Bell slowed down as they reached the gate. The lodge keeper was there parleying with some people who had driven up in a large saloon car. Lady Agatha caught a glimpse of a youngish woman and a little huddled figure beside her.

When she got home she asked for her nephew and was told that Lord Haringdon had not yet returned. She had a bath and lay down on the sofa in her dressing-room until it was time to go down to dinner. David came in to her a few minutes before the hour.

"All right?"

"Yes. I've had adventures. I'll tell you afterwards."

"You look fagged," he said remorsefully. "I ought not to have dragged you into this."

"Rubbish! I—well, I won't say I enjoyed it, but I was interested."

Later, in the library, as they drank their coffee by the fire, she related everything that had occurred. He listened closely and with an increasing gravity.

"It was a bit of luck that you should be mistaken for an incoming patient," he commented. "You certainly would not have got in otherwise. This fellow Saigon seemed worried about something, you say?"

"Worried is hardly the word. The expression on his face shocked me when he first came in. Then he seemed to pull himself together. Of course he made it very clear that I was intruding. But, after all, if it's a home for mental cases they wouldn't want strangers—"

"Did you notice the time?"

"Yes. I looked at my watch several times while I was shut up in that room. It was about twenty minutes to four when he came in."

David nodded. "How was he dressed?"

"Oh, rather dapper, in well-cut grey flannels."

"He's rather above the average height, six feet or over, and has sleek black hair growing thin on top?"

"Yes. How do you know? I thought you'd never seen him!"

"I saw him this afternoon—to be exact, at twenty-seven to four. He was crossing the paved yard at the back from one outbuilding to another, and he was wearing a white overall and rubber gloves."

Lady Agatha stared. "Where were you to see that?"

"Farther up the hill. I was exploring Alderslea copse. Saigon is right. One gets quite a good bird's-eye view of his back premises. I don't wonder he wants to buy the land. I should in his place. But I shan't sell—just yet. Pettigrew will have to temporise. Yes. My afternoon was not wasted. Of course I took field glasses."

His aunt finished her coffee and set down her cup. She looked bewildered and slightly disapproving.

"It does not sound very nice," she remarked. "I don't know that I am particularly proud of my own performance. I am not in the habit of spying on my neighbours. But I trusted you, David. And now you are going to explain."

"Yes," he said slowly. "I can't tell you quite everything. I am not allowed to. I promised some one who had the right to make conditions. You'll still have to take me to some extent on trust, Aunt Agatha."

"Are you referring to Diana Culver?" inquired his aunt. She had suspected from the first that that very forward and designing young woman was involved.

But David first looked blank and then laughed. "Diana. Good Lord! No. Whatever made you think of her?"

Lady Agatha felt relieved. It was so obvious from his tone that Mrs. Culver had been far from his mind. And yet when she left Spinacres on Sunday to motor down to Wiltshire he had been half in love with her. Lady Agatha knew enough of men to be sure of that.

"Never mind," she said rather drily. "Get on with your story."

He told her then of his meeting with Linda Merle.

"It was raining hard and she was standing there by the roadside a little beyond the lodge gate by which you went in this afternoon. There was a little man with her whom she'd met just before I came along. She'd frightened him rather. She was very excited and indignant. A dog had been run over and left in the road. He was too big for her to carry and she wanted to find some one to help her. The little man was discouraging. He said it would be worse than useless to try Black Ridge, and that it was not his fault as he was only a servant there, and when I offered to carry on and do what I could he jumped at it and slunk off. Rather a little worm, in short. Well, I went along the road with her but when we got to the spot where she had left the dog there was nothing but a smear of blood in the place where he had lain. She was certain that he was too badly hurt to move by himself. I looked for and failed to find any signs of a motor having stopped and turned round there, and no car had passed us. She had a girl friend with her who had gone in the opposite direction and we went as far as the crossroads to look for her. She was not there and it was getting late. We both assumed that she had been picked up by some passing motorist and given a lift back to Jessop's Bridge. I couldn't let Miss Merle walk three miles to the station in the gathering darkness and torrents of rain alone, so I went with her."

"I see," said Lady Agatha. "What sort of girl is she?"

"Well, I should say impulsive, good-natured, very fond of animals—"

"I mean, what is she like to look at?"

"Oh, that." He seemed at a loss. "Not a raving beauty, but pleasant. Eyes that look at you straight, and seems to use soap and water mostly. A lady. I believe you'd like her, Aunt Agatha."

She let that pass. "You went on with your walking tour? You were at Winchester the next day."

"Yes. And I came home to see Pettigrew. Then, this morning I ran in to Jessop's Bridge to make sure she was all right. I'd been thinking it over and I wasn't satisfied—"

"Well?"

"I went to the café in the High Street where the two girls have been playing to the customers. I heard there that the other, the one I hadn't seen, had not turned up. The woman I interviewed, the proprietress or manageress, was angry about it and was going to give her the sack when she did show up. Miss Merle came in while I was there and we had a talk. She's worried to death and does not know what to think. She's younger than the other, but I imagine she's got a good deal more sense, and she seems to feel herself responsible."

"Was it the Tudor Café?" asked Lady Agatha with interest. "I go in there for a cup of tea sometimes and I remember noticing the violinist. She does not play very well but she's remarkably pretty, with copper-coloured hair. I quite enjoyed watching her."

"That would be the girl," said David. "Miss Merle said she was wonderful to look at. Her name is Violet Hunter."

"And she did not come home on Sunday night?"

"No."

"It sounds rather strange," mused Lady Agatha. "Young women of attractive appearance often do vanish nowadays, but they usually take a suitcase."

"Exactly. And they don't disappear in the middle of a walk, some miles from a station, on a wet Sunday night. Still, it is just possible that she's gone off with friends, or a friend, whom she had arranged to meet without telling Miss Merle anything about it. They had quarrelled earlier in the afternoon."

"What about?"

"Well, Miss Merle has bought a cottage farther down the road and is going to run a wayside tea place and she thought this other girl was coming in with her, but on Sunday Miss Violet announced that it wasn't good enough and that she had a chance of something much more in her line up in Town, though she would not say exactly what it was."

"Oh," said Lady Agatha, "surely that accounts for everything! Poor silly child! It sounds like the white slave traffic."

David lit a cigarette and threw the match into the fire. "It does rather. It's a possible explanation and I'm bearing it in mind. But it does not account for the dog."

"Oh, you never found him. I forgot that. But the poor thing may have crawled away into the wood to die."

He nodded. "There's the park wall on one side of the road, but on the other the woods aren't fenced properly and there's plenty of cover. I noticed that and I'm going to spend tomorrow morning quartering the ground."

Lady Agatha hesitated. "Is it wise to involve yourself, dear? Wouldn't it be better to leave it to the police? After all, it's no business of yours. These two young women are perfect strangers"—she paused—"aren't they?"

Her nephew glanced up at her, struck by her tone, and smiled. "They are, Aunt Agatha, or rather they were. I feel I know one of them fairly well now. It was a long walk to the station and we talked quite a lot."

"Has she asked you to try to find her friend?"

"Well, not exactly. I offered. As a matter of fact I'm keen on criminology—"

"David! You don't seriously think that a crime has been committed? That would be too terrible! Almost at our gates!"

"Doctor Saigon's gates," he corrected her. "Nearly four miles from ours."

"The doctor! You say he's mixed up in it!"

"I don't. I'm only wondering. I have arranged to meet Miss Merle again on Saturday. In the meantime I'm working on the case. Honestly, Aunt Agatha, it isn't advisable to call in the police too soon or to let the newspapers get hold of a story like this. It makes it more difficult for a girl to change her mind and come back if she's bolted with somebody."

"Yes," she conceded, "I see that."

"You're not sorry you took a hand by going over to Black Ridge this afternoon?"

He saw her shudder. "No. But I don't want to go again, David. There's something horrible about that house. None of the people I saw were normal."

"You didn't meet any of his patients."

"No. But the lodge keeper had such a brutal face and yet he seemed flurried and cowed somehow, and the manservant who opened the door couldn't keep his hands still. And the doctor himself looked ghastly."

"Was he fairly civil?"

"Oh, yes."

"I'm glad of that," he said thoughtfully.

"Why?"

"We don't want to put him on his guard." He looked at her and his conscience smote him. "You're dead beat. We've talked enough tonight."

She got up rather slowly and stiffly. "When one is over sixty any extra excitement tells. But I want to go on helping if I can be of any use."

"Thanks awfully, Aunt Agatha. You're a brick!"

She smiled. "You called me that once when you were about ten. I had given you a cage of white mice. Good night, my dear."

As she went up to her own room she sighed. If it was for the girl's sake that he was doing all this she must try to see her before long. But was it? She knew—he had admitted—that his explanation was incomplete. He was a little afraid of her and of what she might think. She had seen that. He did not realise how fond she was of him. "Some day," she thought wistfully, "he'll tell me everything."

Chapter VII

PICKING UP THE THREADS

The manageress of the Tudor Café was in the shop below the tea room when David entered a little before noon. She frowned, but before she could speak the waitress to whom she had been giving an order whispered, "That's Lord Haringdon—"

"Are you sure?" she whispered back. This was the young man who had been in the day before inquiring after Miss Hunter. She had been short with him then, supposing him to be one of the frequenters of the bi-weekly dances held upstairs. If he was really the new Lord Haringdon she would have to be careful. She composed her features as he came up to her and received him graciously.

"Have you any news of Miss Hunter?"

"None whatever. Her place is filled. You will understand, Lord Haringdon, that we have to carry on—"

"Oh, quite. Of course," he said confidentially; "between you and me, you have a pretty shrewd idea where she's gone and with whom, eh?"

"I have not indeed," said the manageress.

"She told Miss Merle that she had been offered a splendid position in London."

At this point the waitress who had been standing by joined in. "I saw a customer—a gentleman who comes in his motor most weeks, talking to her in the street the week before last. They went into the cinema together."

David turned to her quickly. "Do you know who he is?"

"No. He's tall and big with a red face and wears a fur collar on his coat. I think he goes somewhere for the week-end and comes in here on his way, for I've always seen him either Friday or Monday afternoons—"

"That will do, Miss Miller," said the manageress icily. "I am sure you are mistaken. Miss Hunter was not the sort of girl to go to the pictures with a perfect stranger. Will you kindly do what I asked you just now—"

The waitress reddened and retired in evident confusion and the elder woman turned to David. "I always discourage irresponsible gossip," she said austerely. "What is—forgive me—your *locus standi* in this matter, Lord Haringdon?"

The question was an awkward one and he had no answer ready.

"Damn my lordship!" he thought irritably, "it's a millstone round my neck. It gets in my way when I'm on a job."

Aloud he said, "I haven't one. But you've heard from Miss Merle how we met on Sunday night?"

"I heard her account," said the manageress with the air of one who reserves judgment.

"I was curious to know what happened," he said easily, "but you're right. It's no business of mine. Good morning—"

He went into the Precincts. The bench on which he had sat with Linda was occupied by a couple of nursemaids with their charges. He chose another and sat looking across the sunlit space of turf at the grey front of the Abbey church.

Why was that woman at the café so anxious to convince him that the customer described by the waitress had nothing to do with Violet Hunter's disappearance? He had seen her face change when the man was mentioned and he felt tolerably sure that she knew more about him than she chose to say. He sighed. He had been out in the woods since six o'clock that morning and had searched the undergrowth thoroughly for a quarter of a mile in each direction, beginning from the spot where the dog had been run over, and had found nothing. It had rained since Sunday night which made things more difficult. Perhaps he was on the wrong tack. He smoked a cigarette and then another and was about to go when he saw Linda herself coming down the broad flagged path. She had been to matins at the Abbey and was coming out with the rest of the scanty congregation. She looked tired, he thought, and worried, but her downcast face brightened when she saw him and they shook hands like old friends.

"Have you found out anything?" she asked as he fell into step beside her.

"You must give me a little more time. I heard this morning that she was seen about with a man, an occasional customer at the café." He told her what had passed at the shop. "I fancy the chap may be a friend of the manageress," he added. "I didn't care for her manner."

"She's a beast," said Linda bluntly, "and the man may be the person who offered Vi some post up in Town. But she was willing to go and there was nobody to stop her. He wouldn't pick her up on the road, without any luggage—"

"That's true."

"And we had left the main road. It was my idea that she should go back and try to stop a passing car," said Linda. "She didn't want to. Oh, dear! How I wish I had not persuaded her!" There were tears in her voice. "We ought to have kept together."

"You weren't to know," he tried to console her. "Besides she may be all right." But he spoke without conviction. "I think we'll try a few advertisements. I'll just draft one or two. Here's an empty bench." They sat down and he produced a notebook and a fountain pen.

He had taken off his hat and Linda, watching him, noticed that his crisp brown hair was beginning to turn grey. He was older than she had fancied at first, nearer forty perhaps than thirty. There were lines about the firm lips and at the corners of the steady blue eyes. She flushed a little as he turned his head suddenly and became aware of her inspection.

"Here's one. 'Violet H. are you all right? Very worried and anxious. Do write or send word. Linda.' That can go in the Personal columns of all the dailies tomorrow. And I think we'll have this too. 'Reward Offered. Any person bringing information regarding the present whereabouts of Miss Violet Hunter, last seen on the road to Laxworthy at about seven o'clock on the evening of the twentieth of May to'—let me see—there's a firm of lawyers in the High Street—I'll get the exact address—'will be rewarded.' Now I want you to go to them, Miss Merle, and ask them to undertake to receive any information that may be forthcoming. I shall pay their charges and the reward—say, five pounds—but you are not to mention me. I must not appear in it. Do you get that?"

"Yes," she said doubtfully.

"It's a nuisance that the manageress should have known who I was. She didn't the other day, but this morning she tried to be smarmy."

"You are sure she knows?"

"She called me Lord Haringdon. If she's in this game my number is up. Anyone who has anything to hide will shut up like an oyster when I come along. Have you seen the woman Miss Hunter used to live with yet?"

"Miss Coleman? No. I simply can't face her. She hates me and she is certain to think it is all my fault."

"Well, I don't see how I can butt in with her," said David. "I'm sorry, Miss Merle, but if you really want to find your friend I don't think you ought to leave any avenue unexplored, as the politicians used to say. She may know something. If she dislikes you she won't go out of her way to set your mind at rest, but she can hardly refuse to tell you if you go to her about it. Where does she live? On the outskirts of the Town? I'll drive you to the corner of the road and wait for you. You'd better go there before you see the lawyers."

"Blow!" said Linda. "I don't want to. You're rather good at ordering people about, aren't you?"

He smiled. "Rotten bad habit, isn't it? Are you coming?"

There was a pause. Then—"Very well," she said resignedly. "It will be pretty ghastly, but if you say I must I will—"

David beamed at her. "Good girl!"

He drove her to the corner of Linden Road and waited for her to return. She was away ten minutes.

"Well?" he said, as she rejoined him. He noticed that she was flushed.

"Miss Coleman came to the door. She didn't ask me in. I asked her if she had heard from Violet. She said that she hadn't, and then she was horribly insulting and rude. I can't tell you all she said. She told me it was only what she expected would happen when I induced Violet to leave home and that she held me responsible for everything. She's mad, I think. Her face was working, and then she burst out crying and banged the door in my face. I could hear her sobbing as she went down the passage. I'd be sorry for her, but she isn't fair to me—"

"Of course not. Don't you worry. You're doing your best." He looked at his watch. "Nearly two. I wish we could lunch together, but we should be seen by the wrong people. Are you dying of hunger?"

"No. I'm upset," she confessed. "She said such things."

"Never mind her." They shook hands. "Take care of yourself," he said. "Don't forget to eat. That doesn't do." He wished he could take her back to Spinacres. He was struck by her friendlessness. Apparently she knew no one in Jessop's Bridge to whom she could turn for sympathy or advice.

"You must eat," he repeated.

"I'll go home presently," she said, "when I've been to the lawyers. I've got some sardines. When shall I see you again?"

"Tomorrow."

He had decided to go up to Town by the 2.17 to see a friend of his who was an analytical chemist. He caught the train with three minutes to spare, and a couple of hours later was having tea with his friend and his friend's wife at their house in Balham.

"I've got a job for you, Gibbons."

"I thought you'd gone too high up in the social scale to know anything about jobs," said Gibbons facetiously. "My Lord, the carriage waits! That sort of thing. We'd have hired a butler to hand round the cakes if we'd known you were going to honour our humble abode, wouldn't we, Gladys?"

"Don't mind him, David," said Mrs. Gibbons.

David grinned. "I don't. Look here, G." He took from his pocket a small tin box and opened it, revealing a disk of dried mud.

"What is it?" inquired Mrs. Gibbons, "or mustn't I hear?"

"It's a lump of earth dropped from a circular rubber heel. I want you to find out all you can about its ingredients."

"What are you looking for?" asked the chemist. He had dropped his joking manner.

David looked at him. "I found this in the grass by the roadside within a few paces of a door in a park wall. Can you analyse it without dissolving all of it?"

"I'll try."

"How long will it take?"

"Half an hour."

When he had gone David helped Mrs. Gibbons, who did not keep a maid, to clear away the tea. "I did not think we should ever see you again," she said.

"Why not? As a matter of fact, I've been wondering if I should ask the Chief to take me back. You know he didn't accept my resignation? He gave me six months' leave."

"Wouldn't your people be upset?"

"There's only Aunt Agatha. She would be, I suppose. She's a good sort, but Victorian in her ideas."

"Does she know what Sir Henry thought of you?"

He shook his head. "The Chief hinted that the less said the better."

"You ought to marry," she said, "then you'd settle down all right in the country. That's George calling you—"

David went to the door of the room Gibbons used as a laboratory. The chemist came out to him with the box in his hand.

"Here you are. I found a trace of blood. Did you expect that?"

"I thought it possible. Was it—animal—"

"Yes."

"I see. Thanks."

"Anything else I can do?"

"Not just now. Wait a bit though. Have you ever heard of a Doctor Saigon?"

"Can't say I have. I can look him up."

"He's not in the register. I've ascertained that. It's probably a foreign degree. He's partly if not altogether foreign himself. He's bought a large estate in the country near me and is taking patients."

It was nearly nine when David got back to Jessop's Bridge. He had left his car in the garage of the Station Hotel and he was crossing the road to fetch it when he passed a girl whose face seemed familiar. He had nearly reached the curb when he passed her. It was the waitress at the Tudor Café who had told him of the man in the fur coat. He turned abruptly and hurried after her, coming up with her just as she reached the pillar box where she stopped to post a letter.

"I beg your pardon," he began, "I saw you this morning—"

"Yes, and I wish you hadn't," she said resentfully. "I've been fired. Mrs. Dutton said things and I answered back. It was true what I said about seeing Miss Hunter going to the pictures with that old man. How was I to know it wasn't to be mentioned?"

"I'm awfully sorry," he said.

She remembered that this was Lord Haringdon and became coquettish. "It's not your fault," she assured him, "I don't blame you. She's an old cat and I shouldn't have stayed there much longer anyway. Miss Hunter's well out of it. I don't wonder she did a bunk, though it was a bit sudden. Well, I must be getting on home—"

"Wait a moment," he said. "You're not leaving for a few days, I suppose?"

"I'm sticking on until the end of the week."

"Will you do something for me?"

"That depends," she said brightly.

"I want to meet this man with the rabbit decorations. I think you said he came most Fridays?"

"Yes. But I don't fancy he will this week."

"Why not?"

"Well, I happen to know that Mrs. Dutton went to the telephone after she'd finished with me, and rang some one up. It must have been a trunk call, for she was so long getting through. It's in her own room and I couldn't hang about and listen, naturally. I had to serve a customer. But as I was passing a little later I heard her say something about a lot of questions and possible unpleasantness and then I suppose the person at the other end said something for she answered, 'I've warned you. Good-bye,' and hung up the receiver."

"That's very interesting," said David. "You think she knows this man and was giving him a tip to keep away?"

"I saw her stop at his table once and he spoke to her then, but I didn't hear what passed."

David thought a moment. "If he comes on Friday I want you to come to the window that is farthest from the door of the tea room upstairs, the one that faces the tailor's shop and—and powder your nose. Will you do that?"

She tittered. "Oh, Lord Haringdon, you are a caution! You don't mean it, do you?"

"I do." He wondered how far he could trust her and decided that as he had gone so far he must go a little further. "It will be a signal. I shall be somewhere about. But you must not breathe a word of this to anybody. Do you understand?"

She nodded. "You're going to ask him straight out, as man to man, what's become of Miss Hunter."

"Something like that," he conceded, "and you're going to help?"

She made an impudent little face at him. "And what do I get for it?"

"Wait and see!"

The town clock struck the half-hour. "Gosh!" she cried in exaggerated dismay. "Half past nine. I shall catch it! Good night, Lord Haringdon."

As he drove home along the winding country lanes under a moon now just beginning to wane, in a silence broken only by the hooting of an owl in the woods on his right and the steady running of his engine, he asked himself what progress he had made in the last twelve hours. There was almost certainly something wrong about Doctor Saigon's household. The extraordinary discomposure of the two menservants and of the doctor himself, noted by Lady Agatha, was, at present, unexplained, and Violet Hunter had last been seen within a hundred yards of Doctor Saigon's park gates. On the other hand, there were grounds for supposing that the man in the fur-trimmed coat, with the possible collusion of the manageress of the Tudor Café, had been trying to get hold of the girl, and, if he failed to appear on Friday, it might almost be taken for granted that he was involved.

But why abduct her, under circumstances that were almost certain to attract attention sooner or later, when she was willing to go with him of her own accord?

"I've got hold of some pieces of the puzzle," thought David, "but none of them fit."

The appeal he had drafted that morning would appear in all the daily papers. Would it be answered? And, if not, what could he do next?

He found Lady Agatha in the library. She laid down her novel as he entered. "Anything fresh?"

"Nothing much. I'll tell you tomorrow."

The letters that had come by the evening post lay on the table. He turned them over. A couple of bills, a bulb catalogue, and a large envelope with the Jessop's Bridge postmark. He picked up the last and opened it.

"Miss Merle promised to send me this, Aunt Agatha. It's a photograph of the missing girl."

He took it over to her and they studied it together.

"A lovely face," she said.

"Yes, but not a strong one. Look at that mouth and those eyes. Her friend was right. She'd want a good deal of looking after."

Lady Agatha sighed, and quoted, half to herself:

"'Elle était de ce monde ou les plus belles choses
Ont le pire destin—'

"What can have happened to her, David? Whatever it was you must have been within a quarter of a mile of her. You heard nothing? No cry?"

"Nothing"

Chapter VIII
MR. SMITH IS ANNOYED

The tea room of the Tudor Café was crowded when Mr. Smith came in on Friday afternoon, but there was an empty table in the far corner and he went over to it, moving with his usual heavy deliberation. The waitress who attended to the customers at that end of the room paused a moment by the window to apply a dab of powder to a pert little nose before she came forward to take his order. He eyed her critically. She was not really pretty but she had the grace of youth and the attractive impudence of a sparrow.

"You're wasted here. I could find you a better job," he remarked as she set down a toasted tea cake before him.

"Could you? I'm leaving this hole anyway—"

His face hardened slightly. So this was the girl Mrs. Dutton had told him of. He would have to teach her that it did not pay to interfere with him. But the moment was not propitious, so he smiled amiably. "We'll have a little chat presently—"

She moved away to attend to new arrivals. Mr. Smith poured out his tea and added four lumps of sugar. As he replaced the tongs something made him look up. His eyes met those of a younger man of slight but active build who was just sitting down at his table. Mr. Smith's light lashes flickered. He moistened his lips which had gone dry.

"Some time since we last met, Ebermann," said the other pleasantly.

Mr. Smith cleared his throat. "You—you're looking well, Inspector."

"Thanks. I was three months in hospital after that chat we had two years ago."

"I had nothing to do with that," said Mr. Smith earnestly. "I hope you don't think I had. I hate violence."

The other smiled. "Yes. You generally get some one else to do those little jobs for you, don't you? All right, Ebermann, I'm only ragging. What's your lay just now? Theatrical and film agent?"

Mr. Smith, who also answered to the name of Ebermann, shook his head. "No. That trouble was due to my partner. I trusted him. It is a mistake to trust people. It has always been that with me. I am too easy-going, I listen. I believe—" Under the stress of excitement Mr. Smith's intonation was becoming more guttural. "I am ze victim," he concluded.

"Quite. Then what are you doing now?"

Mr. Smith was cornered. It was apparent that sooner or later he must give a straight answer to a straight question.

"I am in the catering business with my brother-in-law, Enrico Alfieri. I own this place, the Tudor Café. It was not paying and I bought it cheap a few month ago."

"And put in a manageress. I see. You run other places in Town?"

Mr. Smith replied reluctantly in the affirmative.

"A night club? Of course. The Romilda, isn't it?"

"See here, Inspector—"

"Did you take the girl you had here to play the violin up to Town last Sunday night?"

Smith's large frame relaxed. His relief was unmistakable. "I did not. I'll be perfectly frank with you as regards that young woman. She can't play the fiddle for nuts, but she's a looker and no mistake, and I did want to get her at the Romilda. No harm meant. I was going to stand her a course of dancing lessons and give her a job, a well-paid job, as dancing instructress. I knew she'd be a draw. It was practically fixed up and she was to give notice here this week, and now she's gone the Lord knows where and left me on the mat."

The man whom he addressed as Inspector eyed him hard. "It wouldn't pay you to lie to me about this, Ebermann," he said.

"That's right. I know that."

The other rose. "All right. We'll leave it at that. I'll look you up if I want you." He nodded carelessly and lounged off.

Mr. Smith had lost his appetite but he drank the remainder of the tea in his cup and smoked a cigar before he found his way unobtrusively into the manageress' office. She was there, sitting at her desk, busy over her accounts, but she rose as he entered. "You had a long talk with Lord Haringdon."

"Lord Haringdon, nothing!" he said irritably. "I've known that chap for years, and he's put a spoke in my wheel more than once. I got back a bit of my own though when Carrotty Sam and the Slasher—" He checked himself. "Never mind that. Lord Haringdon!" He laughed coarsely. "He's Inspector Chant of the Criminal Investigation Department at the Yard."

"There must be some mistake," she said. "I assure you, Mr. Smith, he is Lord Haringdon, of Spinacres. He came into the property and the title when his uncle died. I didn't know him by sight until the other day but of course I've heard about him. He lives at Spinacres with his aunt. They are almost the principal people about here though they aren't well off and don't entertain. Lady Agatha comes in to Jessop's Bridge to do her shopping. She opened a bazaar last month for St. Jude's. Lady Agatha Chant—"

"Chant!" The man pursed his thick lips to whistle. "Maybe we're both right. His Lordship! Damn him, in any case. But wouldn't he leave the Force when he stepped into his uncle's shoes? And wouldn't the papers have been yapping about an amazing romance, policeman and a peerage? Did you ever hear a word about his having been a busy?"

"No."

"Well, he must be out of it now. If he tries his third degree business with me again, hanged if I don't call his bluff. I wish I hadn't been so civil. I thought he had Scotland Yard behind him."

Mrs. Dutton gave her employer an odd furtive glance. "I suppose he was still inquiring about Miss Hunter? It does seem strange that she should have gone off like that," she said.

"Some man," said Mr. Smith curtly. "I'm not worrying. There are plenty of girls about. I don't say she wasn't pretty. I made her a fair offer." He sat down at the desk. "I'll have a look at the books now I am here."

Meanwhile David had turned out of the High Street and was making his way through a maze of narrow alleys to the row of tall old houses whose gardens sloped down to the towing path. The entrance to Number Nine adjoined a small newsagent's shop and the ground floor rooms were let to a coal merchant who displayed in the front window samples of Derby Brights and anthracite. He climbed the stairs to the top landing and knocked on the door that bore Linda Merle's name, neatly written on a card and tacked to the upper panel. Linda came out with a jug in her hand.

"Oh, I thought it was the milkman," she explained. "Come in, won't you?"

He followed her into the sitting-room. A kettle was simmering on a gas ring and he noticed other preparations for a frugal tea.

"I've finished the curtains," she said. "Now I'm making cushions for the chairs. But honestly, Lord Haringdon, I don't see how I'm to run the cottage by myself."

"You had better put it in the agent's hands," he said.

"I may have to, but I'll hang on for a bit yet. Vi may come back."

"Yes," he said. His voice was noncommittal. "Are you going to give me a cup of tea?"

She smiled at him.

"If you want one, of course. I'm afraid I've only got biscuits—"

"I'm really here," he said, after a short pause, "to ask if you'll come to dinner with us tonight. My aunt would like to meet you. We can put you up for the night. In fact, my aunt hopes you'll stay over the weekend. I shall probably be away and she would be glad of your company."

"It's most awfully kind of her." There was more colour than usual in Linda's cheeks and her grey eyes were shining. "I should be delighted. I've been miserable alone here these last few days, wondering about Vi—"

"I'll run you home in the car as soon as you're ready," he said. "I've got one or two things to get in the Town yet. Shall we say the end of the bridge in half an hour's time?"

"I will be there."

It was dark when they reached Spinacres. Linda could just see the high roof and chimney stacks black against the starlit sky and the formal lines of the clipped yew hedges beyond the paved terrace. A middle-aged housemaid took charge of her and left her in a vast bedroom panelled in old oak and faintly illumined by a solitary candle, after telling her that dinner would be ready in ten minutes. Her only evening dress was the brown velvet frock she had worn throughout the winter and spring when she played the piano at the dances given three times a week at the Tudor Café and she was painfully conscious of its shabbiness. "But they won't expect much from me," she reflected philosophically as she went down to the hall where her host awaited her.

"Aunt Agatha, this is Miss Merle—"

Lady Agatha, with diamonds gleaming on the rusty black lace of her prehistoric tea gown, was a formidable figure, but Linda, looking up rather shyly at the lean ugly strong-featured face, was reassured by the kindly smile in the deep-set eyes that met hers as they shook hands.

It was not until after dinner, when they were all three together in the library, that they approached the subject that was uppermost in their minds. Lady Agatha had led the girl on to talk about herself. She suspected that this was what David wanted and she felt some curiosity on her own account.

"You have no relations in this neighbourhood, Miss Merle?"

"Neither here nor elsewhere," said Linda, and perhaps because she was overtired she failed this time to convey the impression that she was glad to be so free of all ties. "Violet Hunter and I are alike in that. My father was a general practitioner in the Midlands. He and my mother both died during an influenza epidemic when I was about ten. When everything was sold there was just enough money to keep me at a boarding school, where they took me on reduced terms because the principal had known my mother, until I was eighteen. She wanted me to remain on to teach music, but I hate teaching. I got a job as pianist at a little cinema at Eastbourne and then at another in Chiswick, and then I came to Jessop's Bridge to the Tudor Café. This spring a cousin of my father's out in New Zealand died and left me five hundred pounds, and I thought it would be lovely to have a little place of my own. I've always dreamed of a home."

"Your friend was to join you?" said Lady Agatha. "Was it on a fifty-fifty basis? Has she invested her savings in the scheme?"

Linda seemed amused at the notion. "Vi? She hasn't saved a penny. I hadn't either. It was only this legacy. Furnished rooms are very dear, and one has to be decently dressed."

"All silk underneath, I suppose," said Lady Agatha tartly. It was her opinion that too much was spent on clothes by the modern young woman. "In my day cotton was good enough."

Poor Linda looked abashed and David, taking pity on her, suggested that she should play to them. She glanced rather timidly at her hostess.

"Yes, my dear. I should like to hear you if you play good music. I decline to listen to jazz or that tuneless new stuff."

Later, when the girl had gone up to bed, aunt and nephew sat on by the fire.

"What do you think of her?" he asked presently.

"She seems to be a lady according to my rather old-fashioned standards. She's simple and unaffected. She's civil to her elders and she does not use a lipstick."

"I may have to be away for a few days," he said. "I'd like you to keep her here with you while I'm gone. Would you do that?"

"If you wish it. Where are you going?"

He was silent for a moment. "I'd rather not say. Nothing is settled. The man who owns the Tudor Café has been mixed up in the white slave traffic. He used to run a bogus theatrical agency. He was trying to get hold of Violet Hunter, but I don't think he had any hand in her disappearance."

"Then you're no nearer a solution of the mystery?"

"I won't say that."

"David,"—she laid her hand on his knee—"why are you mixing yourself in this business? Is it for Miss Merle's sake?"

"Not altogether."

"Wouldn't it be better to give it up and advise her to go to the local police?"

"You don't understand, Aunt Agatha. The police could broadcast a description of Violet Hunter through their stations all over the country and through the B. B. C., but they can't search a private house or arrest anybody not actually caught in the act of committing an offence, without a warrant. The machinery of the law is tolerably efficient but it is cumbrous and it takes time to set it in motion. We may go to them eventually, but I think we'll carry on a bit longer."

"What will you do next?"

He hesitated a moment. "I can't tell you. I haven't really decided. I'm going up to Town to see a friend who may be able to make some useful suggestions. You'll keep the girl here?"

"Yes."

CHAPTER IX
THE SECRET OF BLACK RIDGE

DAVID'S FRIEND was a man named Trask. He had been many years in the Criminal Investigation Department at Scotland Yard, was already an Inspector and was marked for further promotion when he was set upon by a race course gang and so badly injured that he had to leave the Force. He had been given an adequate pension which, with his savings, enabled him to live in comfort. He occupied a small flat in a block in Battersea, overlooking the river, and occupied his leisure very profitably both to himself and others by collecting and classifying press cuttings. He seldom went out, for he walked with difficulty and only with the aid of crutches, but he received a great many visitors.

His manservant, who had come to him after serving a sentence of five years for manslaughter, was devoted to his interests, kept the flat spotlessly clean, and was an excellent cook. He opened the door to David and greeted him with a beaming smile.

"It's a long time since we've set eyes on you, Inspector. I did hear that you'd come into a bit of money and left the Force."

"Lots of rumours about, Green," said David, "you've not run out of salt, I hope. How's Mr. Trask?"

"Fine, sir. He'll be pleased to see you. Step this way—"

He ushered David into the cheerful sitting-room where Trask sat in a spate of newspapers, clipping busily. He laid down his scissors as David entered and they shook hands.

"Well, Chant—or I suppose I should say Lord Haringdon—are you tired of vegetating yet? Are you coming back to the Yard? The Chief still thinks you will. He came in to see me the other day and we were talking about you."

The other shook his head. "I do feel rather dull at times, but I'm getting fond of the place. My father was born there and his father before him, you see. It's in my bones, I expect. But I'm on a case now, Trask, not officially, of course."

"Mysterious disappearance," said Trask.

"How did you know?"

"A firm of lawyers at Jessop's Bridge is advertising for news of a woman who vanished last Sunday night on the road to Laxworthy. It's been in three mornings now and I've got it filed with an appeal in the Personal columns addressed to Vi. The missing woman's name is Violet."

"Quite right," said David. "I drafted them both. This is what happened—" He proceeded to relate his adventure of the previous Sunday evening and all that had occurred since.

Trask listened closely and was silent for a while after David had finished.

"It looks bad," he said at last. "Gosh! I envy you, Chant. It's just the sort of case I should have enjoyed handling. Ebermann. You've tackled him. I agree with you that he can be counted out. The dog. If we knew what had happened to the dog—"

"You think that's important," said David. "The poor brute might have crept away to die, but I've gone through the covert by the roadside pretty thoroughly."

"You found the disk of mud from a rubber heel by the door in the park wall, and Gibbons got a trace of blood in his analysis—" Trask made his points slowly and thoughtfully, ticking them off with a pencil on the back of an old envelope. "What became of the manservant Miss Merle spoke to?"

"We didn't see him again. He may have gone in either by the big gates or the door in the wall a couple of hundred yards farther on."

"There was some blood on the road, you said. He might have trodden in it."

"Yes. But that does not help us much. He seemed a timid spiritless little chap, a bundle of nerves."

"And he said it would be no good applying to his employer, in fact, worse than useless?"

"Exactly."

"That does not sound as though your doctor friend was a noted humanitarian, does it? Saigon. I know the name. Will you get down from that shelf the scrap album marked with a capital S?"

He made room on the low table beside his sofa for the book and turned over the pages. "No. It isn't here. Wait a minute. It will come back to me. Wait—" He covered his eyes with his hand.

David waited, and after a minute the older man looked up "I've got it!" he said excitedly. "Petroff! Get me the book marked P, Chant, there's a good fellow!" He was eager as a terrier in pursuit of a rat. "Here we are!" He read aloud. "Grafting a new brain. 'Doctor Petroff, who under the Soviet Government has been given special facilities for experimental surgery, claims to have effected complete cures in mental cases. It is reported that he practises a system of grafting, but the process is a secret which has been revealed only to a few. Doctor Saigon, Professor Petroff's assistant in his laboratory, informed our correspondent that the new treatment, if it proved successful, would completely revolutionise the present methods, but added that it was too early to dogmatise. Doctor Saigon, who is of mixed parentage, for his father was an Armenian and his mother an Englishwoman, is the husband of the beautiful Mrs. Saigon, and they have a house in Paris where they entertain a good deal in the season.'"

"What's the date of that cutting, Trask?"

"Two years ago. And now he's running a nursing home of sorts in Hampshire. It doesn't sound too healthy to me. But I've seen the name quite recently. Give me the book marked F, Chant. We'll see if France helps us. No, nothing here. Saigon. Another attempt to fly the Atlantic! That was it. We shall find it in the first book on the shelf under Aviation. I cut it out only ten days ago. Captain Vandeleur with a group of friends come to Croydon to see him start on his hazardous voyage. Reading from left to right Mrs. Culver, Mrs. Saigon, and so on. What's the matter?"

"I know Mrs. Culver," said David. He was looking at the picture. Diana and the woman beside her were both laughing.

"If she's a pal of the Saigon woman she may be able to help you."

"I shan't ask her," said David. Could it be only a week ago that he had fancied himself in love with Diana Culver? He had been too fully occupied since she left Spinacres to nurse the flame that she had fanned, and it had died. He could think of her now quite coolly. Old Culver had left her very well off and she had drifted into a set where money was spent like water. He wondered if Mrs. Saigon had means of her own or if it was her husband who paid her dressmaker's and her hotel bills.

"The doctor told my aunt that his wife was up in Town," he said. "I don't think she's been at Black Ridge since he bought the place."

Trask filled his pipe with his favourite mixture and struck a match. "You say your aunt only got in because she was mistaken for a new patient?"

"Yes. The gates are kept locked and the tradespeople leave their provisions at the lodge, which is half a mile from the house. The park wall has been raised and furnished with spikes."

"And Saigon is trying to buy the strip of land on the hillside that overlooks the place from the back?"

"Yes. A mistake on his part. I should never have known I owned that bit if my attention hadn't been drawn to it."

"You've refused to sell?"

"Not definitely. I've told the lawyer to play for time."

Trask drew at his pipe. "Your aunt said the doctor and the two menservants looked frightened. That's interesting. But it might be just her fancy."

"I don't think so," said David. "She's a very downright sort of person."

Trask looked at him contemplatively. "Have you come to me for advice, Chant—I mean, Lord Haringdon?"

"Blow Lord Haringdon!" replied that peer. "Yes, I have."

"The prudent course and the only one that is not certain to get you into trouble," said Trask, "is to report Miss Hunter's disappearance to the Jessop's Bridge police and then go away for a bit. There's fishing in Norway, I'm told, and some mountains in Switzerland. You can work off your superfluous energy going up and down them."

"The oracle has spoken," said David; "and now tell me what you would do in my place."

"Don't ask me."

David took a photograph from his pocketbook and passed it over. "That's the missing girl's picture," he said.

Trask looked at it. "Yes," he said. "Poor child. It's a foolish face."

"Foolish," said David, "and young and helpless. The kind that goes down—and I'm to spend a week at lovely Lucerne?"

"You're not going to, eh? Well, I didn't think you would," Trask admitted, "and I should have thought less of you if you had. Though you'd be wise."

"Never mind that!" said David impatiently. "I can take care of myself. You'd concentrate on the doctor's place, wouldn't you?"

"I would. Does he know about you?"

"What do you mean know about me?"

"Does he know that the new Lord Haringdon joined the Metropolitan police when he left the Army and was promoted to the C.I.D. after serving his apprenticeship in the uniformed branch?"

"I should say not. The Chief wanted it kept dark. I didn't even tell the family lawyers who advertised for me when Uncle Ambrose died. There was no need. I had all the necessary papers for my identification, and my aunt knew me though we hadn't met since just before the War."

"How was that?" asked Trask. He had often felt curious about his friend's past.

David shrugged his shoulders. "I was engaged to a girl. She jilted me for a man old enough to be her grandfather. He was rich and I hadn't a bean. I went off at the deep end. The Kaiser saved me from making a complete ass of myself. He gave me something to do. I joined up at once. Aunt Agatha and I have always been pals, and she used to write and send me parcels—but she lived at Spinacres with my uncle, and my uncle and my father had quarrelled so I never went there, and after I was demobbed I thought I'd cut loose altogether."

"I see," said Trask thoughtfully. "Chant, I take back what I said just now about thinking less of you. It's not as if you had any personal interest in the girl. Call in the police and wash your hands of the business. I foresee frightful complications if you don't. You've no standing."

David grinned. "None whatever." He got up with a glance at his watch. "And no time to waste. I wish you were coming with me."

Chapter X
DIANA INTERVENING

"Of course I'm going to pay you, darling," said Elena Saigon with well simulated surprise. "I just happened to be rather short of funds. That beastly woman at that little hat shop I've been going to was so insulting that I had to give her something on account. I've told heaps of people about her shop, but that class is so ungrateful. I make a point of paying my friends on the nail, but really I should have thought you could have afforded to wait a few days. You're not poor, are you?"

"No, darling, but I do like to know where I stand," said her companion. They were lunching together at the club of which both were members. "I shouldn't dream of dunning you, of course, but honestly, if it bothers you to settle up, you'd be wise to give up playing bridge." There was an edge to Diana Culver's voice. At any other time she would have let Elena off more easily, but she had been nervy all the week and, as it happened, she had been staying with people whom she had no wish to offend so that she had been obliged to control her temper. It was a relief to vent her irritation on some one who was not in a position to hit back.

Elena Saigon winced. There was a letter in her handbag from her husband, received that morning. Usually he wrote at great length for he was still in love with her, but this time there had been only one sentence scrawled in haste. "I can send you no more money at present. Manage as best you can."

"It doesn't bother me in the least," she said. "I'll pay you in a day or two." She would have to see Michael and have it out with him. Letters were no use. He would give her anything she wanted if she was nice to him. Men were like that. "I'm going down to Hampshire for the week-end," she improvised.

Diana Culver pricked up her ears. "Hampshire? Oh, of course. Your husband runs a posh nursing home or something down there, doesn't he? Lily Walsh told me they'd got him to take her husband's aunt. Well, my dear, all I can say is, you ought to be rolling! I know what the fees are in those places. You'd better ask him for a bit more than you owe me while you are about it, and we'll fly over to Paris and you can help me choose some new clothes. I haven't been over since Easter. Come as my guest and we'll stay at the Meurice."

Elena's dark eyes sparkled. Diana was rich and could be generous when she was in the mood. Elena was willing to put up with a good many humiliations in return for material benefits.

"*Cara!* I should love that. How sweet of you!"

Diana ate her ice thoughtfully. Hampshire. It would give her a perfectly good excuse for calling at Spinacres.

"What part of Hampshire is Doctor Saigon's place?" she inquired.

"My dear, I can't tell you. I've never been there. I hate your English country. So green and wet. The post town is Jessop's Bridge."

Elena saw that for some reason this information was satisfactory. Mrs. Culver's ill humour had vanished.

"I'll run you down in my new car," she said. "I've got friends in that neighbourhood. I spent last week-end with them. They'll put me up and I'll call for you on Monday and bring you back to Town." She looked at her wrist watch. "It's a good thing we lunched early. If you can be ready at a quarter to three I'll call for you."

"That will be ripping!" said Elena with factitious heartiness. She would save the railway fare, which was a consideration. On the other hand, she was not sure that she wanted to spend a week-end with Michael in his present mood, and he had never encouraged her to join him at Black Ridge. He had referred to it more than once as his workshop. "I want to keep you apart from all that side of my life, my beautiful!" He was always rather mysterious about his patients. Of course he was not English and he had not an English medical degree, and the English doctors were jealous.

Probably if Diana Culver, looking about sixteen in a white jumper suit with white fox furs, and a Basque beret pulled well down on her golden head, had not called for her at the hour appointed and whirled her away her courage would have failed her and she would have spent the week-end in London trying to borrow money enough to pay her more pressing debts. As it was Doctor Saigon's lodge keeper, disturbed at his solitary tea by a series of impatient hoots from a motor horn, came out to parley and learned that one of the would-be visitors was his master's wife. The man's hard little eyes, set like pebbles in the red granite of his broad face, wandered from the slim dark young woman in the orange silk frock who said she was Mrs. Saigon to her friend at the driving wheel, and took note of the long clean lines of the racing car.

"The doctor's not expecting you," he said doubtfully. "He said nothing to me, and I'm not supposed to admit chance people on account of the patients."

"What a fuss!" said Diana irritably. "Can't you understand that this is Mrs. Saigon? You really ought to have rung the doctor up, Elena, to prepare him. How far is it from here to the house?"

"About half a mile," he said.

"Too far to walk. Besides, there's your suitcase. I'll run you up to the door, and then I must be getting on. Please keep the gates open," she added, raising her voice as the lodge keeper prepared to admit the car.

"I can't do that," he said gruffly. "I may get into trouble over this. But I'll be here to let you out."

The car shot forward up the avenue into the dense shade of the trees whose branches met overhead. The ground beneath was still sodden with the recent rains.

"It's very shut in," remarked Elena. "I should not have thought it was good for mental cases."

"Heavens!" The car swerved dangerously as Diana turned her head to look at the other. "Are they mental? I hadn't realised that. How gruesome. Some of them may be prowling about, and I've got to drive back to the gate alone!"

Elena giggled. "Don't be absurd, darling. They are properly looked after. Michael's awfully good at his job. I do know that. Professor Petroff thought a lot of him."

Diana stopped the car at the front of the steps that led up to the pillared entrance.

"Won't you come in and meet Michael?" said Elena Saigon rather wistfully. If her husband was angry with her a third person might be rather useful.

"Not now, darling. It's later than I thought. I'll fetch you Monday morning unless I hear to the contrary. I shall be staying with Lady Agatha Chant at Spinacres."

A white-faced manservant had opened the door. Diana backed the car into a bed of geraniums, sounded her horn twice, and was off down the avenue. Half an hour later she was being shown into the library at Spinacres. Lady Agatha, rising to receive her, did not conceal her surprise.

"Mrs. Culver—"

"I was driving down to Bournemouth and something's gone wrong with the car," said Diana glibly. "Isn't it sickening! I left it at a wayside repair shop a couple of miles down the road and the young man in charge was kind enough to bring me here on the pillion of the grubbiest motor bike I ever struck. I must be black all over. The worst of it is that he couldn't promise to put the thing right before Monday. Shall you hate me too much if I inflict myself on you for the week-end?"

"Of course not. But I'm afraid you'll find it very dull. My nephew is away from home." Lady Agatha's shrewd old eyes twinkled as she observed the effect of this announcement.

"Where's he gone? When will he be back?" Diana glowered at her like a spoiled child deprived of a toy.

"He didn't say."

"I thought he was such a model nephew and told you everything."

"Did you?"

Linda Merle had been picking up a stitch Lady Agatha had dropped in her knitting. She had risen too when Mrs. Culver entered but she was partly screened from the door by a high-backed chair, and Diana had only just noticed her. She glanced at her and was averting her eyes indifferently when Lady Agatha intervened.

"I have a young friend staying with me. Miss Merle, Mrs. Culver—"

Diana acknowledged the introduction with a short nod. "May I have the same room I had last week? Good. Then I'll go up and change."

"I'm sorry," said Lady Agatha when she had left the room. "We were so comfortable together, you and I. But Mrs. Culver is an old friend of Lord Haringdon. They were even engaged for a time. But she married some one else. Now she's a widow."

"She's very pretty," said Linda, trying to speak cheerfully. Lady Agatha was right. They had been very comfortable together and she had been looking forward to a quiet evening during which the old lady might tell her some more anecdotes of her nephew's boyhood. It was plain that she was devoted to him, and Linda liked to listen. But this old friend of his, so beautiful and so beautifully dressed had contrived, without a word, to make her feel that she was an intruder. She realised, as she had not done before, that she had entered a world to which she did not belong and which she must soon leave. Lady Agatha liked her and, she thought, Lord Haringdon did, too, but the fact remained that they were members of the leisured moneyed class while she had to earn her living. If she gave up the cottage she must look for another job as a pianist in a café or a cinema. The prospect depressed her and her spirits were not raised when Diana came down, after keeping them waiting twenty minutes for dinner, in a shimmering frock of silver lace with a trail of water lilies down the skirt.

"Charming!" said Lady Agatha, with real appreciation.

"This rag?" said its wearer negligently. "I really haven't a thing to wear. I must fly over to Paris soon and do some shopping. I shall take Elena Saigon. She's got very good taste and her French is better than mine. She's Italian by birth."

"A Doctor Saigon bought an estate a few miles from here last year. It's an unusual name," said Lady Agatha.

"That is her husband. I brought her down with me this afternoon and left her there."

"Do you like him?" asked Lady Agatha.

"I've never met him. I dropped her and came on."

"Of course. You were going on to Bournemouth," said the older woman, "and that reminds me, oughtn't you to let your friends know that you have fallen by the way?"

"I wasn't going to friends. I generally put up at the Mont Dore."

Linda took no part in the conversation at dinner. Once or twice her hostess tried to include her but she did not avail herself of the openings given her. She was sensitive to impressions and felt that Diana Culver was inimical and that anything she said would be taken amiss. Afterwards, presumably in Mrs. Culver's honour, they sat in the huge chilly dimly lit drawing-room instead of the smaller and cosier library with its lighted fire on the open hearth. Lady Agatha asked her to play and she sat at the piano, dutifully working her way through the rather old-fashioned pieces which her hostess had got out for her earlier in the day, while the latter fumbled impatiently over her detested knitting, and Diana, tired after her drive down from Town, yawned and finally went fast asleep on a sofa. The wind had got up and rain pattered on the windows. Later, when Linda was undressing to go to bed, she drew her curtains and looked out at the sky, covered with clouds, ragged and torn, like the banners of a defeated army, flying before the south-west wind. A week to-morrow since Violet vanished. Where was she now?

Chapter XI
NIGHT WORK

David's lair in Alderslea copse was on the edge of an old sand pit. From the top where he lay hidden in a tangled growth of hazels and briars, bracken and heather, he had a tolerably good view of the back premises of Black Ridge, with the outbuildings, which were numerous, surrounding the brick-paved stable yard. He had been supplied with a rough plan by Lady Agatha, who had been intimate with the family who had the place when she was a young girl. On the left were the stables and coach house, now converted into a garage, as were also the wash house and the dairy. It was the dairy that had been turned into a studio by a former tenant with artistic tastes. David recognised it by the large skylight let into the roof. It was from this building that he had seen the doctor emerge, wearing his white overall and rubber gloves, on the afternoon of Lady Agatha's visit. When he arrived at nightfall on Saturday the yard was deserted and the door was shut. He set about making his preparations for the night. He had brought a rubber ground sheet and a blanket and some tinned provisions so he would not attract the attention of the household to his presence on the hill above them by lighting a fire. He was wearing an aged and moth-eaten blue serge suit which Trask's servant had bought for him with a pair of disreputable boots at a second-hand clothes shop in the Vauxhall Bridge road. The only article in his possession which would betray the fact that he was not an ordinary out-of-work, on the tramp in search of a job, was a pair of night glasses, for the ground sheet, though fairly waterproof, was torn and shabby and the blanket exceedingly dingy.

It began to rain soon after he had finished his supper of tinned tongue and biscuits. He cursed the British climate and his own officiousness.

"Why the devil am I here instead of minding my own business? Hallo—"

The back door of the house had opened and some one had come into the yard. The night was very dark with the moon hidden behind clouds and the person who had emerged carried an electric torch. David saw the ray of white light through the mist of falling rain cross to the door of the building which was now, he assumed, a laboratory, or possibly an operating theatre, and vanish for a while. After an interval of about ten minutes it reappeared and bobbed away in the direction of the wash house. At the same time he heard a metallic clanking which suggested that a zinc pail was being carried or possibly even a wheelbarrow pushed along. Once more the light disappeared. Time passed. David, who was growing stiff, changed his position and getting out his clasp knife, cut away some briars that impeded his view. He became aware of a peculiar acrid smell and peered about uneasily, wondering if he had set fire to anything with the last match he had used to light his pipe. Then the moon shining for a moment through a rift in the clouds enabled him to see a volume of black smoke pouring from the wash-house chimney. Apparently something was being burned there that had been brought from the building with the skylight. David looked down into the yard again. The wash-house door was still closed but the house door was open and a man stood on the threshold, his figure clearly visible against the lamplight in the kitchen behind him. It was not the man to whom Linda had appealed to help her with the dog. He had been noticeably small with narrow shoulders and a shambling gait. This man was big and burly. David fancied he might be the lodge keeper. He wondered if there was anyone else in the kitchen. So far he had seen no sign of any women servants.

The man stood with one hand on the knob of the door and leaning a little forward. There was something threatening in his attitude, but when, after what seemed a long time, the other man emerged from the wash house and joined him he moved aside to allow the latter to pass in before him.

"One of the servants," thought David, "and was that the doctor?"

He could hear the closing of the door, and, after a moment he saw that the light had been put out in the kitchen. There was still some smoke coming from the wash-house chimney, but not nearly so much. Evidently the fire that had been lit was dying down.

He had left his watch at Trask's flat. He could tell the time within a few minutes from the stable clock. He waited until it had struck twelve and then rolled himself up in his coverings and went to sleep. He was awakened by the sun shining in his face, and sat up with a groan, conscious of aching bones. He would have given a good deal for a hot cup of tea but he dared not risk lighting a fire. He breakfasted on hard-boiled eggs and oatmeal biscuits, felt his bristling chin approvingly—a two days' growth of beard would help him to look the part he had set out to play—and sat down to smoke a cigarette and consider his position.

It was Sunday morning and he could hear, far away, the tolling of a church bell calling the people to an eight o'clock service. He wondered if Linda Merle would be going with his aunt. Saigon was not likely to be a churchgoer. What had he been doing in his laboratory the night before? There was no sign of life about the back premises yet. The windows and doors were all closed. It was past ten when the butler—David, recalling his aunt's description, was sure he was the butler—came out with a bowl full of potato peelings and other refuse which he threw on a rubbish heap by the gate that led into the kitchen garden. That, in itself was queer. The preparing of vegetables for a meal was no part of a butler's work in a normally constituted household. Apparently cooking was done on an oil stove for no smoke issued from any of the chimneys.

"There can't be many patients just now," thought the unseen watcher.

The time for him to move was not yet. Usually, in the cases that had been allotted to him during the years he had spent in the Criminal Investigation Department at Scotland Yard he had been chary of forming any theory until all the possible scraps of material evidence had been gathered up, and he was trying to follow his normal course now. But it so happened that he had never had to deal with a disappearance before. It was like being given a loom with only a few threads hanging from it and being asked to recreate the pattern with those.

The dog had last been seen, and the girl too, within a few yards of a door in the park wall of a place euphemistically described as a nursing home owned by a foreign doctor who had studied under the notorious Professor Petroff. The professor was rumoured to have effected some remarkable cures with mental cases. He was a surgeon and had been granted special facilities for his work by the Soviet Government. An ominous phrase, that. Saigon, settling down in England, might be missing these facilities. No! That was too far-fetched. Impossible. And yet the strange facts remained and could not be explained away.

An Airedale, Linda Merle had described it, and he himself had seen the stain of blood on the road where it had lain, a dog—and the girl whose photograph he had left, with everything else in his possession that might betray his identity, with Trask at his flat. Where were they now? From the moment that Linda Merle had left them and gone running down the road to the spot where she met the manservant from Black Ridge they had vanished. David, recalling the little man's evident uneasiness and his earnest assurance that it would be "worse than useless" to apply to his employer for help, felt almost certain that he was on the right track.

The day passed slowly and without incident. He saw nothing more of the inmates of the house, and during the afternoon he slept for a couple of hours. When darkness had fallen he resumed his watch, but the yard remained deserted and no one came either to the laboratory or the wash house.

It was past midnight and the few lights that glimmered here and there in the wooded valley beyond the park had been extinguished when the self-appointed investigator into the mystery of Violet Hunter's disappearance became active. He had provided himself with a coil of rope and had fastened one end to a stunted but firmly rooted fir tree that grew close to the brink of the old sand pit.

With the aid of the rope he was able to scramble down the almost sheer face of the pit and land on the roof of the laboratory within a couple of feet of the skylight. If there had been anybody within he must infallibly have been discovered, for he had miscalculated the distance and had come down with a thud. For a minute he lay spread-eagled on the rather steep slope, feeling the rough lichened old tiles, wet with dew, under his hands. His heart was in his mouth, but the silence was unbroken. Apparently no one had heard him. He was about to resume his descent, scrambling down the roof to the gutter pipe and dropping from thence to the yard when the kitchen door was opened. He dared not raise his head to look but he heard footsteps and then cautiously lowered voices. They could scarcely fail to see him if they lifted their eyes as they crossed the yard. Fortunately the moon had gone behind a bank of cloud. They were coming towards the laboratory. They stopped and he heard the key being fitted into the lock.

"You've finished now?"

"Yes, last night. Thank God! I wouldn't live through this week again, Abbott. I'm just going to look round to make sure there's nothing left—"

They went in, closing the door after them. A moment later a dull yellow glow irradiated the skylight. With infinite precautions and moving an inch at a time the watcher on the roof crawled forward until he could, by craning his neck, see into the room beneath. Only a corner was visible but he caught a glimpse of shelves laden with test tubes and retorts behind glass doors and an earthenware sink with a tap that dripped, and a carrying chair fitted with numerous straps. The butler was standing still holding a small oil lamp raised so that the light fell on his bald head and left his face in shadow. His companion was doing something beyond the watcher's range of vision. After a moment the butler set the lamp down, drew forward a chair, and seating himself, proceeded to fill a blackened clay pipe.

David could hear the murmur of their voices. It seemed that they might be there for some time. He began to consider his own position. The moon had emerged from the clouds and was shining full on him and the chances of his escaping notice when the two men came out were remote. And he was beginning to feel very cramped. It seemed to him that if his journey of exploration was not to end ignominiously when it had scarcely begun he must move on. He shifted his grip on the wooden frame of the skylight, slithering very gently down the slope towards the gutter pipe. He was wearing rubber-soled canvas shoes. He was lying full length along the broad shallow gutter when the door was opened within three feet of him and he saw the butler's head thrust out and heard Saigon's voice.

"Well? What is it?"

"Must have been a rat. I caught two in the trap yesterday."

The door was closed again very gently and David drew a long breath of relief. That had been a narrow squeak. He dropped to the ground and edged his way along the old dairy, keeping well in the shadow. The first door he came to was that of the wash house. It yielded at a touch and he slipped inside and found himself in impenetrable darkness. The fire that had burned so fiercely had been out for nearly twenty-four hours and the place struck cold with a vault-like clamminess and chill after the night air. He dared not switch on the torch he carried in his pocket for fear the light should be seen from outside but, after a good deal of fumbling about, he found the iron chimney of the furnace. Presently he was on his knees, scrabbling at the furnace door. It opened rustily and his questing fingers sank into soft powdery ash.

Chapter XII
THE WEEK-END AT BLACK RIDGE

David heard a clock in the hall below strike two as he stood behind the curtain that screened the window on the first landing. Finding that Saigon and his servant had left the kitchen door open when they went out he had taken the opportunity to slip into the house. Evidently the rest of the household had retired for the night, for there was no light anywhere and the silence was profound. David felt his way out of the kitchen and up the back stairs to the first floor. Here was a corridor, running the entire length of the building, with doors on either side.

He opened one door, at random, very gently, and listened for a moment to the even breathing of the sleeping occupant of the room before he shut it again. He moved very carefully, but there seemed little danger of his making a noise. The firm of upholsterers who had prepared the house for Doctor Saigon had done their work thoroughly. These were carpets everywhere, carpets so thick that his feet seemed to sink into them. He would not have heard the two men come in if one of them had not coughed as they crossed the kitchen. Thus warned he realised that they were probably coming up as he had come by the back staircase. Hr stopped hurriedly behind the window curtain on the landing, and he was only just in time.

"Share and share alike. That's only fair. I'm glad you've seen it, sir." The butler's husky whisper was distinctly audible not more than a foot away.

"Yes. But don't forget the story of the goose and the golden eggs, Abbott. Don't press me too hard, that's a good chap."

"That's all right, doctor. He's safe for tonight, I s'pose?"

"I gave him a double dose of bromide and locked him in. We must not take any risks while my wife's here. She leaves in the morning."

"Good night, doctor."

"Good night, Abbott." There was a pause and evidently the butler had gone when the same voice, the voice of Saigon, added, "damn you!"

An hour had passed when David ventured out of his curtained recess. The conversation he had overheard was intriguing. It was also far from reassuring. He felt that the sooner he got out of the house the better. May nights are short and in another couple of hours it would be light and his escape would be cut off. He tiptoed down the corridor to the back staircase and here he met with his first check. The door at the top of the stairs had been locked, by the doctor, doubtless, when he came in, and the key was gone. There was nothing for it but to try to leave by the front way.

David retraced his steps along the corridor to the landing and, leaning over the banisters, peered into the hall below. It was in darkness, a black void in which the only sound was the steady ticking of the clock he had heard striking the hour. He took one step down and stopped. He had heard, quite distinctly, the sharp ping of an electric bell. While he hesitated the door of one of the rooms he had just passed was opened and the corridor was flooded with light. He turned and saw Doctor Saigon in a silk dressing-gown coining towards him. He was holding an automatic.

"Hands up!" said the doctor crisply.

David obeyed, cringingly. "All right, guv'nor. It's a fair cop—" His mind worked quickly. Everything depended on his playing his part successfully. So long as the doctor took him to be a vagrant who had somehow found his way in he was fairly safe, for he did not think Saigon was likely to call in the police. But if he aroused the doctor's suspicions—

"You put that pistol down, sir. I wouldn't 'urt anybody, I wouldn't—"

Saigon's restless dark eyes were like jet beads in his white face, his black hair was rumpled. Evidently he had been aroused from sleep. David remembered a click be had heard soon after the two men had parted in the corridor. He divined that there was some electrical arrangement which caused a bell to ring by the doctor's bedside when anyone set foot on the top stair, a device that would only be switched on the last thing at night.

"How did you get in?"

"I been 'angin' about them woods on the 'ill for several days, sir. I got a kind of cramp like." David always told the truth as far as possible. They could verify his story for he had left his stuff on the hillside, hoping to return in safety, though he had been careful to hide the night glasses. "There didn't seem to be no dogs about the 'ouse so I thought I'd try me luck—"

"H'm. Well, I'll have to consider your case. Just step into this room here—" still keeping his automatic levelled at the intruder, he stepped back and opened a door on his left—"quickly—"

"Look 'ere, guv'nor."

David, purposely, had slightly raised his voice. Saigon, frowning, signed to him to make less noise.

"I don't want anyone disturbed. Oh, hell!" he said helplessly, as a very pretty girl in a pyjama suit of primrose brocade came out of his room. She was smoking a cigarette and appeared to be quite at her ease.

"A burglar, Michael? How frightfully thrilling." She looked David up and down. "Not one of the swell mob, is he, not a bit like Raffles."

"You shouldn't have left your room, Elena," said her husband irritably.

"Why not? I can help you. What are you going to do with him? Now you see how much better it would be to be on the telephone. We could ring up the police at once. As it is, I suppose you'll have to tie him up and send one of the servants to the nearest town in the morning."

"I don't know," said Saigon. "Somehow I hate the idea of giving the poor beast in charge. Probably he's never had a chance—"

David thought it time to intervene. He was prepared to play into Saigon's hands up to a certain point, far he did not want the police either just yet.

"That's right," he whined. "I never 'ad none. You let me go and I'll say Gord bless you! I 'aven't done no 'arm nor touched a thing."

"We'll make sure of that," said Saigon curtly. "Turn out your pockets. Put everything you've got down there on the floor—"

David obeyed. A battered clasp knife with one blade broken, a tangled mass of string, a packet of fags, a cherry wood pipe of grimy aspect and a small tin box containing tobacco, the stub end of a pencil and one shilling and two pence halfpenny in coppers. There was nothing there to betray him—unless the box was opened.

Saigon's opaque black eyes were unpenetrable, but he seemed satisfied. "You can keep that junk," he said. "I'll think it over. Get in there." Again he indicated the room on the left. "If I let you out before anyone is up, let you go scot free, will you try to run straight in future?"

"I'll try, sir, I will indeed—"

"What a soft-hearted old thing you are, Michael!" remarked his wife. "I think you're all wrong. Of course he'd promise anything."

Saigon was turning the key on his prisoner. "I don't trust him," he said. "I may send for the police in the morning. I probably shall after you have gone. Leave it to me and run back to bed now, my darling. You'll catch a cold."

"You're not afraid of his smashing the furniture or anything?" she said.

Saigon smiled for the first time. "There is no furniture in there—and no window to break. It is the padded room."

"Oh!" she shivered. "How gruesome! I don't like this place—"

"You came," he reminded her gently, "of your own accord."

"Couldn't you do something else?"

"My God!" he said, with a sudden vehemence that startled her. "You say that—you, who write always for money, and more money. You came for that, didn't you?"

"Oh, Michael!" She began to cry.

"Never mind." He slipped an arm about the childish figure in its finery of pale yellow brocade. He could never bear to see her in tears. "Forget it! The padded room is quite comfortable. He'll be warmer and drier there than he would have been on the hillside. I'll let him out some time tomorrow. Meanwhile you'd better get off to sleep again."

Soon he heard her regular soft breathing at his side, but he lay awake himself until it was time to face another day.

It was nearly noon the next day when Mrs. Culver stopped her car at the foot of the steps. Elena came out, followed by her husband, carrying her suitcase. Diana greeted her.

"Hallo, Elena, you look as if you'd dropped half a crown and picked up sixpence. I know I said I'd be here about ten, but I was detained at Spinacres. My dear, such a scene! I'll tell you later. Is this Doctor Saigon? How do you do? Can't say you keep open house. That lodge keeper of yours was quite sniffy about letting me in just now. I'd be sorry for the burglar who tried to annex your teaspoons—"

Her friend emitted a little shriek of triumph. "My dear! One broke in last night! Wasn't it too thrilling! Michael caught him on the stairs, and he was rather young and had nice eyes, I thought. Blue, with unusually long lashes for a man. But he was very ragged and dirty and covered with bristles."

"Evidently the country's the place for a really hectic week-end!" commented Diana. "Did he show fight?"

"No. Michael had him covered."

"It sounds like a film! What did you do with him?"

"Well—" Elena hesitated. Saigon had warned her to say nothing of the padded room.

"One has to be rather careful," he explained. "None of my patients have been certified, and one is not supposed to use co-ercive measures or even to lock them in their rooms. The English laws are very complicated and troublesome—" His foreign accent had become more marked when he said this as it always did when he was nervous. He intervened now, covering his pretty feather-headed wife's silence. "The poor chap was down and out. I should have no mercy on a professional burglar, Mrs. Culver, but this fellow was obviously an amateur. What he needed was a bed and a breakfast and a shilling or two to help him on his way."

"You're quite a philanthropist, I see," said Diana. She was thinking that he did not look the part. Handsome, in that rather exotic style, but inclined to be jumpy. "Get in, Elena. Good-bye, doctor—"

"Well?" she said, when the high iron gates were closing behind them. "Did he shell out?"

Elena answered ruefully. "I'm awfully sorry, *cara*. I do hope you won't mind waiting just a little. He was quite decent. He adores me. Simply! But he's had an awful lot of expenses lately. But he's promised to let me have something to go on with in a week or two."

"Oh, all right," said Diana. After all, the small sum Elena owed her meant nothing to her, and just now she was thinking about something else. "I must tell you what happened this morning. We'll lunch at Ye God Begotte at Winchester. They give you quite good food there. My dear! It was priceless! Quite a new experience for law-abiding little me."

CHAPTER XIII
THE WEEK-END AT SPINACRES

ON SUNDAY MORNING Lady Agatha and Linda Merle had walked together across the park to the tiny church in the village. The uninvited visitor came down, yawning, just in time for the old-fashioned midday dinner of roast beef and Yorkshire pudding.

"We have a cold supper on Sundays, as you know," Lady Agatha remarked as she carved the sirloin. "Mrs. Pringle, who has been with us thirty years, sings in the choir in the evening."

"How sweet!" said Diana. "I wondered last Sunday why you had such a weird arrangement. This is another world, isn't it,

Miss Merle? We think our maids aged retainers if they've stayed with us three months, don't we?"

Linda, who was perfectly aware that the other was trying to make her feel uncomfortable, smiled. "Mine never dream of leaving me."

Lady Agatha gave her a quick look. She had thought the girl so sensible. Surely she was not going to try to impress Dima Culver by any silly boasting. Diana was far too sharp to be taken in. She was the kind of woman who knows to a penny the price of other women's clothes, and judges them accordingly.

Lady Agatha, who had been taken by the girl's pretty deferential manners to her hostess, did not want to see her placed in a false position and would have changed the subject, but Mrs. Culver was already speaking.

"Don't they? How ripping for you! How many do you keep?"

"Ten," said Linda, and then laughed outright as she held up her hands.

Lady Agatha laughed too, relieved. "Your fingers. Of course. They serve you well at the piano, my dear."

But Diana was not easily disconcerted. She gazed at the girl's hands with the mild curiosity of a visitor to the Zoo inspecting the animals. "I see," she said, in a voice that indicated that she was not amused. "You were joking. How did you get all those scratches?"

"Those? I was trimming a quickset hedge. I hadn't any gardening gloves—"

Lady Agatha, meaning well, intervened with an explanation. "Miss Merle has bought a cottage on the main road beyond Jessop's Bridge and is going to run it as a wayside tea house. There is a strip of garden and she hopes to make it bright and attractive with flowers and serve dainty little meals. It would be kind of you to tell your friends about it."

Linda flushed. She wished Lady Agatha had not said that. She did not want to feel obliged to Mrs. Culver for her patronage. In any case she felt sure that she would not get it.

"How romantic!" said Diana perfunctorily. "I hope you make your fortune." But she did not say that she would come to tea or bring anyone she knew.

The rest of the day passed slowly for all three. Lady Agatha dozed in the library after asking Linda to play to her. Diana left them and sat in the orangery with a novel which she did not read. She had generally managed to secure the thing she wanted throughout her life. She had let David go because she could not face the prospect of poverty. Now that she was a free woman, with ample means, she could please herself. It was all to the good, of course, that he was now Lord Haringdon, but she told herself that she would have had him even if he had still been only Mr. Chant. Like so many people who behave heartlessly or meanly, she was incapable of appreciating the reactions caused by her conduct, and it had never even occurred to her that David might not have forgiven her for jilting him.

"Why didn't he ask me to marry him last week?" she wondered irritably. "I gave him plenty of chances. He's very dense."

It was most annoying that he should be away. She had let herself in for a week-end of unmitigated boredom, and she would not be able to work the broken-down car stunt again. Lady Agatha did not like her. That did not matter, but what was this Merle girl doing at Spinacres? She was not pretty and her clothes were simply terrible according to Diana's standards, but a man might not notice that, and she seemed to be a pet of the old lady's and firmly established under her wing.

Diana Culver would not admit, even to herself, that she might be jealous of a creature so inferior to her in everything that mattered, with nothing in her favour but her youth and some not very marketable talent as a pianist. She made no admissions but she decided that the girl needed watching and in pursuance of this theory she made a special effort and came down at an unusually early hour on Monday morning.

She was early—for her—but Lady Agatha and Linda had already breakfasted and gone out together. Diana lit a cigarette and stepped out on the terrace. A burly man in a brown tweed suit was coming up the avenue to the front door. She wondered idly if he was the new vet whom David had been talking of last week, and then decided that he could not be the vet for, seeing her, he turned aside and came up the terrace steps to speak to her.

"Miss Merle?" he said.

She stiffened. "You are making a mistake. Hadn't you better inquire at the door?"

His keen eyes had by now taken in every detail of her appearance, noting the fine string of pearls about her white throat and the flash of the diamonds in the engagement ring that had been given her by old John Culver. His manner changed slightly. "I beg your pardon, madam," he said. "I see you're not Miss Merle. Perhaps you would be good enough to tell me where she is? It would save time and I am rather in a hurry."

"I think," she said, "the best way would be for you to come into the house and wait while one of the servants goes to fetch her. She is somewhere about the grounds, I think."

"Very good," he said.

She led the way through the open window into the breakfast-room. The parlourmaid was there clearing the table and he addressed her without waiting for Diana.

"Will you find Miss Merle and tell her she is wanted. I would be glad of a few words with his lordship too."

The maid looked at him doubtfully, impressed by his air of authority. "His lordship is away just now."

"Lady Agatha then—"

But there was no need. Before the maid could reply, the door was opened and Lady Agatha came in with a basket of freshly cut flowers, followed by Linda with a tray with vases to be filled and a jug of water.

Lady Agatha looked at the parlourmaid reproachfully. How many times had she been told not to show people in just because they asked for her at the door! Really, Parker was a nuisance. Only last week half a morning had been wasted in trying to get rid of a plausible young man who wanted to sell a vacuum cleaner. But the stranger proffered his card. She took it, reluctantly, glanced at it, and stood for a moment, motionless. She had received an unexpected and very unpleasant shock. Parker, somewhat flustered, was trying to explain.

"I—I didn't show the—the gentleman in, my lady, he came in from the terrace with Mrs Culver—"

"Very good, Parker. It's all right. We'll go into the library and leave you to finish here." She looked at her visitor. "Did you wish to see me alone?"

"No, my lady. I wanted to ask Miss Merle a few questions—"

"I see. Come with us. Linda—"

Diana, who by this time was bursting with curiosity, followed, and Lady Agatha was too much agitated to notice her presence. The police! She had never had anything to do with the law, though her brothers, of course, had been on the local Bench and David would be too when he had had time to settle down in his new position. If only David were here now to deal with the situation!

"Linda, come here, my dear, and sit by me. This is Superintendent Lamb. Won't you sit down?"

"Thank you, my lady, I prefer to stand," replied the Superintendent, taking up his position on the bearskin hearth rug and holding his brown Homburg hat with both hands as if it had been a concertina. He was looking at Linda Merle. "I've come from Jessop's Bridge. I daresay you can guess on what business." He waited, still looking expectantly at the girl.

She faltered a little, daunted by his loud voice and by that hard gaze. "Is it about Vi—I mean Miss Hunter?"

"That's right."

"Have you—has she been found?"

"Not yet." He laid down his hat on a chair and got out a notebook. "She's been missing since last Sunday. You left your lodgings together that morning. It came on to rain in the afternoon. Your landlady, who had been to the pictures, saw you come in alone at about half past ten. Is that correct?"

"Yes. I missed the train we had meant to catch at Laxworthy Junction and had to wait for the next. I hoped to find that she had reached home before me."

"How was that? Didn't you spend the day together at the cottage you bought on the main road a couple of miles out of Brent Green? You've been doing the place up, painting and distempering and so on, yourselves, haven't you?"

"Yes. We were walking to Laxworthy and had turned into the side road through the woods when we found a dog that had been run over. He was badly hurt but I thought he would recover if he was properly looked after and I persuaded Vi to go back to the main road and try to stop a car while I went the other way to see if I could find anyone who could help. I met a man who was a servant in a big house near but he couldn't do anything, and then Lord Haringdon came along. He walked back with me but when we came to where the dog had been it was gone. We went on to the crossroads but we saw no sign of Vi. It was raining hard and we both thought she had been given a lift back to Jessop's Bridge by a passing motorist. Lord Haringdon saw I was upset and very kindly walked back to Laxworthy with me and saw me off by the train. And both he and Lady Agatha have been most awfully good to me—"

Superintendent Lamb looked thoughtfully at his boots. He had heard this story already at second-hand both from Linda's landlady and from the manageress of the Tudor Café. Both women had prefaced the narrative with a significant "She says"—which had made it clear that they doubted Miss Merle's veracity, but when questioned neither had anything very damaging to relate regarding her. She was a quiet well-behaved girl, so far as they knew. Her work at the café, during the time she had been engaged there as a pianist, had kept her out late three nights a week, but on other nights she was always home early and—again, so far as they knew—she had no men friends. And he liked the look of her. Simple, unaffected, no nonsense about her. You couldn't go by looks, though. The Superintendent did not forget that.

"You and Miss Hunter were great friends?"

"Yes."

"You were going to live together at this cottage of yours?"

"Well, I thought we were—but that fell through. Vi changed her mind."

"Were you upset about that?"

"I was rather."

"You've a quick temper, Miss Merle, flare up if you're annoyed, eh?"

"No," she said, "I don't think so. Not specially."

"Well, never mind that now." He closed his notebook. "I'll be glad if you'll come back to Jessop's Bridge now with me. We need your help."

She rose rather uncertainly. Lady Agatha got up too. "Is it usual for the police to take up this sort of case unasked?" she inquired, remembering what David had said on this point. He had been so certain that they would not move until their assistance was invoked.

Superintendent Lamb turned to her. "No, my lady. Miss Hunter, it seems, has no near relations, but the lady she lived with until recently, a friend of many years' standing, came to us."

"Annie Coleman," said Linda. Her heart sank, she hardly knew why. It was natural that Annie should be worried over Violet's disappearance, and perhaps she had done the right thing in going to the police. It was what she—Linda—would have done if Lord Haringdon had not dissuaded her. He had meant well—she was sure of that—but people might wonder. They might even think that she was indifferent to her friend's fate.

Lady Agatha looked troubled. She was wishing more than ever that her nephew had been present. "Will Miss Merle be back for lunch?" she asked.

The Superintendent answered very decidedly. "No, madam."

"I am coming to Jessop's Bridge to do some shopping this afternoon. I can pick her up if you will give me some idea of the time."

"I'm sorry, my lady, but at this stage in our inquiry it will be best for Miss Merle to remain within easy reach. We should be glad if she would return to her lodgings for the present."

"You mean that she is not to come back here?" said the old lady with dignity.

"Well—if you like to put it that way."

Lady Agatha was trembling with indignation. "I never heard of such a thing! This young lady is my guest. I promised Lord Haringdon—"

"Is that so?" he said very drily. "I'm looking forward to a little chat with his lordship when he comes back. You couldn't tell me where he's gone, I suppose, my lady? It might save time in the end."

Lady Agatha drew herself up. "I don't know where he is. But I will inform him of—of everything when I see him, and he will probably take action."

Linda had slipped out of the room to put her things on and pack her suitcase. When she came down into the hall Lady Agatha was there alone.

"That man is outside waiting for you," she said hurriedly. "My dear, what does it mean?"

Linda looked white but she answered steadily. "I don't know. But I've nothing to fear. I've done no harm. Dear Lady Agatha,"—tears came into her eyes—"you've been heavenly to me. I—I'm rather alone. I can't tell you what it meant to me to be here these last few days—"

"You must come to us again." Lady Agatha drew the girl to her and kissed her. "You are not without friends, remember."

While they were all in the library a man from the way-side repair shop where Diana had left her car on Saturday evening had brought it to the door. Diana had seen him arrive for she was nearest the window but she was far too much interested in the Superintendent and his methods to move before she was obliged and it was not until Lamb had gone out to smoke a pipe on the steps while he waited for Linda Merle that she joined Lady Agatha.

"How too exciting!" she said. "But, dear Lady Agatha, what has she done?"

"Nothing."

Diana smiled. "How loyal and splendid of you! I do hope you'll stick up for me like that if ever I get into a scrape. I couldn't quite make out what it was all about but really it almost sounded as if David had run away."

"Rubbish!" aid Lady Agatha angrily.

"Oh, of course. I only said that it sounded like that. Well, my car's outside and I must be off. Good-bye, Lady Agatha, and thanks for everything."

She took advantage of the fact that her hostess had not come out to see her start to speak to the Superintendent, who was smoking his pipe and keeping a wary eye on the exits. It would be possible, as he had noted on his arrival, to slip out by way of the stables.

Diana paused beside him while she drew on her gloves. "Do tell me if all this is what they call making an arrest?" she said softly.

He glanced at the lovely face framed by the silvery fair curls. "No. Just getting information, as you might say. Are you a friend of the family, miss?"

"Yes." She paused. "Dear Lady Agatha is too kind-hearted. She's getting old." She smoothed out a crease in the back of her white doeskin glove. "Of course I know nothing of Miss Merle," she said casually. "I noticed the scratches on her hands—"

The Superintendent gazed after the high-powered car as it vanished down the avenue. He took off his hat and rubbed his head.

It had been so quickly done that he felt almost as if a little knife had actually flashed by him and stuck, quivering, in the door at his back.

Chapter XIV
DAVID COMES HOME

Doctor Saigon saw his wife well away in her friend's car before he paid his customary morning visits to his patients. David, watching from the hillside above, had seen no woman about the place, but there was a nurse, a middle-aged person with a thin worn face and a timid deprecating manner, who accompanied Saigon to the room of old Miss Walsh, the patient who had arrived on the afternoon Lady Agatha had called. She was in bed and seemed drowsy, answering the doctor's questions with murmured monosyllables. When they were out again in the corridor he turned to the nurse.

"She's not to get up."

"But—doctor—isn't it rather weakening? When shall you operate?"

"Not for a few days. Perhaps not at all."

"But—she expects the treatment."

Saigon silenced her with an impatient gesture. "Give her the medicine regularly. That will keep her quiet. Mr. Craddock and Mrs. Lennox too. I want them all to remain in their rooms for the present."

"Very well," she said submissively. She glanced past him towards the farther landing. "What about—am I to—"

"Don't go near!"

She bowed her head. "No."

He waited until she had gone back to Miss Walsh's room and closed the door after her before he went on alone down the corridor.

It was nearly an hour later that David was awakened from a sound sleep by the entrance of his captor. Saigon set the tray he had brought in on the floor, for there was no furniture in the padded room, and relocked the door before he addressed his prisoner.

"You're a good sleeper," he said with a touch of envy.

David sat up and then scrambled to his feet. "Try a night on the Embankment with a couple of *Daily Mails* for blankets," he said grimly. "Well, guv'nor, wot abaht it? You're not going to be 'ard on a poor chap, are you?"

"No, I'm not. I might have sent for the police, but I'm going to let you off. But if I catch you lurking about here again—"

"You won't, guv'nor. I'd be getting along if I 'ad a pair of boots ter fit me. These 'urt my poor feet somethink cruel—"

This was perfectly true for Trask's man, when buying him a pair at a wardrobe dealer's, had miscalculated the size he wore. They had served his purpose, being rubber-soled, but they cramped his toes. Saigon smiled, not pleasantly. "No, my friend. I'm not going to let you out. You can eat that bread and cheese, and drink that glass of beer. Then, as I'm going out in any case, I'll take you a few miles on your road and drop you."

He pointed to the tray. "You must be hungry if your story is true."

David felt a sudden and very unpleasant qualm of doubt. He suspected that something very terrible had happened recently under that roof. If he was right Saigon would stick at nothing to avert discovery. And he was a doctor with, of course, access to deadly drugs. Suppose that, after all, he had seen through his captive's disguise and was playing with him as a cat plays with a mouse before dealing the sharp blow that would make him harmless?

These thoughts passed through his mind as he squatted awkwardly on the floor and took his first bite of the lunch provided for him. It seemed to him that the cheese had a faintly bitter taste but he dared not reject it. He felt Saigon's dark black eyes peering into him and he took pains to play his part, munching noisily and drinking with his mouth full. When he had finished Saigon beckoned to him to follow and took him down the back stairs and out by the butler's pantry.

A closed saloon car had been brought out of the garage. David noticed that newspapers had been placed on the seat so that he should not soil the cushions and also that his dingy camping kit had been found on the hill and packed in a bundle.

Saigon ran the car five miles in the direction of Winchester and then, stopping on a lonely stretch of road, ordered his passenger to get out.

David obeyed. The car was backed and turned and he was left standing on the roadside, dirty, unshaven, ragged, burdened with an unwieldy parcel of dingy bedding, and with only a few pence in his pockets. He had buried his money with his night glasses in a rabbit's burrow before he started on his nocturnal adventure. It was not a pleasant predicament. On the other hand, if the bread and cheese or the beer had been poisoned he would surely have felt some ill effects by now. It was something to have got away from that house with a whole skin. He sat down in the ditch and filled his pipe with the shag tobacco in the tin box that had been displayed with the rest of the contents of his pockets when Saigon bade him turn them out but he did not strike a match. He had remembered what lay hidden underneath. Never mind! He looked up at the blue sky and noticed the towering honeysuckle in the hedge with quiet satisfaction. It was good to be alive.

He had experienced similar sensations more than once during the War, when his battalion was resting in a village behind the lines.

If he had succeeded in getting back unobserved to his camp on the hillside he had meant to return to London by train and shed his disguise at Trask's flat, where he had left his clothes, but that was no longer feasible, and obviously the only thing to be done was to get back to Spinacres and effect an entry without attracting too much attention. A bath and a shave and a change of linen would all be very welcome. He got up with a sigh, for he was stiff and weary and his feet ached, and started on his return journey.

"Good gracious!" Lady Agatha was in the library, having her tea by the fire when her nephew came in. Her knitting, a hopeless mass of dropped stitches, lay on a chair beside her. "I never heard you arrive, David. How tired you look!"

She rang and asked the parlourmaid to bring another cup and saucer.

"Did you know his lordship had come in?"

"No, my lady, not till I heard the bath water running—"

"I'll blow a trumpet next time," said David good-humouredly. He drank his tea with manifest enjoyment. "The first hot drink I've had since Saturday." He set the cup down. Mac, his Aberdeen, scrambled up on to his lap and proceeded to lick his hands industriously all over. "I tell you, Aunt Agatha, it's jolly to be home again. Where's Miss Merle?"

Lady Agatha's cup rattled in the saucer as she replaced it on the tray. "Oh, David, I did so wish you were here. You would have known what to do!"

He looked up quickly, struck by her tone. "What's happened?"

"She's gone. She went this morning. A police superintendent came from Jessop's Bridge and fetched her away."

"Took her away? Why? What for?"

"It seems some other friend of the missing girl has been to the local police and they've taken up the case, and they want Linda to be at hand. I suppose it's all right, but I miss the child, and I could see she did not want to go."

David took a cigarette from the box on the mantelpiece and lit it thoughtfully.

"The superintendent wanted to know where you had gone. He seemed very anxious to meet you."

"He'll meet me all right. I'll buzz along to Jessop's Bridge now."

"I don't like being mixed up with the police," said Lady Agatha. "Policemen are all very well in their place, holding up the traffic at dangerous crossings, and, of course, after a burglary, picking up clues and all that. I had to bring him in here—" She glanced about her as if she was wondering if a spring cleaning would be necessary.

David grinned in spite of himself. "Too bad," he murmured.

"Heaven only knows what people are going to think us. Not that I have ever cared what people thought."

"Nobody need know," he said soothingly.

"Diana Culver went back to Town gloating. She was here the whole time sitting in that chair. I never noticed her until afterwards."

David was startled. "Diana?"

"Of course! I forgot I hadn't told you. She came Saturday night. Her car had broken down on the road very conveniently. She expected to find you here and was extremely annoyed at having let herself in for a Sunday with me and Linda. And, by the way, David, she actually knows Mrs. Saigon. She brought her down and left her at Black Ridge for the week-end."

He nodded. "She's very pretty, Aunt Agatha."

"Who?"

"Saigon's wife."

"You've met her?"

"In a sort of way. I wasn't introduced. It was last night. She was wearing very dinky pyjamas. Yellow satin."

Lady Agatha gasped. "David! You've been there at Black Ridge?"

"Hanging around," he admitted cheerfully, "as a tramp of burglarious proclivities. Saigon caught me but he didn't smell a rat, fortunately for me, and as he didn't quite know what else to do with me he gave me some excellent advice about running straight in future and let me go."

"My dear! Was it necessary to run such frightful risks? If he had called in the police and you had had to admit your identity it would have been a dreadful scandal. The papers would have been full of it. Think of the posters! Arrest of Lord Haringdon!"

"Oh, I knew I was pretty safe with Saigon," he said lightly. "He loves the police even less than you do, Aunt Agatha."

"You think he is mixed up in this mysterious affair? Did you find out anything?"

"I don't know—yet." He threw the end of his cigarette into the fire and stood up. "Don't wait dinner for me."

"Bring her back if you can, David."

He had been turning away but be stopped. "You like her?"

"I do."

"I'm glad," he said quietly. "No, Mac, old fellow. I can't take you."

Chapter XV

THE POLICE AT WORK

Superintendent Lamb was not in when David called at the Jessop's Bridge police station. The subordinate who was in charge during his absence asked him to wait and was obviously disconcerted and uneasy when he declined. "The Superintendent won't be long, my lord. He's just stepped out. He'd be sorry to miss you—"

"That's all right," said David easily, "he won't miss me. I shall come back later."

The police station was in a narrow side street near the busy shopping centre of the town, and David, turning to the right, found himself almost at once opposite the Tudor Café. The shop was closed, but it was one of the nights when dances were held in the room above and he saw lights in the windows and groups of young people, shop girls and typists and clerks, going in by the side door. He passed on and, leaving the crowded High Street for the older quarter of the town, came to Rosemary Passage and the house where Linda Merle lodged. As he stopped at the door he glanced over his shoulder and noticed a man standing in the shadow of the arched gateway to a stone mason's yard opposite, and another man coming along the street behind him.

He rang the bell, after trying the door and finding that the latch was down. The door was open when he came before. The landlady, a stout red-faced woman a suspicious manner, admitted him grudgingly. It was clear from her manner that she had a grievance. "Seventeen stairs up from my kitchen, and the sooner it's done with and I'm quit of such the better I'll be pleased. I've kep' this 'ouse as it should be kep' all these years. No carryings-on, and no bobbies nosing round neither, and if you're one of them you can tell your boss I said so."

"Too bad," said David sympathetically. "Were they here long?"

"Best part of an hour, and a Sunday evening too. They wouldn't have got past the doorstep if I'd been in, but I was at chapel. I didn't half give it to our Gladys for being so silly-like. Who have you come for?"

"Miss Merle."

The woman, who had grown almost friendly, became hostile at once. "Best go up then," she said offensively. "You'll find her packing. She leaves in the morning."

As David went up the three flights to the top floor his lean brown face was graver than usual. Evidently Linda's rooms had been searched by the police while she was it Spinacres. He had seen for himself that a watch was being kept on the home, and be rather suspected that he had been followed from the police nation. There had been the scene in the library described to him by Lady Agatha, and there was the angry landlady. "A rotten shame!" he muttered. He had reached the top landing. Her door was dosed. He had been about to knock but he checked himself and listened. The sound of a stifled sob and a long-drawn pitiful sigh of fatigue and misery, and then the scraping of a box being drawn along the uncarpeted boards.

He waited a moment and then rapped gently. He heard footsteps retreating to the inner room and then returning, and a key was turned in the lock.

"Lord Haringdon! Oh, do come in!" Linda said thankfully.

He looked down at the tear-stained face, touched by her eager welcome. "I got back this afternoon," he said. "I'm afraid you've had rather a thin time. The local police have got hold of some mare's nest apparently. Don't worry. I'm going to have a heart to heart talk with this Superintendent chap. You're busy"—he glanced about the disordered room.

"I've got to leave in the morning. The landlady says I've disgraced her house. The police came here yesterday evening and went through all Violet's things and mine too. I"—her lips were trembling—"that man frightens me. He kept me all day at the station asking questions. It seemed as if he didn't believe me. It was Annie Coleman went to the police. I know she thinks it was somehow my fault that Vi disappeared."

"Never mind," David said soothingly. He saw that she was worn out and he was not surprised for he had been present often at the informal examination of witnesses by the police and he knew what an ordeal it might be. "He's on the wrong tack at present, I fancy. I think I can promise you that it will be all right after I've seen him. Aunt Agatha sent her love and I'm to bring you back with me if I can."

Linda's tired eyes filled with tears. "Really? She's too kind. She's been an angel to me. You—you haven't found out anything about Vi?"

"Nothing definite, but there's something very queer about the house that little man came from."

"You haven't come across him again?" she said.

"No, I haven't." He looked at the watch on his wrist. "I'll go back to the station now. If I'm not back by ten you go to bed and get a good night's rest. I'll come for you in the morning in that case."

"I don't know how to thank you—"

"You needn't. This is doing me good. I was getting rusty—" He gripped her hand hard and was away again, leaving her to wonder what he meant.

On his way back to the police station he amused himself by darting off up side streets and going round by a churchyard. If he was being followed he would give his attendant shadow a run for his money. He was received, with evident relief at his appearance, by the subordinate official he had seen before and shown directly into the Superintendent's room.

Superintendent Lamb, large and somewhat plethoric, eyed him curiously. "Lord Haringdon? Will you sit down? Been away for the week-end, I understand? May I ask where?"

"You may ask certainly," said David genially. "It's chilly for the time of year, isn't it? I'm afraid we're going to have another wet summer."

The Superintendent frowned. "I wouldn't advise you to take that tone, Lord Haringdon. This is a serious matter."

"I quite agree," said David. "When you brought Miss Merle away from Spinacres this morning, did you inform her that she was not compelled to come? You needn't answer me. I know you didn't. If I'd been there you wouldn't have pulled it off."

The Superintendent listened quietly and seemed to be weighing his words. "Is that so? Well, it's true that I couldn't have fetched her away without a warrant, but if the young lady is really as anxious as she says to find her friend, why should she object to giving us all the assistance in her power?"

David looked at him squarely. "You treated her as a friendly witness? I found her just now crying. It looked to me as if you'd been putting on the screw a bit."

They were not alone in the room. A young constable in uniform had followed David in and seated himself unobtrusively near the door. David glanced round at him. "Are you taking it all down in shorthand? Good."

The Superintendent cleared his throat. "What is your interest in this affair, Lord Haringdon? How long have you known these two girls?"

"I met Miss Merle for the first time Sunday week. I don't know the other at all."

"And yet Miss Merle tells me that you have been actively engaged these past few days in trying to trace her missing friend."

"Yes."

"And Miss Merle has been staying at Spinacres with Lady Agatha Chant. A girl who has been employed at the Tudor Café."

David nodded. "Yes. I thought she'd be safer there."

"Safer from what, Lord Haringdon?"

The young man shrugged his shoulders. "There you have me. I don't quite know—yet. But I'm motoring her back there tonight."

"No," said the Superintendent.

David jumped up. "What the hell do you mean by that?"

"What I say, Lord Haringdon. I can't lose sight of Miss Merle at this stage in my inquiry. You don't seem to realise the seriousness of your own position. Why didn't you come to us before? We shall require a full account of your movements on Sunday week. You were noticed at Laxworthy Junction seeing Miss Merle off. You were with her that evening. That is indubitable."

"Of course it is," said David irritably. "She's told you what happened, I suppose."

"Yes. She says you've been extraordinarily kind and helpful. Do you always exert yourself so much for comparative strangers?"

David had recovered his temper. After all it was natural that the Superintendent should be puzzled. It was time to enlighten him.

"No," he said, "but the problem—for it is a problem—interested me professionally. I'll tell you a secret, Lamb, and I rely on you to keep it, at any rate for the present. After I was demobbed in nineteen eighteen I joined the Metropolitan police and presently was drafted into the Criminal Investigation Department. When my uncle died the family lawyers advertised for me. I saw my Chief and talked it over with him. I did not want to give up my job but he seemed to think it might be my duty. The end of it was that I came down here to see if I could stick it. Sir Henry was very good about it. I haven't actually resigned, I'm only on leave at present. He only stipulated that I should keep it dark. Obviously, if I came back to my work at the Yard a newspaper stunt about a peerage for a policeman would cramp my style. A few of my personal friends know, but they can be relied on to say nothing."

"Your name was Chant. Not the Chant who caught the woman who stole the Beraardine pearl pendant?"

"That was a bit of luck really," said David.

"Luck be blowed!" said the large man emphatically and he extended a hand like a leg of mutton. David shook it. "That was a smart bit of work."

"You see now? I was settling down at Spinacres, or trying to, but when this happened on my very doorstep, so to speak, I simply had to have a go at it."

"I understand. You've been keeping an eye on her. But it would have been better to come to us sooner."

"Perhaps," said David. He looked at the other. "You've got a man watching the house where she lodges tonight. What's the idea? Don't you believe her story?"

"It lacks corroboration," said Lamb.

"Oh, come! What about mine? I met her along the road. She was evidently distressed about the dog. She was talking to a little fellow employed at Black Ridge. He told her it was no use applying there. In fact he said worse than useless—"

"That's all right," said Lamb. "But you didn't see the dog, and you didn't see the other girl. How do you know there was a dog? She might have invented the whole story."

"I saw the smear of blood on the road."

"A road through the woods. A rabbit might have been killed there by a hawk or a fox."

David bit his lip. "Possible, of course. But the girl's as straight as a die."

The older man grunted. "See here, Lord Haringdon, before we go any farther I'd like to ring up Sir Henry and verify your statement. You won't be offended, I hope. I don't doubt you. It's just a matter of form."

"Quite right," said David. He took a cigarette from his case and lit it while the Superintendent waited for his call to be put through to Victoria 7000. The ensuing conversation was brief but it sufficed to satisfy Lamb. He hung up the receiver after replying with a deferential "good night, Sir Henry, and thank you—" to his interlocutor at the Yard.

"I'm glad," he said frankly. "I—well—I hardly knew what to think. I couldn't find an atom of evidence to connect you with the violinist at the Tudor Café. Of course when a girl is as pretty as she was, poor soul, there'll be men of all sorts after her."

"The owner of the Tudor Café was one. He calls himself Smith but his real name is Ebermann. I saw him on Friday and he admitted that he had persuaded her to leave here and go up to London. He has an interest in several places up West. I suspected him for a while, but she was coming to him of her own accord."

"That meant letting Miss Merle down," said Lamb. "Yes"

There was a knock at the door and a constable put his head in.

"Miss Coleman is here, sir. Will you see her now?"

"Yes."

"May I stay?" asked David.

He saw that the other hesitated, but he answered, "Yes, if you like. If you sit back there in the shadow and seem to be writing she won't notice you. I don't want her attention distracted. She's not easy to manage."

It had been growing dusk in the room while they talked. Now the Superintendent switched on the green shaded lamp on his desk.

"Good evening, Miss Coleman."

She came in briskly and took the chair he indicated. She had been doing her shopping and carried a string bag full of groceries which she placed on the floor beside her.

"Well," she said, "have you got her?"

"Miss Merle? She is at her lodgings."

"She'll slip between your fingers if you're not careful."

"We must be sure, Miss Coleman, more sure than we are now, before we make an arrest."

"What more do you want?" she demanded. There was a fierce impatience in her voice and manner that betrayed how her nerves had suffered. "I can't sleep at night for thinking of my poor little Vi. She was safe with me. I waited on her hand and foot and took care of her, and then that Linda Merle came along and enticed her away and led her into temptation. Dancing, late nights. The primrose path. The primrose path to everlasting fire! And she had the nerve to come to me—to me!—to ask if I knew what had become of her! I told her off, I can tell you. But it set me thinking. I said to myself 'You can't throw sand in my eyes, my lady! You went off in the morning with Vi and you came back at night without her. If anyone on this earth knows where she is now it is you!'"

"Yes, yes," said the Superintendent. "So you came to the police. Quite right, Miss Coleman. Now—no need to get excited. I want you just to look at this. Do you recognise it?"

He took something from a drawer of his desk and laid it on a sheet of notepaper. She rose and bent over the desk to peer at it through her spectacles. The broad, rather flat face was twitching with nervous agitation.

"Oh, dear! Oh, yes! That was Vi's engagement ring. She was engaged two years ago to a veterinary surgeon here—Mr. Lovell. After his death she took to wearing the ring on a thin gold chain round her neck. She always wore it. Always. The stones were valuable. Opals and diamonds. It was an old ring that had belonged to the young man's mother. Where did you find it?"

"Never mind that at present, Miss Coleman. You are quite sure of your facts?"

"Absolutely. I could swear to that ring. Besides, if you look inside you'll see he had her initials engraved inside. V. H."

"Thank you," said the Superintendent. "Then that will be all tonight, Miss Coleman. We'll notify you if we need any further help in identifying—anything."

"You've no news—no good news for me?" she said huskily.

"Nothing at present. You'll hear in time. We're obliged to you—"

She sighed heavily as she stooped, a thick ungainly figure, to pick up her bag of groceries. "Those that are responsible should be punished. That's what I say. And I won't rest until they are. You've only to send for me. I'll come any time."

When the door had closed behind her David returned to the circle of lamplight. "Where did you find the ring, Lamb?"

The Superintendent looked at him gravely. "When I searched Miss Merle's rooms last night. Hidden among her handkerchiefs at the back of one of her drawers."

"Are you certain they were not the other girl's?"

"Certain. They occupied separate rooms."

"She'll be able to explain!" cried David.

Lamb shook his head. "I showed it to her this afternoon. She denied all knowledge of it—that is, of how it came to be where I found it. She admitted that she knew Violet Hunter wore it on a chain about her neck. I'm sorry."

David was silent for a moment. Then he said: "After all, we don't know that the girl has come to any harm. It seems to me quite likely that if she planned to go off with some man or other she would stop wearing this ring, the reminder of a past affair, and she might leave it in her friend's drawer as a parting gift. That's a working hypothesis."

"Yes," said the Superintendent grimly, "but it doesn't square with Linda Merle's own story. Is it likely that any girl in her senses would arrange to be picked up and carried off in the clothes she stood up in—which were not even her best clothes—at a place which she had already passed and to which she only returned by chance? But I admit that we can't make an arrest until we have more material evidence that there has been foul play." David began to speak and checked himself. He dared not show his hand until he knew a little more about the cards he held. He rose. "I wish you'd let me take Miss Merle back with me to Spinacres. I believe in her and so does my aunt. I give you my word that she'll be there if you want her. She won't run away. I don't like leaving her at those lodgings. The landlady's antagonistic and has told her to clear out tomorrow anyway."

The Superintendent looked annoyed. "That won't do. She'll have to keep her for a day or so. I'll send a man round to talk to her."

"Mayn't she come to us?"

"No." The Superintendent spoke more curtly than he had done since the beginning of the interview. "And, see here, Lord Haringdon. The local police have got this case in hand. We see no necessity to call in the Yard, at present at any rate. I shall see the Chief Constable in the morning and I fancy he'll agree. I'm not complaining, Lord Haringdon. You happened to be on the spot and naturally you were interested, but I must say quite frankly that from now on I hope you'll leave me to carry on my own way."

"I understand," said David. He would have liked to have closed their interview on a friendlier note, but it was clear that Lamb resented the fact that it was not he—Haringdon—who had called on the local police. And he had not gained his point and got leave to take Linda home with him. He hated to leave her where she was, with a hostile landlady and under police surveillance, hut there was no help for it. In any case it was past ten when he left the station and she would have ceased to expect him.

Late as it was he found Lady Agatha sitting up for him. "You haven't brought her? My poor boy, how tired you look!"

"Oh, I shall sleep like a log," he said. "I shall be off again tomorrow. I rely on you to do what you can for her, go and see her."

"If you wish it, David."

"I do wish it. That local fellow is a dunderhead. He warned me off but I'm hanging on whether he likes it or not. Be nice to her, Aunt Agatha. Tell her I'm doing my best. She—she'd been crying when I saw her tonight."

He said nothing of the ring, but while he was speaking he seemed to see it still sparkling on the Superintendent's coarse and calloused palm. Opals. The unlucky stone.

Chapter XVI
THE DARKEST HOUR

Linda was up and boiling a kettle for her tea on the gas ring when the woman of the house appeared. She looked up quickly, mindful of what the landlady had threatened to do if she had not left by nine o'clock.

"I'm packed and ready, Mrs. Biggs. My friends will be fetching me. But what about Miss Hunter's things? Will you take charge of them until she comes back or sends for them?"

"There's some one waiting below for you now," said Mrs. Biggs coldly. "You'd better leave your suitcase and box. They'll be called for later, it seems. My 'ouse is not my own nowadays, nor my wishes considered."

Linda drank her tea hastily, put on her hat and coat, and ran down the stairs. Lord Haringdon was so good, she must not keep him waiting. But the car outside was not his but a hired taxi, and a young policeman who was standing by the curb opened the door for her.

She shrank back. "The station again? I told them all I knew yesterday—"

"Step in, please."

She glanced up at his impassive face and realised that it would be futile to argue. He had to carry out his orders. She got into the taxi and he followed. The little crowd of idlers that had collected scattered as the driver sounded his horn.

"Where are you taking me?"

"I wouldn't talk if I was you, miss. The less you say the better."

"Oh—very well—"

They had turned down the High Street and crossed the bridge. Some time before they reached their destination the girl realised that they were going to her cottage, the place that for weeks past had been the centre of all her activities. The taxi stopped at the garden gate. Superintendent Lamb himself was there to open the door and help her out.

"Thank you for coming, Miss Merle. I shall be glad of your assistance." He unlatched the gate she had painted green the last time she was there and they walked up the brick path to the cottage together.

"You expect to find a clue to Vi's disappearance here?" she said rather faintly. This man had bullied her yesterday. She feared him as she had never feared anyone in her life before. He seemed in a more genial mood this morning but she knew that at any moment he might bark out one of those questions she had found so hard to answer.

"You came here every day last month, painting, distempering the walls, and so forth," he said, "saving the wages of a handy man, eh?"

"Yes. I had to be careful—"

"But you haven't been since the day you and Miss Hunter quarrelled, Sunday week, that is. The green paint you were using has dried in the pot," he said conversationally.

"No. I haven't been since," she admitted.

"How's that? You wanted to get the place ready and move in, didn't you? Why waste ten days?"

"Lord Haringdon asked me not to come for a while."

"Why?"

Her colour faded. He was beginning again. "I—I don't know. He seemed to think there might be danger—"

"Danger?"

"On the road. It's a lonely road. Until we knew what happened to Vi—" She faltered.

He stopped in the little trellised porch, with his hand on the latch of the door, and looked down at her with—yes—with unmistakable aversion.

"We know what happened to Violet Hunter, Miss Merle."

She began to tremble. "You—you—"

"Come in," he said. He opened the door and motioned her to pass into the living-room before him. She looked about her. There were the two packing cases which she and Violet had used as chairs, and a row of paint pots and cans of distemper, and on a shelf a tin of biscuits and the spirit lamp and some odds and ends of crockery that had sufficed for their picnic lunches and teas. The door leading into the kitchen at the back was closed.

"If you know"—she said—"where is Vi? Is she—all right?"

"Miss Merle," he said, "on Sunday—this last Sunday—you wrote to the local house agents from whom, or rather through whom, you bought this cottage, to inform them that it was again for sale. Why was that?"

"I didn't feel I could carry on alone. Vi told me before she—before that night—that she had changed her mind about living here and helping me. She wanted to go to London. I told you yesterday that that was what we quarrelled about."

"You've nothing more to tell me, Miss Merle?"

"No."

"Then I will tell you something," he said. "Violet Hunter is here. She is in this kitchen, on the other side of this door. It's locked, you see, and I've got the key. I thought we might find her not so very far off, and we did!"

The young constable who had brought the girl was standing just outside on the brick path. Linda, looking from one to the other in her bewilderment, met his solemn gaze. Violet—found—and waiting in the kitchen! But—how queer to lock her in! And why did both these men stare at her like that, with a kind of awful curiosity? Her lips had gone dry and she had to moisten them before she could speak again. "I—I don't understand—"

"You dug up the patch of garden at the back, didn't you? We found the new spade you bought at Broughton's in the High Street in the shed and a bag of grass seed."

"Yes—"

"Two of my men dug over the garden again this morning. They started as soon as it was light, and they found her a couple of hours ago. Graves must be dug deeper than that if the dead are to sleep sound."

The young policeman started forward. "Look out! She's going to fall—" He was in time to catch her as she stumbled. "What shall I do?"

"Lay her down on the floor. There's a well at the back. Go and draw some water to sprinkle over her face," said the Superintendent gruffly.

As Linda returned to consciousness she could hear their voices, sounding far off but distinct.

"Perhaps I shouldn't have said that, but she don't deserve to be pitied. Clever, but not quite clever enough, like most of them. That story about the dog never went down with me."

"She's coming to. Her lips are not so blue. I needn't have made her hair so wet, but my hand shook. You—you're quite sure she did it?"

"That's enough now. Stand back—"

Linda was trying to get up from the floor. He helped her to her feet and made her sit on one of the packing cases. "Better now? That's right. Now you needn't say anything if you don't want to, and anything you do say will be taken down by the constable in his notebook and may be used in evidence against you; but it always pays to tell the truth, and I'd advise you to make a statement," said the Superintendent.

Linda shivered. The young policeman, in his agitation, had drenched her with water. "I'm cold," she murmured.

"Do you want to see her?"

She looked up at him dimly. "See her? I thought—I thought you said she was dead. Vi! She was only twenty-three. And so pretty!"

She fumbled for her handkerchief to wipe away the tears that were running down her face. "She went back to the crossroads to get help from a passing motorist, and I went on and met that little man who seemed frightened and wouldn't do anything, and then Lord Haringdon."

"You stick to that?"

"That's the truth! Ask Lord Haringdon."

"He only knows what you told him. Very well. The taxi's there, Barlow? Take her back to the station. You'll be detained, Miss Merle, pending the issue of a warrant for your arrest."

"Arrest! What for? I haven't done anything!" she cried. Instinctively she looked towards the door. Oh, to get away from these men, to be free!

"No use," he said. "You'll have to go through with it now. See that she has some dinner, Barlow, and a cup of tea—"

He watched them go down the path together and enter the taxi before he unlocked the door to the back kitchen and went in. The police surgeon had just finished his examination and replaced the piece of coarse sacking over the still figure that lay in the middle of the room. The little lattice window faced east and the morning sunshine was streaming in. The brick floor was covered with the muddy footmarks of the men who had carried what they had found in from the garden. There was a strong smell of carbolic.

"You've done, doctor?"

"As much as I can here. You're having her removed to the mortuary? What about the inquest?"

"Tomorrow, if I can get the coroner."

"Right. I can carry out the post-mortem this afternoon."

"What was the cause of death, in your opinion?"

"There are finger marks on her throat. Some one tried to strangle her. I don't say she was strangled. Death was probably due to heart failure caused by shock."

"Murder," said the Superintendent.

"Oh, yes." The doctor had been washing his hands in a bucket of water. He wiped them carefully on his handkerchief. "Some one will hang for this, I imagine, Lamb. You'll see to that, eh?"

"I'll do my best," said the other grimly.

Chapter XVII
THE UNWELCOME VISIT

The sun had set when Colonel Bellingham turned in at the gates of Spinacres. His usually cheerful face wore a worried expression, for he had come on a disagreeable errand. He was accompanied by Superintendent Lamb.

The grey-haired parlourmaid who answered the bell glanced quickly from one to the other as he asked to see Lord Haringdon. "His lordship is not at home."

Lamb intervened. "Where is he?"

"I couldn't say. If you'll step in, sir, I'll inform Lady Agatha." She addressed herself pointedly to the Colonel, ignoring his companion. Lamb grunted his dissatisfaction. He detested well-trained servants and their habit of taking refuge from him behind formulas.

They were not left long in the hall. The maid came back and showed them into the drawing-room. The lamps had not yet been lit or the curtains drawn. Lady Agatha was standing by one of the windows opening on the lawn, watching the stars that shone out, one by one, in the quiet dusk, over the wooded hills. They had no means of guessing her thoughts, for her face, when she turned to meet them, was but a pale colour in the growing darkness.

"Colonel Bellingham—won't you sit down? And you too—" The Superintendent took the chair indicated.

He had noticed as he crossed the polished floor between the rugs that his boots creaked.

The Colonel cleared his throat. He and his wife had generally dined two or three times a year at Spinacres and he had sometimes been asked to shoot over the coverts with the late Lord Haringdon. He had not yet met the nephew. They had exchanged calls but neither had been at home, and he and Mrs. Bellingham had been considering the advisability of giving a luncheon party and inviting the young man and his aunt.

"It was Lord Haringdon we wished to see—on a matter of business—"

"My nephew went up to Town this morning. He did not say when he would be back."

"Do you know where he's staying?"

"I do not."

"That's awkward," said the Colonel. "The inquest opens tomorrow and he'll be wanted as a witness—"

"What inquest?" she asked sharply, "a witness to what?"

"I beg your pardon. Of course you don't know. It's extremely unpleasant, Lady Agatha. I'm afraid I'm going to give you a shock—"

"Go on," she said.

"I understand that you have been very kind to Miss Merle and that she spent a couple of days under this roof at your invitation."

"Yes. What of it?"

The Colonel coughed again. "The body of the girl who lived with her, the girl who disappeared ten days ago, has been found buried in the back garden of the cottage—Miss Merle's cottage. Naturally there must be an inquest, and as Lord Haringdon met Miss Merle farther down the road on the Sunday evening—the last day on which the other girl was seen alive, and heard her account of what happened he will be wanted to give evidence."

"I see," she said. "Then the poor thing was actually murdered? How horrible! Then David was wrong—"

She checked herself.

"Your nephew? What about?"

"He had a theory of his own," said Lady Agatha. "Miss Merle had asked him to help find her friend, and he has been trying to. That is why he has gone up to Town. I wanted him to go to the local police some days ago, but he preferred to work independently."

"An amateur sleuth, eh?" said Colonel Bellingham.

"Not exactly that, sir," said the Superintendent unexpectedly. "He asked me to keep it dark and I said I would but it's only right you should know as things are turning out. Lord Haringdon joined the Metropolitan police force in nineteen eighteen, after he was demobbed, and when his uncle, the late lord, died a couple of months ago, he was an Inspector in the C.I.D. He told me yesterday when I asked him why the hell—begging your pardon, ma'am—he was butting into this. I rang up the Yard and verified it."

"Dear me!" said the Colonel. "You knew, of course, Lady Agatha."

She shook her head. "No. He never told me what he had been doing. Now I understand why he laughed yesterday when I said I didn't like policemen."

The Superintendent's chair creaked under him protestingly.

"We haven't called in the Yard, and if we had I presume that his lordship has left the Force now. We want him, and we're going to have him as a witness. No more than that."

There was a pause. Lady Agatha sat very upright on the settee, with her hands folded in her lap. Colonel Bellingham was evidently anxious to be friendly but she was not so sure of the Superintendent, and she had long since learned the value of silence as a weapon of defence.

The Colonel coughed again. "There will be some account of this dreadful business in the local press tomorrow, and, no doubt, in the London papers. It has unusual features which will give it prominence. That should bring him home even if we can't reach him by any other channel." He paused again. "This is a very serious matter, Lady Agatha. Are you sure you can't get at him?"

"He will come back, as you say, when he sees the papers," she answered. "I suppose the inquest can be adjourned if he does not return in time to give his evidence."

"We must leave it like that then," said the Colonel, rising.

Lady Agatha bethought herself. "That poor child! She was out this morning when I called at her lodgings. Does she know about this?"

"She knows."

"It must have been a fearful shock. Colonel Bellingham, you really must let me have her here while the inquest is being held. I'll bring her in punctually at the time agreed upon."

The Colonel was startled. "My dear lady—"

"You are the Chief Constable! if you say she can come—"

"My dear Lady Agatha, I am afraid you have not grasped the situation. The thing is *sub judice* and I don't want to prejudice you, but, if you take my advice, you won't identify yourself in any way with Miss Merle."

"What on earth are you talking about?"

It was Lamb who rejoined with his accustomed bluntness. "She's being detained on suspicion, my lady."

"You imagine she had something to do with her friend's death?"

"We're not satisfied with her story."

"Absurd!" said Lady Agatha scathingly. "I never heard of anything so ridiculous!"

The Colonel stiffened. "Appearances are not in her favour." He did not relish this plain speaking. He took a step towards the door. "Come, Lamb. Good evening, Lady Agatha."

"One moment," she said. "Can't you trust me if I make myself responsible for her? I promise she won't run away. Think of what this means to her, the stigma if she is innocent, as I am convinced she must be. I want to save her that!"

"My dear lady, are you wise? Would Lord Haringdon approve of this quixotism? It will mean very unpleasant publicity. And you met this young woman less than ten days ago and have only heard what she chose to tell you about herself. Ask yourself if it isn't possible that you have been deceived?"

"It is possible," she said slowly. "I wish David were here, but as he is not I must do what I think right. Please, please let me have her. I give you my word of honour that you will not regret it."

Bellingham hesitated. He would have been glad to oblige Lady Agatha. "What do you say, Lamb?"

"No," said the Superintendent.

The Colonel acquiesced. "I'm sorry, but I think the Superintendent's right. The matter is too serious. I may say the young woman will be kept under medical supervision while she is in our—ah—charge—for her own sake, you know. She will be kindly treated, I assure you."

"Is there nothing I can do for her?"

"You can engage a solicitor to look after her interests and represent her at the inquest and the police inquiry."

"I'll do that. Of course. Why didn't I think of it before? I'll ring up James Pettigrew. Good night, Colonel Bellingham." She rang the bell. "Parker will see you out. Good night, Superintendent."

When she had seen the visitors safely off the premises the parlourmaid brought in the lamps. The events of the last few days had been eagerly canvassed in the servants' hall. All agreed that there was something wrong, and Parker and cook were of opinion that it was "all along of that Mrs. Culver." Parker, who had been thirty years with the family, was genuinely fond of her mistress and there was real feeling in her voice when she exclaimed, "You do look bad, my lady—if you'll excuse my mentioning it. Can I get anything for you?"

"I am a little upset," Lady Agatha admitted. "My sal volatile, Parker. You'll find the bottle on my dressing-table." She leaned back and closed her eyes. "I'm an old woman, too old for this sort of thing. I wish my nephew had not gone away just now."

"Could I telephone to his lordship to come back, my lady?"

"No. But you might ring up Mr. Pettigrew presently. You know his number. Tell me when you have got through—"

She shivered a little as she sat, after drinking the sal volatile, drawing the white woollen shawl Parker had been thoughtful enough to bring down, more closely about her shoulders. She had faced the two men bravely but now she was feeling the reaction. Murder. The word reminded her of the splash of a stone dropping in a deep well. Out of light into darkness. That poor young thing with her pretty face and her bright hair. The loveliest red, Linda had said. And now they thought that Linda—

She shivered again, glancing about her involuntarily. The farther end of the long room was in shadow. She would ask Parker presently to bring another lamp, and perhaps even to come and sit with her. Linda! Impossible. Women did not do such things. And yet, years ago when she was quite a girl she had been taken to Madame Tussaud's. She seemed to remember that there had been women in the Chamber of Horrors. A woman called Manning. She had been hanged in black satin, and black satin had been banned for a generation. And there were others. Not impossible, therefore. But the motive—she sighed impatiently—jealousy—but Linda had never shown a trace of it. A generous nature, or she—Lady Agatha—was no judge.

Parker came in. "I've got through, my lady. Will you come?" Lady Agatha went out to the telephone in the hall.

CHAPTER XVIII
THE INQUEST

THE NEXT MORNING there were columns with scare headlines in most of the London papers, and the local weekly, the Jessop's Bridge *Gazette*, which happened to come out on that day, displayed a poster on which "Tuttleford Flower Show. Sweetpea Awards" had been left out to make room for "Tragic Discovery in Cottage Garden. Girl's Terrible End." It became known that the inquest was to be opened at the old Guildhall at two and a large crowd collected some time before the doors were opened to admit the few who could find places in the narrow space allotted to the public. Mr. Pettigrew eyed that jostling throng coldly. He had come because Lady Agatha was one of his oldest friends and a highly respected client of his firm, but this sort of thing, as he told himself, was not in his line. A hatchet-faced young man approached him tentatively.

"Mr. Pettigrew? I am Stephen Hargreaves. I understand that you want me to represent Miss Merle here and later, if need be."

"Yes."

"I haven't had a chance to see her yet—" He broke off. "Here's the coroner—"

The jury were sworn in and the coroner addressed them briefly.

"You have been called here, gentlemen, to inquire into the circumstances under which the deceased young woman, Violet Hunter, met with her death. There is no possible doubt that she was the victim of foul play. Her body was found yesterday morning by the police in the garden of a cottage on the main road to Southampton about half a mile beyond the spot where another, a by-road, branches off through the woods towards Laxworthy. According to one of the witnesses whose evidence we shall hear presently Miss Hunter was last seen alive on this road at dusk, that is to say, at about seven o'clock, the Sunday before last. I have an ordnance map here which we may find useful when we try to visualise the—ah—background of this tragedy. And now it is our painful duty to view the body—"

The jury, shepherded by two of the policemen on duty in the hall, retired through a door at the back and presently reappeared with pale shocked faces. The proceedings were resumed, but now Mr. Pettigrew could hear through intervening doors a sound of hammering which he had no difficulty in interpreting.

Evidence of identification followed, the first witness called being Miss Annie Coleman, who deposed that she knew the deceased well. The deceased had come when she was quite a little child with her mother to lodge with Miss Coleman and her mother and had remained in her house until the previous autumn. She was then engaged to play the violin at a local café and a young woman who had come there as a pianist persuaded her to leave home and share lodgings with her.

"It was against my wish," concluded Miss Coleman. "The deceased was delicate and needed care, which she had from me. I knew it would turn out badly."

Annie Coleman had left her handbag and umbrella on the bench where she had been sitting with the other witnesses. In her ready-made mourning, with her broad face discoloured and swollen with crying, she gained the sympathy of all who knew how devoted she had been to the dead girl, and the coroner spoke kindly to her as she turned to leave the witness box. "Your distress is very natural. We are sorry for you, Miss Coleman."

The next witness to be called was one of the policemen who had searched the cottage and dug up the plot of freshly turned earth at the back. He described the finding of the body of Violet Hunter.

The coroner glanced up from his writing now and again to ask a question. "Was it far below the surface?"

"No, sir. Barely two feet down."

There had been some shuffling and scraping of chairs at first in the court, but now the silence was absolute. "What was the position of the body?"

"Lying on its left side, sir, with the knees drawn up and the hands clenched. The head and shoulders were wrapped in a holland overall."

"A holland overall." He paused a moment. The coroner's pen scratching over the paper was distinctly audible, that and an occasional sharply drawn breath. "It's here, sir, if you or the jury should wish to see it. It's stained with earth and smeared with the paint that had been used on the doors and windows of the cottage, and it's marked L.M."

"Leave it there, please, on the table. We will now hear the medical evidence. Call Doctor Hallett."

The evidence of the police surgeon was listened to with an equally close attention. He had examined the body of the deceased and had found bruises on the arms and wrists and on the throat. The latter was considerably swollen and discoloured. Death was due to heart failure from shock caused by what he should describe as attempted strangulation.

"She was not actually strangled?"

"Not quite, I should say. The case seems parallel with that of Desdemona."

"How's that?"

"Desdemona was not smothered. She was able to speak after the attack upon her. She—too, died of shock resulting from injuries."

"I see. Thank you. Could you form any idea of when death took place?"

"It is difficult to say, but certainly some days ago. A week or more."

"There were no other marks of violence than those you have mentioned?"

"None."

"Thank you. That will do, Doctor Hallett. Call Linda Merle."

Linda had been sitting a little apart from the other witnesses at one end of the bench reserved for them in the well of the court. Hargreaves rose hastily, and, leaving his place beside Mr. Pettigrew, went over and spoke to her in low tones. She looked up at him and her pale face brightened perceptibly. "It's very kind of Lady Agatha, but I only have to tell the truth—"

She was visibly eager to enter the witness box, and Hargreaves, realising that her obvious willingness to speak might make a good impression, said no more but returned to his seat. It was evident both to him and to Mr. Pettigrew that, in spite of the fact that she was virtually under arrest, she had not yet realised the awful danger in which she stood and clung to the illusion that she had but to tell her tale to be believed.

When she had taken the oath the coroner kept her waiting a moment while he fixed another nib in his pen.

"Now," he said, "you spent Sunday week at your cottage with the deceased?"

"Yes."

"Will you tell us what happened?"

"I did some painting of the doors and window frames, and Vi fixed on some of the hooks for the window curtains. We had a picnic lunch and tea, and left soon after six to walk to Laxworthy Junction."

"Were you on good terms?"

"I'm afraid not very. We had had a quarrel, and we had not made it up, but when we found the poor dog on the road we forgot about that—at least I did."

"What was the cause of the quarrel?"

"Vi told me she had changed her mind about helping me run the cottage as a tea garden, and that some one had offered her a post in London. I was angry because I thought she might have told me before and that she had been sly about it. I'm awfully sorry now, but I know I lost my temper. There was another reason, too. I had rather persuaded her to leave Miss Coleman's house and I felt more or less responsible for her."

"You lost your temper," said the coroner. "What then, Miss Merle?"

"We had walked about a mile on our way and had left the main road when we found a dog which seemed to have been run over lying on the road. Its forelegs were hurt but I thought something could be done for it. It was too heavy for us to lift and I thought the best thing would be for Vi to go back to the main road and stop the first car that passed, while I went on to see if I could get help that way. I never saw her again."

"Yes," said the coroner. His tone was noncommittal. "About the overall. Was it yours?"

"Yes. I had been wearing it. I left it rolled up in a corner of the kitchen."

"The dog was the occasion of your parting from the deceased. I understand that when you returned to the spot where you had found him he was gone?"

"Yes."

"So that no one but yourself actually saw the animal?"

"Vi did. She was upset too, though she was not so fond of dogs as I am—"

"I meant no one living, Miss Merle. That will do, I think. It is growing late, and I gather that the police would be glad of a little more time. We will adjourn, gentlemen of the jury, until next Tuesday at eleven."

He rose, and the court rose with him. There was a rustling of papers and a subdued murmur of conversation as the doors were opened. Hargreaves turned to the old lawyer. His thin face looked anxious. "Lord Haringdon met her on the road, didn't he? He will corroborate her story, I suppose."

"We don't know where he is."

A rather dour-looking woman in a close old-fashioned bonnet and cloak was shepherding Linda through a side door. Hargreaves hurried after them and came back in a few minutes.

"That was a wardress of Aylesford prison for women. They are taking her there tonight. She is to appear before the Bench on Monday, the Superintendent tells me, charged with murder."

"Oh, Lord!" groaned Pettigrew.

"I'm to be allowed to see her tomorrow," pursued the young barrister; "meanwhile I'd like to hear a little more about the case."

"Of course. I'm staying at Spinacres. Lady Agatha asked me to bring you along. This is a black business, Hargreaves. I wish to heaven I could keep my clients out of it. Not a soul in that court believed her!"

They were out in the market square now. He saw one of the young men who had sat scribbling at the reporters' table bolting into the post office and groaned again. "The publicity! Dreadful!"

"People don't mind that now," said Hargreaves consolingly.

"Lady Agatha will. Where did you leave your bag? At the Station Hotel? They'll make you comfortable. But Lady Agatha expects you to dinner at eight. Come with me now and we'll talk things over. I am hoping Haringdon may have returned—"

But when they reached Spinacres it was to learn that no word had come during the day from his lordship. Parker, who admitted them, showed them into the library. Lady Agatha, she said, was resting but would be coming down immediately. When she had left them Hargreaves turned to the older man. He had been given an outline of the case, so far as it was known to Mr. Pettigrew, during their five-mile drive. "Is she to be spared?"

"You mean from disagreeable facts? Certainly not. Lady Agatha Chant is one of the pluckiest women I know, and one of the cleverest, though she didn't have the educational advantages girls have nowadays. She has always been devoted to this nephew, the only child of her favourite younger brother who quarrelled with the rest of the family. The present Lord Haringdon was never at Spinacres until he came into the title and estates a couple of months ago. We had to advertise for him. Ah, here is Lady Agatha. . . . This is Mr. Hargreaves. He has consented to represent Miss Merle—"

Lady Agatha, who looked tired but held herself very erect, gave Hargreaves her hand. "Is the inquest over?"

"No. It was adjourned. Lord Haringdon will have to be present next time."

"I made sure he would come back," she said, "when he saw this morning's papers. How is Linda, James?"

Mr. Pettigrew cleared his throat. "She—she was removed in custody."

"That Lamb!" said Lady Agatha, as who should say "That serpent!" . . . "I'm not surprised. She's innocent, Mr. Hargreaves. My nephew is working on the case. James, did you know that he'd been a policeman all these years?"

Mr. Pettigrew looked rather bewildered. "Who? Superintendent Lamb. I had a short talk with him before the inquest opened—"

"No, no. David. My nephew. It seems that he was at Scotland Yard, in what they call the C.I.D., after he was demobilised. I only heard it yesterday. The Superintendent told me when he came with Colonel Bellingham."

"Dear me!" said the old lawyer. "He never mentioned it to me. Well, he might have done worse, eh? That accounts for the interest he has taken in this case, doesn't it?"

"Partly, I suppose," she said, "but he likes the girl, James—"

"He must come back," said Pettigrew, with a touch of irritation. "He can't leave us here in the dark."

At this point dinner was announced, and no further reference was made to the subject until they were back again in the library.

Parker had served the coffee and left the room. The curtains had been drawn and the fire blazing on the hearth mitigated the dreariness of the wet June evening. The two men were smoking, and Lady Agatha had lit a cigarette. The firelight flickered over her rusty black lace gown and was reflected in the diamonds that gleamed on her bony old fingers. Her rather equine countenance was turned to Hargreaves and her shrewd eyes were observant of him.

"Have you much experience in criminal cases, Mr. Hargreaves?"

"Not much," he confessed, "but I'm keen."

"You are undertaking Linda Merle's defence? My nephew and I will bear the expense. You understand that?"

"Yes." He hesitated. "Forgive me, Lady Agatha—is it a fact that Lord Haringdon met Miss Merle for the first time ten days ago?"

"He says so. I do not think he has ever told me a lie."

"But on certain points he has been—reticent—" he reminded her.

"You mean about his previous employment? That is not quite the same thing."

"No. And the dead girl?"

"He never even saw her."

"She played the violin at the Tudor Café. A good many people must have seen her there."

"David was never in the café until he went there to make inquiries after her disappearance. Are you suggesting that there is anything discreditable to him in this case, Mr. Hargreaves?"

"No, no! Certainly not. I gather that he has a theory which does not coincide with"—he checked himself on the verge of saying "with the facts" and amended his phrase to—"that held by the local police."

"Naturally!" she said, with a fine contempt. "What do they know! He was taking something up to London for analysis, and—now I remember—he said something about consulting the Chief. I did not know what he meant."

"His former Chief at Scotland Yard probably. That would be either Sir Henry Blunt Gaynor or Sir Roland Lord, unless he meant his immediate superior in the Force. That might help us to get in touch." He looked towards the old lawyer. "Do you happen to know either of them personally, Mr. Pettigrew?"

"I met Sir Henry not long ago at a dinner party. He is a widower with an only daughter who runs his house. A very charming young lady, I believe."

"You are on the telephone here?" said Hargreaves.

"Yes. Do you suggest that I should try a trunk call?" said Pettigrew doubtfully. "What do you think, Lady Agatha?"

"I wish you would," she said. "I can't imagine why I have not heard from him. I am beginning to fear that something may have happened to him."

"Very well." He rose. "You must be patient. I may be some time getting through."

The telephone was in the hall. He went out, closing the door after him. The two he had left sat silent, waiting.

Chapter XIX
MR. PETTIGREW IS SHOCKED

When Pettigrew came down to breakfast at eight o'clock Lady Agatha had already been to the stables. He saw her from the window, crossing the lawn to intercept the postman who was coming up the avenue on his bicycle. Parker was just bringing in the bacon and eggs. Pettigrew turned back to the table, and a minute afterwards his hostess entered with a bundle of letters and circulars which she laid down beside her plate.

"Nothing from David—"

She sat down and poured out the tea. Pettigrew made no comment. He was beginning to share her evident alarm. He had not rung up the Yard the previous evening. His native caution had suggested that it might be best to make his inquiries sound as casual as possible, and he had looked up Sir Henry Blunt Gaynor's private telephone number and got through, after a long wait, to his house in Swan Walk. Their colloquy had been short and not very fruitful. He recalled it word for word.

"Hallo. Is that Sir Henry Blunt Gaynor?"

"Yes. Who are you?"

"I am Pettigrew, James Pettigrew. I had the pleasure of meeting you at the Barlows'. I am staying with Lady Agatha Chant at Spinacres. Her nephew has been up in Town. Have you seen anything of him? Her nephew . . . Lord Haringdon . . ."

"Yes. He rang up. Said he wanted my advice. I asked him to dinner. He came, but we never had a talk. I fancy he changed his mind. We had other guests and that may have put him off. Nothing wrong, I hope. He didn't seem quite himself."

The lawyer, instead of answering, had asked another question. "Do you know where he's staying?"

"No."

"Thank you, Sir Henry . . ."

Lady Agatha, gaunt and mannish in her old tweed skirt, woollen sports coat and muddy brogues, had torn open her letters, glanced through them impatiently and pushed them aside. She drank her tea and refilled her cup. "No. No bacon, thanks. I'm going off my feed with this, James. That boy—it's not like him to be inconsiderate—he knows I get worried. And besides, there's this inquest—"

"Do you know what his theory is, Agatha?"

"Partly. I've been reluctant to mention it even to you," she explained. "It implicates other people, and he may have abandoned it."

"I think I had better hear all that you can tell me," he said.

"Very well—" She rose. "Come into the library—"

When they were seated and the old lawyer had lit a cigar she began. "When you came down last Monday week to see David regarding the sale of a strip of land over beyond Black Ridge he asked for time to consider Doctor Saigon's offer, didn't he?"

"Yes."

"You remember that when David first saw Linda Merle on the road she was talking to a man who appeared to be in the doctor's service. He was plainly anxious to get away from her and he warned her not to try to get help from Black Ridge. David was unfavourably impressed, though, to my mind, that is all explained by the fact that Doctor Saigon takes slight mental cases. Still, I must say that when I called there—I wanted to help David and he asked me to go and spy out the land—it struck me very forcibly that the doctor had something on his mind. David was convinced that the mystery of that poor girl's disappearance was no mystery to Saigon, and he spent last Saturday and Sunday watching the house from that copse on the hillside the doctor is so eager to buy. In fact, he went further, and got into the house when the inmates had retired to rest—"

Mr. Pettigrew was profoundly shocked. "My dear Agatha! How reckless! How foolhardy! If he had been caught the scandal would have been resounding. Resounding!"

"He was caught."

"He was caught? But—"

"He was dressed like a tramp. Apparently the doctor failed to penetrate the disguise."

"Didn't he hand him over to the police?"

She leaned forward, looking him in the eyes. "No, James, he didn't. He shut him up in a padded room for several hours and then he took him some miles along the Southampton road in his car and dropped him."

Pettigrew grunted. "Lucky to get off so easily."

"James—he found something. I don't know what it was, but he was taking it up to Town to be analysed."

"Saigon," said Pettigrew slowly. "I think I've heard rumours of some remarkable new treatment for nervous troubles. But he has no English degrees, I believe, and I fancy the medical profession over here have cold shouldered him. I obeyed Lord Haringdon's instructions and wrote him that we were considering his offer for that bit of land." His cigar had gone out. He got up and walked about the room. "I might call on him to discuss the matter. No harm in that, eh? That wouldn't commit us to anything."

"They may not let you in," she said.

"What do you mean?"

"I was admitted by mistake. The man at the lodge gate thought I was a new patient. When the doctor discovered his mistake he got rid of me as soon as he decently could—a little sooner, in fact."

"Thc bounder!" said Mr. Pettigrew indignantly.

Lady Agatha was fondling Mac. The old dog was restless and uneasy in his master's absence, continually pattering up and down stairs and whining at closed doors.

"David didn't confide in Sir Henry," she said. "I have a feeling that he may have come back to Black Ridge. If there is really something in his theory the doctor is a man who would not be hampered by scruples. I tell you, James, I am frightened."

"But, my dear Agatha, the poor girl's body has been found buried in Miss Merle's garden! Surely that clears Saigon. Haringdon was on the wrong tack. He'll be the first to admit it."

"Not necessarily," she said. "Where's the ordnance map of this district? David was studying it the other day. I think he put it back in this drawer. Here it is—"

Pettigrew joined her and adjusted his glasses while her bony forefinger prodded swiftly here and there.

"These are the grounds of Black Ridge. There are the cross-roads. The cottage is here, on the main road. The land at the back is Saigon's. She may have been killed in his house and brought to the place where she was found, carried across the park and lifted over the wall at the end of the cottage garden. I drove round that way yesterday while you were at the inquest and saw for myself. I don't say it was so, but it's possible."

"We shall have to tell Hargreaves and see what he thinks," said Pettigrew. "He promised to come here and report progress after lunch. He was to have an interview with Miss Merle at the prison. Dear me! If she is innocent—"

"You have had your doubts?" said Lady Agatha quickly.

He took off his glasses and polished them with his silk handkerchief. "To be frank, my dear, I have. I liked her face and I liked her manner in the witness box, but as a lawyer I have learned that—well—that appearances may be deceptive. I shall be extremely sorry if—especially as you say that Lord Haringdon—"

"But you will go to Black Ridge—"

"If it seems advisable, certainly. But I think we should wait for Hargreaves' opinion before we move."

"Very well," said Lady Agatha resignedly. She knew him too well to say more. He must have time to—to chew the cud. Slow, cautious, inclined to diffidence, he had never risked a rebuff. If he had been a little bolder he might have won her thirty years ago. She smiled, a trifle wryly, at the recollection. Poor James! She could hardly expect him to become dashing so late in the day.

He looked after her as she left the room and shook his head sagely. Dear Agatha! What a brilliant girl she had been. A little alarming to some people, perhaps, her wit like the flash of a rapier, and terribly headstrong and imprudent. And she had not changed in essentials. Wrinkles, grey hairs, the wearing of the scabbard, the blade as keen and bright as ever. She still thought him stodgy, no doubt. A fortunate thing that he happened to be on the spot to restrain her.

He was in the library after lunch when Hargreaves arrived and was brought in by Lady Agatha.

"You saw Miss Merle?"

"Yes. She told me her story. We must get Lord Haringdon to corroborate it. And the other man she spoke to. He must be traced. I asked Superintendent Lamb if he had looked him up and he said he called at Black Ridge the day before yesterday to make a few inquiries."

"That's very interesting," said Lady Agatha, "please go on."

"The doctor was very sorry he could not help him. The man was a kind of under-footman apparently. He wasn't satisfactory and was under notice to leave, and he did leave the day after—the Monday—"

"What was his name?"

"Capper. Herbert Capper. We shall have to advertise for him." Lady Agatha looked at Pettigrew. "Tell Mr. Hargreaves," she commanded, and the old lawyer, having had the time he needed for the assimilation of a new idea, cleared his throat, and began.

Chapter XX
IMPASSE

A voice not his own seemed to be whispering "Get out of this!" David, irritated by its urgency, groaned and rolled over on his side. The place was dark, utterly, and soft, and that softness was abominable. The spongy yielding surface of the walls and floor defined his efforts to attract attention. So might some poor wretch, buried alive, struggle soundlessly, trying to force up the lid of a well-lined coffin. He could not hurt himself, and yet there was pain somewhere, a dull ache—

He groaned again, his brain, warned by that voice, trying desperately to resume its functions. The back of his head. The pain was there. Some one must have struck him a heavy blow. When? Where? He had come down by the last train after leaving the Chief's house in Chelsea, and gone back to his camp in the wood, on his own land. He had not decided on his next step, but anyway he wanted his night glasses. He had left them in a rabbit's burrow when he clambered down to the laboratory roof last Sunday night. He was looking for the burrow in the undergrowth when something had crashed. Evidently he had been stunned, struck down from behind. He had been a fool to come back alone. This might be the end of him. He knew where he was now, of course. This was his former prison, the padded room. He lay quite still for a while, thinking. How long had he been lying here? He had no idea for his watch had stopped, and though they had left his loose change and a handkerchief in his pockets they had removed his matches with his penknife and the pocketbook—containing nothing which could betray his identity—and his fountain pen.

His throat felt dry and he was aware of a sinking sensation which recalled certain of his experiences in the front line during the War. When the door opened he shrank involuntarily, his eyes, accustomed to the darkness, dazzled by the light of the unshaded globe overhead that had been switched on from the passage.

"Don't get up," said Saigon smoothly, but David had scrambled to his feet and was facing him. "You quite took me in, you know, the other day. I really believed you were a tramp. You're quite a good actor, Mr.—"

David smiled. "Mr. A," he suggested.

Saigon shrugged his shoulders. "Oh Mr. S? S for spy, is it not? I was foolish to let you go, but you—you were even more foolish to come back, for, you see, when we searched the camp of the supposed down-and-out vagrant on the hillside we found night glasses that cost much money to buy, and that rather gave the show away."

"I wonder if I might have a drink?" said David.

"Certainly." Saigon went out, and returned almost at once with a glass of water.

David drank it eagerly. "Thank you," he said, "that was decent of you."

The doctor's sallow face twitched. He gave the other a queer look. "I would like to be decent, as you call it. I wish to be, but you have made it difficult. I have others to think of. But perhaps if you will tell me who you are and why you have been spying on us I may be able to arrange something."

"And if I refuse?"

Saigon made a movement of his hands. "I should be sorry—"

David glanced with a faint distaste at those long bony spatulate fingers, stained yellow with nicotine.

"I am not entirely without friends, Doctor Saigon."

"They knew what you were doing?"

"Yes."

"And if you do not return to them they will come and say, 'Where is our dear Mr. S?' And I shall reply that I know nothing, and give them leave to search, and they will find nothing. Nothing."

"How very interesting!" said David. "Well, they do say that practice makes perfect, don't they? Hallo—"

The door behind Saigon was not quite closed. It let in a sound from the outer world. It was the faint whirring of a bell. Saigon evidently heard it too. "I shall come back in a few minutes," he said. "Be frank with me and I will do my best for you—" He slipped out. The door, padded like the walls, closed noiselessly, and the light was extinguished.

David passed his hand across his forehead and found it damp. They would never dare let him go. He knew that well enough. And he did not want to die.

Presently the light was switched on again and Saigon came in. "I was called to one of my patients," he exclaimed. "Now, Mr.—whatever your name is—I must confess to being curious. Come—I will admit that we have something to hide, something that would spell ruin for me if it became known. Will you, in return, tell me why you thought us worth watching?"

"Naturally," began David, "when she disappeared—" He stopped, startled by the change in Saigon's face. What had he said to bring that look of mingled surprise and—yes—relief into those weary eyes.

"She?" said the doctor. "There must be some mistake. We're at cross-purposes."

"I think not," said David, but his tone was less confident. "It's no use—" He broke off as the door opened and a fat man with a heavy white scowling face sidled in.

"See here—" He dropped his voice to a husky whisper. David, straining to hear, caught a few words. "Gate . . . thought it better . . . get rid . . ."

Saigon nodded. "All right, Abbott. I'll come—"

"What about him?"

"He'll keep. I'll see about him later. Don't you interfere, Abbott. I won't have it. You understand."

"You're too soft," growled the fat man. They went out together.

Once in the passage the doctor turned to his servant. "Who did you say it was?"

"Lord Haringdon's lawyer, one of the regular old family sort, with grey whiskers and spats complete. Says he's come to see you on behalf of his client about that strip of land. A damn nuisance to have them nosing about just now, but I think it's O.K., and you should shunt them off easy. No need to get the wind up," he added, with a glance at his master's twitching face.

"No, no. I expect you're right," said Saigon. "Just one moment."

It was all very well for Abbott. The brute had the hide of a rhinoceros. Saigon turned into his bedroom, leaving the butler to wait for him in the corridor. Hurriedly he pulled up his coat sleeve, took a hypodermic needle from a drawer and gave himself an injection. He must steady his nerves before meeting strangers. He settled his tie before the glass and brushed his sleek black hair. Then, before going down, he picked up the framed photograph of his wife that stood on his dressing-table. "Elena! It's for your sake, my darling!" He stood there for an instant, dreaming of her, spoiled, selfish, exacting, but, ah! how sweet! She had left so lately that the scent she used still lingered in the air.

Abbott knocked on the door impatiently.

"Coming," said Saigon.

Lord Haringdon's solicitor and his companion were both standing when the doctor joined them in the drawing-room. He bowed to them formally, not offering to shake hands.

"You wished to see me?"

"Yes. My name is Pettigrew. This is my friend, Mr. Hargreaves. I suppose we may assume that you do not intend to build on the hill, Doctor Saigon?"

"I thought I had made that clear. Is his lordship willing to sell?"

"He is considering your offer."

"Perhaps you will be good enough to let me know by letter when he has come to a decision," suggested Saigon. "I am understaffed just now and exceedingly busy."

"Of course," said Hargreaves rather unexpectedly. It was the first time he had opened his lips but Saigon had been uneasily aware that he was being closely inspected. "Of course! The man Capper. He left suddenly, didn't he? You must miss him. You haven't replaced him yet?"

Saigon licked his lips, which had gone dry. "No I—I haven't replaced him."

"I believe the police were round inquiring after him the other day. You weren't able to give them his address. I don't think they will be bothering you again, but I want him badly."

"You? I'm afraid I don't understand."

"You haven't been reading the papers lately?"

"The papers? I—perhaps not. I've been very much occupied—" stammered the doctor.

"Then it may be news to you that a murder was committed ten days ago quite near here?"

Saigon looked at him in silence.

"I have been engaged to defend the person who has been arrested on suspicion, and I have reason to believe that Capper's evidence may help my client. With your permission I should like to question your other servants. It is possible that Capper may have told them where he was going."

Saigon found his voice. "You can see Abbott if you wish, but I am quite sure he knows no more than I do."

He had turned very white and the other two noticed it and exchanged glances.

Pettigrew spoke. "You are unwell—"

"No, it is nothing. I—I am subject to it. Murder. I—I certainly had not heard. Who—who was it?"

Hargreaves answered. "The victim was a young girl." He was watching the doctor carefully, for by now he was convinced that he had something to hide from them. Saigon, he could see, was a highly nervous subject, the kind of witness who is almost certain to break down under a severe cross-examination, but he was puzzled by his reaction to his last statement. "The victim was a young girl." What was there in that to take a load off his mind?

"Terrible!" said Saigon, "but I can't believe Capper was involved. He was a very"—there was for an instant a queer break in his voice—"a very harmless little man."

"If we might see his fellow servant just for a moment—" hinted Hargreaves.

"To be sure." Saigon rang the bell. The daily paper was still lying folded as when it had been brought up from the lodge, on the table. He picked it up. "If you'll excuse me, gentlemen, I will just see what they say here. A murder! Awful—" His tone was appropriate to the occasion. Hargreaves began to wonder if he had not been mistaken. And yet—they were following Haringdon's lead, and Haringdon had been, as he had learned that morning, one of the most promising of the younger men at New Scotland Yard.

The butler entered. A fat man with small shifty eyes like marbles. "You rang, sir." His manner was deferential, even oily.

"These gentlemen, or rather, one of them, want to ask you if you know where Capper went, Abbott?"

"Capper, sir? I couldn't say. He did talk of emigrating to Canada or Australia."

"I see. Where had he been before he came to you, Doctor Saigon?"

Saigon laid down the newspaper. "He had been out of work for some time. In fact, I picked him up on the Embankment. He was down and out, poor fellow. I took him without a character. A mistake, perhaps."

"I see," said Hargreaves again. "Well, he'll have to be found. I think I'll get the B.B.C. to broadcast an S.O.S. for him. Perhaps you would be kind enough to furnish me with a description.

Then was a perceptible pause, and then Abbott answered. "He was, I mean to say he is a little chap, ginger hair and moustache, pale blue eyes with pink lids, and inclined to be flat-footed. A C3 physique. Will that be all, sir? I've the silver to clean—"

"Yes. Thank you," said Hargreaves. He did not see how the interview could be prolonged. "We will wish you good afternoon, doctor."

"Good afternoon," said Saigon. He was not entirely successful in concealing his satisfaction at their departure. Abbott had left the room.

Pettigrew coughed. "I suppose—" he began, "I sometimes get asked to recommend—you are running this place as a nursing home, are you not, Doctor Saigon? I wonder if, now that we are here, you would show us over?"

"I should have been delighted," said Saigon smoothly, "at any other time, but the fact is I have a very troublesome patient just now. He is in a highly nervous state and the least sound irritates him. The nurse may be bringing him down at any minute now and if he met strangers I'm afraid it would excite him. So I must ask you to excuse me. Another day, if you will make an appointment, I should be pleased—"

He had shepherded them through the hall to the front door and stood at the top of the steps to see them start. Hargreaves was driving Lady Agatha's little two-seater.

"I don't like it," he said in a low voice to Pettigrew, "but what can we do?" He slipped in the clutch. "I—Good God! What was that?"

They had just turned the corner of the house when they both heard a crash and a shout, and a shower of broken glass came tinkling down on the gravel of the drive, one larger piece striking a mudguard of the car. Hargreaves put on the brakes with an abruptness that came near to sending them skidding into one of the trees of the avenue. Pettigrew, looking up when the crash came, had caught a glimpse of a figure gesticulating wildly at a broken window on the second floor. He said so when Hargreaves, having stopped the car, turned to him for further information.

"The deuce you did. I don't hear anything now—"

They both listened, but not a sound broke the silence of the afternoon. The house might have been uninhabited. Hargreaves, glancing back at the front entrance, noted that the doctor, presumably satisfied that he had seen them off the premises, had gone in and closed the door.

"Was it some one trying to attract our attention by smashing a window as we passed? It sounded like a cry for help," said Pettigrew. "I—the fact is, Hargreaves, I am out of my depth. I—I don't see my way—" He broke off. "My dear fellow, what fools we are. That was the patient to whom he referred. No need for us to worry. Poor creature."

The young barrister hesitated. He had no wish to make a fool of himself at the outset of his career. It might be as Pettigrew said. They might suspect, but they had no facts to go upon except the fact that Haringdon should have returned by now. For an instant he sat there, his hands gripping the steering wheel, with a half-realisation that much might hang on his decision. A little thing turned the scale. The fragment of broken glass that had fallen on the mudguard had not dropped off. As it by there be noticed that its sharp jagged edge was streaked with blood.

"I've got to make sure!" he said, half to himself, and he jumped out of the car and ran back up the drive. Pettigrew, thirty years his senior and always a bad starter, followed more slowly.

Chapter XXI
BROKEN GLASS

David did not relax when the two men left him again alone in the dark. He guessed that they would be returning before long. Saigon, he believed, would spare him if he could. He was more afraid of Abbott. If Saigon killed him it would be with the utmost reluctance, but the fat man, he felt, would know no compunction.

He had no means of judging how the time passed and it might have been a few minutes or it might have been an hour later when he heard the click of the lock and the light was turned on again. The door opened and Abbott came in alone. He was carrying a glass nearly full of a yellow liquid on a silver salver.

"The doctor said I was to bring you a whisky and soda."

"Very good of him," said David. He took the glass from the tray and raised it to his lips. It was whisky, but—his mind worked quickly. He had seen the white sediment at the bottom of the glass. With a swift jerk of the wrist he had flung the liquid in the man's face. As Abbott staggered back he leapt forward and reached the corridor. Right or left? There were the front stairs and the back stairs, but there was no time to choose for the butler was at his heels. David fled down the long corridor towards the landing window. He could hear a motor car being started. Desperately he beat at the window panes with his bare hands. The glass shattered. "Help! Help!" he yelled before he dropped, felled from behind by a glancing blow.

Saigon, below in the hall, hurriedly shut the door and shot the bolts before he came running up the stairs. He found his prisoner prone on the landing beside the broken window and Abbott, standing over him, cursing volubly as he mopped his wet face with his handkerchief. "What have you done? How dared you go near him without my leave! If you've killed him—"

"We've got to get rid of the swine, haven't we? Can't afford to be squeamish, not with the mess you've made of things," said Abbott savagely. "I meant to get it over before you come up, but he was too quick for me, blast him!"

"And I tell you I won't have it!" Saigon's voice cracked. "I—I'm finished. There's a limit—"

"Don't be a fool, doctor. It's him or us. Think of your wife—"

Saigon groaned. "Is there no other way?"

"None. And you know it—"

"If—" He started violently. "What's that?"

Some one was knocking, knocking loudly and continuously, at the house door. The two men looked at each other. Both were pale. There was no one downstairs to open it.

"It's those two lawyers come back. They must have heard him break the window," growled Abbott. "You better go down and get rid of them."

"All right. I'll do what I can—"

Saigon went down and fumbled with shaking fingers at the bolts. Pettigrew and Hargreaves were outside and they stepped past him into the hall before he could speak.

"I fear there is something wrong here," began the elder man.

Saigon made a final effort. "One of my patients. But it's all right now. If you'll excuse me—I—I am busy—"

Pettigrew wavered. All this was highly irregular. He and his companion had no *locus standi*. He glanced at Hargreaves. They had no right to insist. But the barrister's blood was up.

"I'm sorry," he said, "but if we are not allowed to see him I shall communicate with the police. I heard a cry for help. You must know that you cannot detain patients who have not been certified, against their will."

"And if I refuse?"

"I wouldn't if I were you."

Saigon made the gesture of one who admits defeat. "Very well," he said huskily. "Come this way."

They followed him up the stairs and along the corridor to the landing. Fresh air blew in through the broken panes. Abbott was gone. David had rolled over and lay on his side. His left hand had been badly cut.

Hargreaves turned to the doctor. "Hadn't you better bandage him up? He's unconscious. What have you done to him?"

"I did nothing. My butler struck him. He was trying to escape. I—I'll get some lint—"

"Do," said Hargreaves curtly. "What's the matter, Mr. Pettigrew?"

"Matter!" Mr. Pettigrew was very red in the face. "This is an outrage! You were right! Thank God we came back! This is my client; this is Lord Haringdon!"

"I thought it might be," said Hargreaves. "Have you any explanation to offer, Doctor Saigon?"

Saigon had brought a roll of lint and a bottle of anti-septic lotion out of a cupboard in the corridor and was banding the injured hand. He answered without looking up from his work.

"Yea. It's rather a long one, but you may as well hear it. Wait a moment—" He laid the bandaged hand down and turned his attention to the head.

Pettigrew, watching those long supple square-tipped fingers, stained brown with nicotine, fumbling about the base of the injured man's skull, found himself wondering how he should break the news to Lady Agatha if—if—

"Is he—badly hurt?"

Saigon had concluded his examination. He stood up, wiping the red smears from his hands with a bit of lint. "No. Slight concussion. Very slight. He ought to be kept quiet for twenty-four hours. He'll be all right by tomorrow evening probably. You say he's Lord Haringdon?"

"Certainly."

"He came here dressed as a tramp a few days ago, and broke into the house," said Sagan bitterly. "We found him prowling about on the hillside after having let him go once. It seems to me that it is I who should be asking for an explanation."

Saigon's restless black eyes were quick to see the old lawyer's embarrassment. He was regaining his self-possession. It might still be possible to explain everything. If only that brute Abbott had hit a little harder he would be safe enough.

"A burglarious entry. A little difficult to justify," he said. "Of course if I chose to make trouble I could hand him over to the police even yet. My wife was here and could identify him."

"Hush!" said Hargreaves. "He's coming round!"

Saigon bit his lip. He had hoped the injured man would remain comatose for some hours longer. David moved his head slightly and opened his eyes. For a minute he stared up at them blankly while they waited. Then—"Hallo, Pettigrew," he said faintly. "Good egg! I'm damned glad to see you. It was getting a bit unhealthy here."

Pettigrew bent over him. "My dear fellow," he said, "don't exert yourself. You're quite safe now. We shall be taking you home to Spinacres. You must rest—"

"Not yet. I must get on with—my job. Saigon. Don't let him go. Where's that fat scoundrel who tried to do me in? I believe—I'm sure they did it—"

For an instant no one spoke. Pettigrew and Hargreaves exchanged glances. The latter broke the silence.

"Did what, Lord Haringdon?"

"Murder." The faint voice was dreadfully distinct "Violet Hunter."

"This is a terrible accusation," said the doctor loudly. "I protest against it. I am innocent. I swear it."

"Liar!" said David.

Pettigrew intervened, "No, no. Haringdon, a great deal has happened that you know nothing of. The poor girl's body has been found."

"Impossible!"

"I assure you that it is so."

"Then what was he burning in his furnace secretly, night after night? And what was Abbott's hold over him? I tell you I heard them—and I got some of the ash. Yes, I did. He made me turn out my pockets but he didn't look in my tobacco box. It was there under a layer of shag. I had it analysed in London. Calcined bone dust! Hold him! Don't let him go!"

Chapter XXII
THE SCENT OF ALMONDS

A SOMEWHAT FLUSTERED constable burst into the Superintendent's room.

"I beg pardon, Superintendent, but the Chief Constable, Colonel Bellingham, is outside and asking for you—"

"I'll come." Lamb pushed the notes he had been studying into his desk and locked it. It was nearly nine o'clock and he had been thinking of going home to his supper, but that would have to wait if the Colonel wanted him. He went into the station yard.

Colonel Bellingham was there in the driving seat of his big saloon car. "Sorry to bother you at this hour," he said, "but I've had an urgent telephone call from Spinacres, Lady Agatha Chant speaking. Something has happened. She wouldn't say what but when I suggested bringing you she made no demur. Better have one of your men with us perhaps—"

Lamb nodded and beckoned to the young policeman who had fetched him out. "You'll do, Gardiner—"

Lamb sat by the Colonel in front. Neither spoke until the car was on the outskirts of the town. It was a dark night, clouds covering the moon, and when they had left the lighted streets behind they could see nothing but the patch of road illumined by the car's headlights. Lamb was the first to break the silence.

"We haven't got to the bottom of this case yet, sir," he said.

"I'm afraid not," agreed the Colonel. "Lady Agatha seemed to be greatly agitated when she rang me up."

"She's very fond of her nephew, they say," remarked the Superintendent in his most expressionless voice.

"Yes. You are not suggesting—"

"Between you and me, Colonel, Lord Haringdon was on that road, within a mile of the cottage, that Sunday night He had left Spinacres directly after lunch, on foot. What was he doing between two o'clock and seven or thereabouts, when, according to his own account he met Linda Merle on the Laxworthy road? I haven't asked him because I don't want him to realise that I've wondered, but it's a question he'll have to answer when he goes into the witness box. The theory of the prosecution at present is that the two girls quarrelled and that Linda killed the other. Her hands were badly scratched, by the way. But, to my mind, it's more likely that she was only an accessory and that the principal was a man."

"Haringdon!" exclaimed the Colonel.

"I've no evidence at present," said Lamb, "and there's the question of motive. But Violet Hunter was a beauty, everyone says to, the kind men go mad about. Lord Haringdon says he never even saw her, but we've only his word for that. They may have met on the sly."

"I hope you are wrong." the Colonel, in a voice that betrayed his perturbation. "Ah, here we are—"

He sounded his horn as the car passed through the crumbling stone gate posts surmounted by their heraldic griffins, scattering the deer that were browsing under the limes of the avenue. Evidently they were expected. There were lights in all the windows on the ground floor and the door was opened as they mounted the steps by the grey-haired parlourmaid who had admitted them when they came before. She looked pale and scared.

"Oh, sir, I'm glad you've come! This way, please—"

Mr. Pettigrew came out of the library as they were crossing the hall. Both the Chief Constable and the Superintendent recognised him from having seen him at the inquest. The parlourmaid slipped away as he advanced to meet them.

"A dreadful business," he began, "I hardly know how to tell you—"

"One moment. You are the legal adviser of the Chant family?" said Bellingham.

"Yes, yes. My firm has acted for them for a great number of years. The business of the estate—"

"Lady Agatha rang me up."

"She did. She is upstairs just now with her nephew. He is in bed suffering from the effects of a blow on the head. Doctor Wynne has been. We sent for him as soon as we got his lordship safely home."

"Do you mean that he was set upon?" asked Lamb. "Is that why you wanted the police?"

"Not altogether. The fact is, gentlemen, that Lord Haringdon, in his eagerness to clear up the mystery of that poor girl's death, got himself into a—a thoroughly false position. He could not plead ignorance. You both know that he was a Scotland Yard detective until he inherited the Haringdon title and estates from his uncle a few months ago. He was perfectly aware of the difficulties that beset the official investigator, and he was determined not to be hampered by them himself. In short"—Pettigrew cast a troubled glance towards the library door—"he was convinced that Doctor Saigon of Black Ridge was somehow involved in this dreadful business. I won't trouble you with details now. I will only say that Mr. Hargreaves and I called on the doctor this afternoon and discovered that Lord Haringdon was being forcibly detained in his house. He was struck while attempting to escape. In the end we brought him and the doctor back to Spinacres. Doctor Saigon, who was in a highly nervous state, was induced by Lady Agatha to write a statement, which he signed and we witnessed. He then asked for a whisky and soda, and after drinking it he collapsed. We—there was nothing to be done. Lady Agatha rang you up."

"You mean that he is dead!" exclaimed Bellingham in a shocked voice.

"Yes. He had left the writing-table and was sitting on the sofa. He slipped down on to the floor. We have not moved him."

Bellingham and the Superintendent hurried into the library, Pettigrew following with unconcealed reluctance. Saigon's body was lying as he had described. Lamb bent over it for a moment.

"The glass fell from his hand and broke, I see. I notice a smell of almonds. Prussic acid, most likely. The post-mortem will show." He straightened himself and stood for a moment, thoughtful.

This development was entirely unexpected. He avoided the Chief Constable's eye. "I'll ring up the station. The police surgeon will have to come out with the ambulance. Who mixed the whisky and soda, Mr. Pettigrew?"

"I did."

"Was there anyone else in the room at the time?"

"Mr. Stephen Hargreaves."

"Not Lady Agatha or Lord Haringdon?"

"No. He spoke to us at Black Ridge when he recovered consciousness but he relapsed after a few minutes. He was put to bed directly we got here. Lady Agatha went up to him directly after she had witnessed the statement."

"We'll have a look at that presently," said Lamb. "Did you see Saigon put anything into the drink?"

"No, I can't say I did. But I turned away after handing him the glass to fill my own. Neither I nor Hargreaves had any suspicion. It never occurred to me that he would attempt to take his own life. I—I am quite unused to violence," said poor Mr. Pettigrew. "I—I am very much shaken."

"Very natural," said Colonel Bellingham sympathetically.

The Superintendent had gone out into the hall to telephone. He came back presently.

"Now about this statement. Do you know what it contains, Mr. Pettigrew?"

"Yes. Saigon read it to us before we witnessed his signature."

Lamb grunted his dissatisfaction. "Seems to me you took a good deal upon yourselves. However, we'd better know what he had to say. We've got to wait for the doctor.

"Perhaps you would be good enough to read the document to us, Mr. Pettigrew?" suggested Bellingham. "I came away in a hurry without my glasses—"

Pettigrew glanced towards the sofa. "Must we remain here?"

"In the next room if you like," conceded the Superintendent. He allowed the others to precede him and lingered himself for a moment to make sure that the window fastenings were secure. When he rejoined his companions Bellingham had lit a cigarette and Pettigrew was adjusting the shade of the reading lamp.

"Now," he said, in a voice that shook slightly, "let's begin. The ink is hardly dry, and yet the hand that held the pen is cold."

It is twenty minutes to seven. I have been persuaded by Lady Agatha Chant to write a full account of the events that have culminated in my being brought to this house. Some things may be hushed up, but in any case I am ruined. No more patients will come to me for Professor Petroff's treatment. I suppose I must think myself lucky that nothing like this happened before. I took frightful risks. I see that now, and, indeed, I realised it at the time, but I wanted to make money for Elena's sake. She was fond of pleasure and of pretty clothes. It was natural. I believe she loves me, but if I could not give her all she wants there would be others—and I could not bear that. But I must begin at the beginning.

I got my medical degree in Vienna and then obtained a post as assistant to Professor Petroff in Moscow. I had an illness and when I became convalescent he arranged that I should go to Italy for a holiday. I was a favourite of his and he was very kind to me. While in Rome I met Elena Olivieri. Her father had a Government post, very ill paid, and she was one of nine children. I fell in love with her and she accepted me more because she was anxious to get away from that dull flat in the Trastevere than because she cared much for me. When I returned to Moscow Petroff was furious with me for having married. He said he would not trust his secrets to a man who had a wife. Perhaps he was right. I am not very squeamish but I do not care to think now of some of the experiments that were carried out under his direction. Still I had to earn my living somehow, and I had already discovered that Elena was extravagant. I went to him and begged him to make an exception in my favour. I can see him now, with his bald head like an egg and his glittering eyes. He refused. We left Russia and went to Paris. There I met a man who had been a fellow student of mine in Vienna. He had some capital and together we started a nursing home for nerve cases. Petroff's famous grafting operation had been talked about and I was known to have been his assistant. An enormously wealthy manufacturer brought his son to me. The young man had been a nervous wreck since the War. They had all kinds of treatments but all in vain. Money was no object. We were doing fairly well, but I knew that Elena was running up bills.

They asked me to perform Petroff's operation. I warned them of the danger. Out of twenty patients who had undergone it eight had died, nine had been cured, and three had recovered but had shown no signs of improvement. The young man declared that he was willing to take the risk and they offered a fee that seemed a fortune to me then. I allowed myself to be persuaded and he was received into the home and prepared for the operation. But, as the moment approached, my nerve failed. Petroff was supported by the Government. He had a free hand, and the human material he had worked on was not regarded as of much importance, sweepings of the streets and the prisons that served as laboratory fodder. But my patient was a person of influence. If I failed with him the consequences would be far-reaching. I talked it over with my partner and he agreed with me. And yet, as he pointed out, if I refused to carry out what I had undertaken the effect would be almost as disastrous. I should be labelled incompetent and we might as well put up our shutters. It was a difficult position, but he was clever, very clever and subtle. Did I mention that he was a compatriot, that is, his father was Armenian, but his mother was Greek, while mine was English. As I say, he was clever, and he found a way out. The nurses were told that as I had promised Petroff to keep the exact nature of the operation secret they could not be present and that they must leave the theatre as soon as the patient was under the anaesthetic. My partner, who administered the ether, would give me any assistance I required. I allowed the time to elapse that was usually required for the grafting and then we rang for them, and the patient, still unconscious, and with his head bandaged, was taken back to his bed. Actually I had merely made an incision of the usual length in the skin of the scalp and sewed it up again. Naturally we expected that the result would be negative. The patient would survive, but without benefiting from my treatment. Meanwhile I should receive my fee, which I had agreed to share with my friend. No one, as you may imagine, was more surprised than we were to find that we had effected a complete cure. The grafting had not been carried out, but the patient thought it had. In fact it was a case of faith healing.

That was two years ago. We did very well for some months after that and effected several more cures. It was a risky game and we often talked of giving it up, but it was easy money. Then my partner died of pneumonia and I got out of the business and Elena and I came over to London. Elena wanted to live in England. She had made friends with an English lady, a Mrs. Culver, who had promised to take her about and give her a good time. She was young and gay, with expensive tastes. I soon saw that to satisfy her I must go on making large profits. There were already several clamouring to be treated. Some were cases that could not be cured by suggestion, but it was understood that there must be some failures, and meanwhile they would have paid their fees. I made a favour of taking any patient and I charged them enormously. I had bought Black Ridge and lured a staff of servants. My nurse was fully trained and competent, but she had made a mistake which had cost her patient his life and done for her professionally. Abbott and Cardew had both been asylum attendants who had lost their jobs, Cardew for being drunk while on duty, and Abbott for maltreating one of his charges. Abbott had been an indoor servant too and was a first rate cook. I never had more than four patients under my care at one time. Abbott complained of having too much to do and a few weeks ago I picked up Herbert Capper, down and out, on the Embankment, and engaged him to help with the rough work. My staff, you will notice, was a job lot. My English colleagues had cold shouldered me from the first. They called me a charlatan, and they disapproved of Petroff and his methods. I do not think I could have secured the services of a nurse who had not a black mark against her name. I don't know. I never tried. But I must say here that none of my people knew that the operations I performed were fakes.

Three weeks ago I received a new patient. I am not going to tell you his name. It is a famous and an honoured name and would be known to all of you. He had been suffering from nerves and depression. It seemed to me one of those cases which can really be cured by suggestion. He was quiet and gave no trouble. On the first Sunday after his arrival we played tennis in the morning. It began to rain in the afternoon but he seemed restless and, after tea, he put on his mackintosh and went for a stroll. None of my patients went outside the grounds. I had had the wall round the park made higher and the lodge gates were kept locked. There was also a door in the wall about a quarter of a mile from the gates which was used by the servants when they went out, but they were supposed to lock it after them. My new patient—I will call him Mr. X—did not appear at supper. I went up to his room. He was not there. He was to have his operation on the Monday and it struck me that he might be worrying over it. I began to be anxious and I went out to look for him. I met him coming up the avenue. He was terribly distressed. He said "I've killed them both. They're just inside the door. I covered them with dead leaves. I don't know why I did it." Then he began to cry. I took him back to the house and left him in the padded room. Supper was over. I got my other two patients off to bed, and then Abbott and I went out to see what had happened. We found the mangled bodies of Herbert Capper and a dog under a heap of leaves just under the park wall. It was Capper's evening off. Apparently he had gone out by the door and had left the key in the lock. Mr. X, strolling by, had opened the door and finding the dog lying on the road, had carried it in. He could not remember himself exactly what had happened, but I fancy he had been startled by Capper's return. The shock had sufficed to throw him off his balance. I see now that I should have sent for the police, but my one idea then was to hush it up. Capper had no friends and would not be missed. I resolved to dispose of his body by burning it in my furnace with that of the dog.

Abbott knew what had happened, not Cardew and the nurse. I did what had to be done in the laboratory at night, after the others were in bed. Mr. X was violent when I went to him. Obviously he would have to be certified. I thought I would write to his people and tell them I could not operate in his case. Fortunately he seemed to have forgotten everything that had occurred. I meant to motor him back myself in a few days' time and meanwhile I could keep him under the influence of drugs. I thought I had provided for everything and was beginning to feel fairly safe when Abbott started to blackmail me. He pointed out that I had disposed of Capper's body and that if I were accused of murdering him I should not be able to prove my innocence. It was too late to go to the police, and I was at his mercy. I gave him hush money. I had to. And Elena was writing for money too. You know the rest. After we caught the alleged tramp on the hillside I dismissed the nurse and sent all my patients back to their own homes, informing their relatives that Black Ridge had to be closed temporarily. I still hoped to be able to surmount my difficulties. And yet—in my heart I knew that the game was up. I should have to get rid of Abbott and of the mysterious spy. As to the girl who was killed that Sunday night I knew nothing. Mr. X might have attacked her if he had come across her, but I am quite certain that he only left the grounds for the two or three minutes that were required to go out by the door in the wall and carry in the dog he found lying on the road.

I have nothing more to say except that I am glad now that you came to Black Ridge today. I have been a fool, and I saw no way out but the one from which my flesh shrank. It is better to be Abel than Cain, after all.

Pettigrew laid down the last of the scribbled pages. "That is all. He signed it in our presence and we witnessed the signature. He asked and received permission to write a note to his wife."

"Where's that?" asked Lamb gruffly. He seemed put out.

"I have it," said Pettigrew. "I will see that she gets it."

"It's a queer story," said Lamb. He turned to the Chief Constable. "What do you make of it, sir?"

"Damned queer," Bellingham agreed. "But I presume it can be corroborated in part at least by Mr. Pettigrew."

The solicitor nodded. "It was evident both to Hargreaves and myself that the doctor was in a highly nervous state, with something on his mind. Lord Haringdon will be able to tell you more when he has recovered from the attack made on him by the man

Abbott. It is a mercy he was not killed. If he had not succeeded in attracting our attention by breaking a window—" He broke off with a shudder.

"There will have to be an inquest," said Bellingham, "but I think that, until we know who this Mr. X is, we must be rather careful, Superintendent."

"I suppose so," said Lamb heavily. "You won't produce the statement?"

"No."

All three men rose as Lady Agatha came into the room.

"Don't let me disturb you," she said.

"How is Lord Haringdon?" inquired Bellingham.

"Better, I think. The stupor seems to be turning into a natural deep sleep. The Chants are very tough. My father used to say that he had had every bone in his body broken at one time or another out hunting." She sat down with a sigh. "I'm tired. Well, Colonel Bellingham. You've read that wretched man's *apologia pro vita sua*. You see now that Linda did not invent the dog. You'll release her at once, of course."

"I'm afraid I can't do that, Lady Agatha." He glanced rather uncomfortably at the Superintendent who hastened to his Chief's rescue.

"We weren't depending on the dog, one way or the other, my lady. We won't dispute that all that happened more or less as she said. It won't help Miss Merle much. The case for the prosecution rests on another basis."

"Rubbish!" said Lady Agatha. "The police can do no wrong. You've arrested her, and therefore she must be guilty."

"My dear?" implored Mr. Pettigrew. There was nothing to be gained, be felt, by antagonising the authorities. He was thankful that just then the doctor arrived with the police ambulance, creating a diversion. The Colonel and the Superintendent returned to the library. He turned to her then reproachfully. "You're a loyal friend, Agatha, but terribly impulsive and indiscreet. If you're not careful you'll do that poor child more harm than good."

"But, James, surely this makes a difference!"

He shook his head. "She's not out of the wood yet. Not out of the wood."

"You've only to look at her face!" she cried.

"Ah," he said, "if it was as easy as that—"

CHAPTER XXIII
THE CASE FOR THE CROWN

ON MONDAY MORNING Lady Agatha herself took up the invalid's breakfast tray. She found him sitting up in bed.

"How do you feel, dear?"

"Right as rain. I could have got up yesterday if you had let me. Where are my clothes? I couldn't find anything. The wardrobe is locked and the key is gone."

"I'll bring it back," she said unblushingly. "You needed a rest."

"Well, I've had it," he said. "Now Aunt Agatha, for heaven's sake tell me how we stand? Pettigrew and another chap came to my rescue, I know, or I shouldn't be here, but the rest is vague. Saigon is a thorough bad hat. I tried to tell them to hold on to him but I was a bit groggy at the time and I may not have made them understand. Our highly respectable family solicitor is a dear old thing, but—or perhaps I should say and therefore—direct action is repugnant to him," remarked David as he poured out his tea.

"I'll tell you everything," she said, "when you've eaten your breakfast."

"Done with you!" he said cheerfully. He whistled softly to himself as he buttered his toast. Lady Agatha looked at him, surprised to see him so light-hearted, and then with a sense of shock, realised that he had not yet heard of Linda Merle's arrest. How would he take it? Perhaps, after all, she thought, it would have been better if he had remained in love with Diana Culver. She smothered a sigh and sat down to wait until he had satisfied a healthy appetite and then took away his tray and resumed her seat at the foot of the bed.

"Now—" he said. He had lit a cigarette. Smoking in bed was one of his bad habits. He was wrapped in the faded old dressing-gown he had brought with him from his Balham lodgings. Mac, who had come upstairs with Lady Agatha, had jumped up on the counterpane, unreproved, and lay curled up, but with one ear cocked, at his master's side.

Lady Agatha described the finding of Violet Hunter's body and Linda's arrest. "The inquest has been adjourned but she is to be brought before the magistrates today, and Mr. Pettigrew thinks she will be committed to trial at the Assizes."

"The damned fools!" said David fiercely, and then, having relieved his feelings—"and yet I don't know that I can blame them. It must look black to anyone who does not know Linda as we do."

"David—" said his aunt hesitatingly.

"Well?"

"We haven't known her—long."

The blue eyes, so very blue in that thin brown face, met hers with a new gravity. He seemed to her to have aged perceptibly in the last half hour.

"You don't doubt her, Aunt Agatha?"

"No!" she said hastily, but in her heart she acknowledged that there were moments when she was not quite sure.

David glanced at his wrist watch. "Will you ring up Hargreaves and tell him I'm coming along? When I've heard the opening of the case for the prosecution I shall know better how we stand."

Half an hour later she was seeing him off. He was driving himself and had resolutely declined to take her with him. The day dragged on. She tried to read but could not concentrate her attention on any book. After lunch, when she made a pretence of eating to please Parker, she went into the garden and did some weeding. It had not rained for twenty-four hours and she had tea brought out on the terrace. Still David did not return, and dusk was falling and the bats wheeling overhead when she heard the car coming up the drive. She lacked the courage to go to meet him and waited for him to come to her.

"Well?"

He sat down heavily in the basket chair facing her. She saw that he was very pale. "The case for the prosecution it that the two girls quarrelled over—over a man, that Linda attacked the other, seizing her by the throat until she collapsed, dying of heart failure, and that then, terrified by her own act, she concealed the body as best she could by digging a shallow grave. They allege that then, knowing that she had very little of her legacy left, she was tempted to take the only article of value wore by her victim, the opal and diamond engagement ring, to raise money on it later on. They called two police witnesses to describe the finding of the body, wrapped in Linda's overall, and the landlady at their lodgings who swore that Violet came home later than usual the night before the crime was committed and that they had a fearful row. She occupied the room underneath and was disturbed by the noise they made and meant to complain but they were off early the next morning, and she never saw Violet again. Hargreaves is badly rattled. From what he said to me after the hearing I rather fancy he wants her to plead guilty to manslaughter."

"David! He thinks she did it then!"

He lit a cigarette. "He does not know her. Of course, there's the ring. She can't explain how it came to be in her possession. And the Saigon business does not help us at all, apparently, unless he was lying in that statement of his—and somehow I don't think he was, do you?"

She shook her head. "It was the truth, I'm sure."

"There was a homicidal maniac at large in the grounds of Black Ridge that evening. He killed Capper, probably while Linda and I were walking down to the cross-roads. It must have happened within a hundred yards of us, on the other side of that park wall. He might conceivably have killed Violet, coming through the door in the wall just as she passed on her way to the main road to try to get help for the dog, but he couldn't possibly have carried her to the garden of the cottage and buried her before the doctor found him. Who dug the grave? I said the owl, with my little trowel. We've got to find the owl." David laughed, and his laughter was not good to hear.

Lady Agatha got up quickly. "My dear boy, don't! Don't!"

CHAPTER XXIV
HERMANN GLIDE

WHEN DAVID CAME UP to Scotland Yard the following day he was not kept waiting. His former Chief was in his private room going through a pile of letters. He rose as David was shown in and the two men shook hands.

"Sit down, Haringdon. There are cigarettes in that box. And now, what's the trouble?" asked Sir Henry kindly. He was shocked to see how ill the other looked.

David took a cigarette. His hands were trembling. "I think you know something about it, sir."

Sir Henry shook his head. "Not officially. The Yard hasn't been called in. But—Saigon was a friend of yours, wasn't he?"

"No, Sir Henry. A neighbour."

"Then I am at a loss," said the Chief. "You rang me up some days ago and said you were going to ask my advice. You came to dinner at my house but you left without seeing me alone. It puzzled me rather at the time."

"Mrs. Saigon and Mrs. Culver were there; they were going on to a dance with your daughter and I had come to tell you that I suspected Doctor Saigon of having committed a murder. It was a bit awkward—"

"Good heavens! I never met Saigon. I've just read an account of the inquest. Financial worry and overwork. Temporary insanity. It seemed straightforward enough."

"There's a lot more to it than that," said David. "But I think Colonel Bellingham, the Chief Constable, is right not to let it come out."

"Well, if I am to be of any use I had better be told," said the Chief.

David embarked on his story, explaining the chance meeting that had led to his efforts to dear up the mystery of Violet Hunter's disappearance. Sir Henry listened carefully and with evident interest.

"It's just as well you didn't spill all this before, young fellow," he said rather grimly when David had done. "You've been sailing pretty near the wind. You had no earthly right to break into Saigon's house like that."

"I know it, but I thought I was on the right scent, and to be quite frank I didn't trust the local police."

Sir Henry thought a moment. "They've made an arrest. You still think they're bunglers?"

David tried hard to be calm and judicial. "They were in too great a hurry," he began, and then cried out, with a passion that startled the older man, "Linda Merit is innocent! For God's sake, Sir Henry, take a hand in this!"

"My dear boy, how can I! You know how touchy these provincial chaps are sometimes. Our assistance has not been required. We can't offer it unasked. Besides the law has been set in motion. The thing will have to be threshed out before the Bench. They shall commit her for trial. I advise you to retain Lander Collins for the defence. He'll get her off if anyone can."

"Then you can't do anything, sir?"

"I'm afraid not. Of course, if you can produce evidence that satisfies the police between now and the opening of the next Assizes at Jessop's Bridge they will drop the case. You can't do much more in the matter yourself. You are one of the witnesses and are altogether too well known by all the people who are mixed up in the business. In your place—" The Chief broke off as the telephone bell rang and took up the receiver. "What? Oh, very well. In a minute." He turned again to David. "I am sorry I can give you no more time this morning. By the way, you are only on leave, you know. I half hoped you might come back to us."

"Thank you, Sir Henry, but I've left the Yard for good. Too much red tape," said David.

The Chief looked at him reproachfully. "I don't deserve that from you, Haringdon."

"I beg your pardon, sir. I shouldn't have said that. I know it's not your fault that when I ask for bread you give me a stone. You were about to say what you would do in my place—"

Sir Henry nodded. "I understand," he said, and his voice was kind. David had been at no pains to disguise the nature of his feeling for the girl whose life might hang on what he did or left undone. "You are too deeply involved to be able to see clearly. You need some one who will come fresh to it, approach it from a new angle. In your place I should try a fellow called Hermann Glide."

David looked up. "I've heard of him. A bit of a mountebank, isn't he?"

"He's clever. I thought you were tired of the official methods," Sir Henry reminded him. "As a matter of fact I believe you are right. He is none too scrupulous about the means he employs to attain his ends, though I fancy he is clever enough to keep within the law. When I advise you to go to him I am speaking as man to man." He scribbled on a half sheet of paper which he passed to David. "That's his address. Yes, we keep in touch with him here. We don't approve of him—but we find him useful."

He rose and walked with David to the door. "I make no promises but I shall butt in if I get the chance," he said as he held out his hand.

David gripped it hard. "Do!" he said. "It—it's a nightmare to me."

Once out on the Embankment David signalled the first taxi that passed. Hermann Glide's office was in Southampton Row and consisted of two small rooms on the second floor. His brass plate on the door below described him as a private inquiry agent. David was admitted by a young woman typist in horn-rimmed spectacles who asked for his card and vanished with it into the inner room. David, waiting, heard a murmur of voices.

"Mr. Glide will see you, my lord."

The inner, like the outer, room was scantily and poorly furnished. Mr. Glide made no effort to impress his clients by the magnificence of his carpets or his chairs. When David entered he was seated at his shabby desk playing with a lump of modelling wax. He was a little man, noticeably frail in appearance, with wistful brown eyes in a small puckered face that reminded David of a monkey on a barrel organ.

"Sit down, Lord Haringdon. You have something to say to me? Have no fear. You can say anything here. It will go no farther than these four walls unless you give permission. You want something. Everyone who comes here brings some trouble for me to put right—if I can. You will not mind if I go on with this while you are speaking? It helps me to concentrate." His long slender supple fingers were busy moulding the wax into fantastic shapes. David watched them fascinated, while, for the second time that day, he told the story of Violet Hunter's disappearance and his part in the ensuing investigation. When he had done Hermann Glide nodded twice. "I have read the newspaper accounts. They do not tell much. Still I could see that the case was unusual. You believe in this girl's innocence. You want me to make further inquiries?"

"Yes."

"My terms are ten guineas a week and my expenses."

"That's all right."

"I shall come down to Jessop's Bridge, naturally. I must have a free hand and not be interfered with. If I want you I will communicate with you."

"There isn't much time," said David.

Mr. Glide smoothed his lump of wax down on the table and prodded it with a delicate forefinger. "It may be that I shall prove her guilt. In that event I shall still be paid?"

"Of course," said David.

"Don't be offended," said Glide. "One makes bad debts in my profession as in most others. People ask for the truth and when they get it they are sometimes very much annoyed. The local police have arrested Miss Merle. You tell me that you have been in the C.I.D. yourself. You must know that for one innocent person taken for murder there are ten who go free because there is not enough evidence to satisfy a jury."

"I agree," said David.

"In this case," pursued Glide, "the circumstantial evidence is strong, but the motive so far remains obscure. Of course the police may know more than we do. We shall see when they call their witnesses at the next hearing." He laid down his lump of wax reluctantly and took a notebook from a drawer. "I'll just jot down the names of the *dramatis personae* so far as we know them.

"Let us resume. The two girls were employed through the winter to play at the Tudor Café. There's a manageress, a Mrs. Dutton, but the owner is a man who calls himself Smith, but is better known as Ebermann. I know of him. He has an interest in several night clubs and was lagged four years ago for running a bogus film artists' agency. He had evidently taken a fancy to Violet Hunter and had offered her a job in London with a better salary than she was getting. Ebermann wouldn't stick at much, Lord Haringdon. The trail may lead to the basement in a back street of Soho where fools with money to burn jig about and drink bad whiskey at famine prices."

David shook his head. "He's a bad lot—but it would be much easier to get rid of her if he wanted to when he had got her up in London."

"Yes, if the crime were premeditated. I doubt if it was. However, it is too soon to dogmatise. We have to add to our list the landlady of the two girls, who has already given evidence for the prosecution, and the woman Violet Hunter lived with before she shared diggings with her new friend. I think you said it was she who informed the police of the disappearance?"

"Miss Coleman. Yes. I believe she practically brought the girl up and was absolutely devoted to her."

"Have you talked to her at all? Has she any theory?"

"I don't think she's worth listening to," said David, "she's an ignorant woman, the sort of person who has violent prejudices and is utterly unreasonable."

"Still she probably knew the girl better than anyone else. I have a notion that to understand what happened three weeks ago we may have to go back quite a long way," observed Glide. "I assume that she believes Miss Merle committed the crime?"

"She's prejudiced," repeated David.

"No doubt. But she may help us all the same. We've got to go back with both these girls. Yes, Lord Haringdon, with Linda Merle too. Has she told you anything about her past?"

"She has. Her father was a doctor in Birmingham. He and her mother both died during the influenza epidemic in nineteen eighteen. There was just enough money left after the sale of their house and furniture to keep Linda at school until she was eighteen. The headmistress would have kept her on as a music teacher, but she hated teaching. She has earned her living ever since as a pianist in cinemas and cafés. The legacy which she spent on buying the cottage was left to her by a cousin in New Zealand."

"Have you verified all this?"

"No. But—"

Glide smiled for the first time. He looked impish, but somehow it was impossible to take offence. "That's all right, Lord Haringdon. What Miss Merle says goes. All the same—I'll get an assistant to check her facts while I carry on at Jessop's Bridge."

"You'll keep in touch with me, Mr. Glide? I shall be at Spinacres."

"You shall hear from me," the little man said, "and meanwhile you will pay me a week's salary in advance with ten pounds on account of expenses. It would be nice to be as vague about money as Mr. Sherlock Holmes, but he, I fancy, had private means."

David produced his cheque book and his fountain pen. "Have you been in this profession long?" he asked when he had written the cheque and Glide had pocketed it.

"Some time," said Glide. "I was brought up as an acrobat but I had a bad accident on a trapeze. I've walked on at the Old Vic, I've been a pavement artist, an agent for sewing machines and a—" He broke off with another of his elfish smiles. "I don't think I'll tell you that."

CHAPTER XXV
THE ANGEL

"I WAS LOOKING for rooms," said Hermann Glide. "You have a card in your window—"

Miss Coleman stared at him. He was very small and insignificant and his clothes, though neat and well brushed, were ill cut and much worn. This was all in his favour. She had a horror of the loud-voiced cheerful young men, bank clerks or shop assistants, who kept golf clubs and hockey sticks in their bedrooms and came home late at night. On the other hand, if she really wanted to let she could not afford to pick and choose.

"Will you come this way?" she said ungraciously.

He removed his hat as he crossed the threshold with a charming little air of deference that was entirely wasted on its object and followed her into the front sitting-room. He looked about him at the overmantel with its china ornaments and framed photographs, at the aspidistra on the bamboo stand in the window, and the framed pictures of "Grandpa's Pet" and "Will Oo Love Me?" on the walls. There was, he noted, a pile of tattered music on the top of the piano.

"It would be this room," said Annie Coleman dully, "and the bedroom over, but I don't know about taking a gentleman. I can't undertake cooking at night and I don't hold with late hours. The gas is turned off at the meter at ten."

"That would be all right," said Glide. "I suppose I could have a candle in my room."

"Lights are extra," said Annie, "and the sitting-room fire and the cruet. Two guineas"—she corrected herself—"two and a half guineas, with extras. You could do your own catering or I could get in what you need. Just as you like." Though her manner was grudging as ever Glide saw that she was really eager to have him.

"I like the position," he said, "but it's rather more than I can really afford. Perhaps I had better try elsewhere."

Annie's broad face reddened. She disliked the idea of having a stranger in the house, but she wanted the money badly for a certain reason. "Would it be for a permanency?"

"That would depend on many things," said Glide.

There was a pause which appeared to be given up to mental arithmetic on either side. Then Annie said "We'll say two and a half guineas inclusive."

Glide brightened visibly. "Then I'll take the rooms. I'll fetch my luggage from the station now. Perhaps you'll be kind enough to get in bread and butter and milk and some groceries—"

He glanced at the black marble clock on the mantelpiece. It had stopped. He consulted his own watch. "Ten to three. Could I have tea at half past four? Shall I leave a deposit?"

She nodded. "A pound. I'll give you a receipt."

When he had gone she put on the hat and the old rainproof coat that she kept hanging in the passage and hurried out with her string bag. She did her shopping in the High Street. Would he fancy eggs or a bloater for his breakfast? Perhaps eggs would be safer until she knew his likes and dislikes. As she bustled from counter to counter choosing rashers of bacon, packing her parcels in her bag, counting her change, she felt more cheerful, more like her old self than she had done for a long time. Perhaps it had been a mistake to refuse to look out for another lodger when Violet left her, but she had been so sure that the girl would come back to her sooner or later. Now "I daresay it will be good for me to have something to do," she thought as she turned into the office of Cullen and Seabrook, the stone masons and funeral furnishers. Mr. Cullen himself was looking through a ledger, and he left a clerk to attend to her. Annie was red and rather breathless for she had been walking fast.

"I've changed my mind," she began. "I won't have that composition curb I decided on for the grave when I came in yesterday. I want something better, much better."

Mr. Cullen, overhearing, closed his ledger and came forward, waving his subordinate away. "Very good, madam. The same thing in Carrara marble, or granite? Or a cross?"

He opened an album full of photographs. "Perhaps you can see something here?"

Annie moistened her lips. Her stubby finger encased in the black cotton glove, turned over the pages. "I want an angel like that one."

"That would cost you fifty pounds, madam," said Mr. Cullen.

Annie knew it. She had looked through these same photographs when she came into the office before, but though she had admired the angel she had passed it over as being far beyond her means. Lying awake between two and three o'clock she had recalled it wistfully at first and then with a growing determination to secure it or something like it for Violet's grave. She would get the money somehow. And when she came down in the morning she had got out the Furnished Apartments card, which had been lying at the back of the sideboard drawer for years, and put it up in the sitting-room window. "It's for you, Vi dearie," she said aloud. She often talked to the girl as she went about her household duties as if she were still there. Latterly her next door neighbours had heard her. "That poor Miss Coleman. She's gone a bit queer since she's been there alone—"

"I thought maybe I could pay fifteen pounds down and the rest in instalments," she said.

Mr. Cullen reflected. "Yes. That might be managed."

"Then I'll have it, please," she said, speaking more quickly than usual.

She thought of the angel with pride and satisfaction as she trudged home. Her lodger had arrived before her and was waiting on the doorstep with his suitcase and a bulging carpet bag.

"I'll have your tea ready in twenty minutes," she promised.

When she came into the sitting-room to clear the table he was doing a crossword puzzle but he laid it aside as she set down her tray.

"About tomorrow's dinner, I should like a bit of loin of lamb with Yorkshire pudding about one if that will suit you—"

"It won't," she said bluntly, "not tomorrow. I thought of leaving you some slices of ham and a salad and a dish of tinned fruit, unless you'd rather get your dinner out somewhere."

"I thought you were prepared to cook," he protested.

"Most days, yes, but tomorrow I have to give evidence at the Guildhall. There's a murder trial going on," she explained. "Haven't you read about it in the papers?"

Glide was satisfied. He was very anxious to hear her version of the story without betraying his own interest in it. The subject had now been introduced in a manner that justified some display of curiosity on his part.

"Of course," he said, "who hasn't! But you don't mean to say you're mixed up in that business, Miss Coleman?"

She had gathered the plates and crockery on to her tray and folded the tea cloth. She stood now by the table, and it was apparent to him that she was glad to unburden her mind.

"Violet Hunter lived with me until that Linda Merle got her away. She was a little bit of a thing, the prettiest you ever saw, when she came here with her mother, and after Mrs. Hunter died she stayed on with us. The money her mother had left was spent, and after that I paid for her music lessons and all. I never liked her going to that Tudor Café, but so long as she was with me I took care of her. She'd be alive today if it wasn't for that other—" She broke off and drew a shaking hand across her mouth. "But she'll pay for what she did—she'll pay."

"You believe in Linda Merle's guilt?" he asked.

"I do, and if you come to the Guildhall tomorrow you'll hear why."

"Do you think I could get in?"

"I don't know. There was a big crowd at the first hearing. Lots were left outside."

"I suppose the ring being found among her things will go against her," he suggested.

"I suppose so."

"It was the poor girl's engagement ring, wasn't it? The young man died, didn't he?"

"Yes."

"Very sad," said Glide sympathetically, "some people seem born to bad luck, don't they? Was he a nice fellow? You knew him, of course."

"He was well enough," she said, "but he wasn't good enough for my Vi. A bit of supper at eight?"

She picked up her tray and prepared to leave the room. Glide sprang forward to open the door for her. She passed him without acknowledgment of his courtesy which she found embarrassing. "Dancing master airs," she thought as she carried her tray down to the kitchen; but it had done her good to have some one to whom she could speak. She was beginning to realise dimly that she had been alone, brooding over Violet's desertion, too long.

CHAPTER XXVI
CIRCUMSTANTIAL EVIDENCE

THE MAGISTRATES present on the Bench, who had been conferring together in whispers, stiffened to attention as the counsel for the Crown rose.

"My next witness will be Annie Coleman."

One of the reporters at the press table dropped a pencil and stooped to pick it up but no one else moved as the thickset middle-aged woman in deep mourning who had been seated a little apart from the other witnesses rose and made her way to the witness box. It had been rumoured that the evidence she had given at the inquest had been incomplete and that what she had to say now was likely to create what journalists call a sensation.

The people who, after waiting for hours outside, had succeeded in pushing to the front of the gallery, craned their necks to get a better view of her. Hargreaves, his lean face impassive, wrapped his gown about him and leaned back in his place, crossing his legs with a well-assumed air of indifference, but he was watching her. The eyes of everyone in that crowded court room were fixed upon her with one exception. The prisoner in the dock was looking out of the window. The view was restricted. A roof of lichen-grown tiles and a patch of sky beyond. But a pair of sparrows who had a nest in the eaves were fluttering about the roof, and the sky was blue.

Lumley, the counsel for the Crown, pushed his wig a little farther back on his head, a gesture which with him signified the clearing of the decks for action.

"You knew Violet Hunter—the murdered girl—well?"

"Yes."

"You might almost describe yourself as her adopted mother?"

"I was very fond of her and she of me until mischief was made—"

"One thing at a time please, Miss Coleman. Answer my questions, yes or no. She left your house last autumn to share rooms with another girl, the pianist at the Tudor Café?"

"Yes."

"Against your wish?"

"Yes."

"But she still came to see you occasionally?"

"Yes."

"Her last visit was made on the very day before she disappeared?"

"Yes."

"Will you tell the Bench in your own words what passed between you?"

Hargreaves jumped up. "I object—"

"Very well," said Lumley patiently. "Was Miss Hunter in her usual spirits?"

"No."

"Bothered and depressed?"

"Yes."

"She told you that she had decided not to cast in her lot with the prisoner but to accept an offer of a post in London?"

"Yes."

"She gave you the impression that she dreaded telling the prisoner this?"

"Yes."

"Would you say that she went in fear?"

"Yes. Looking back now I see she was afraid," said Annie slowly, picking her words amid a tense silence. "I didn't make much of it at the time. I never liked Linda Merle, but I knew no harm of her. Violet had complained to me of her temper—"

Lumley crossed the court room to the witness box and held up a small object. Annie took it from him, looked at it, and passed it back again.

"Have you seen that ring before?"

"Yes."

"It belonged to Violet Hunter?"

"Yes."

"She was engaged to be married two years ago?"

"Yes."

"The engagement only lasted a few weeks as the young man died?"

"Yes."

"She has worn the ring ever since suspended on a thin gold chain about her neck?"

"Yes."

"Would you have been surprised to hear that she had parted with it?"

"She would never have parted with it. I am certain of that."

"Thank you, Miss Coleman. It is sufficient to say yes or no. I have no further questions to ask."

The chairman of the Bench leaned forward. "Now, Mr. Hargreaves—"

Hargreaves shook his head. "I have no questions to ask at this stage."

Annie Coleman looked hot and tired. It was with evident relief that she stepped down from the witness box and returned to her place. Her evidence had made a profound impression on everyone present. It was noticed that not once had she glanced towards the dock and that as she went back to her seat she edged away from it. She made no attempt to disguise a loathing which was natural enough, given the circumstances.

The next witness for the prosecution was Superintendent Lamb.

"About this ring, Superintendent," said Lumley conversationally, after Lamb had been sworn. "Will you look at it before it is put back among the other exhibits? Do you recognise it?"

"Yes."

"Where did you see it first?"

"I found it last Sunday week while searching the rooms occupied by Miss Hunter and the prisoner."

"Where was it?"

"At the back of a drawer in the prisoner's room, among her gloves and handkerchiefs."

It was growing late when Lumley concluded his examination of the Superintendent. The magistrates consulted together. "Another adjournment," whispered Hargreaves to David, who was sitting beside him. The chairman was speaking.

"Shall you be cross-examining this witness, Mr. Hargreaves?"

Hargreaves jumped up. "One moment, please."

Lamb eyed the young barrister with an air of good-humoured superiority. "Anything you like, sir."

"Miss Merle and her friend occupied rooms at the top of the house in Rosemary Passage. The rooms on the lower floors were all let and people were coming and going all day and far into the night?"

"Yes."

"The landlady and her daughter were frequently out, and the house door was left unlatched?"

The Superintendent shifted his feet. "Very likely."

"It would be quite possible for some one to slip in unnoticed and plant this ring in Miss Merle's drawer?"

"Possible," said Lamb gruffly, "but not probable."

Hargreaves reddened with anger. "Come, come, Superintendent, you know better than that. I did not ask your opinion. I want facts. There's a great deal too much hearsay and prejudice in all this. I'll repeat my question. Miss Merle was away for the week-end. It would be possible for some one to come in her absence and leave this ring in her drawer?"

The Superintendent conceded the point. "Any party who had the ring. Yes."

"Thank you," said Hargreaves. It was as much as he could hope for at that stage in the proceedings. David had been anxious that the case should be fought inch by inch before the magistrates, but Hargreaves believed it might be best to reserve the defence.

"They are bound to commit her for trial," he argued. "It can't hurt her to plead not guilty and let them do the talking now. In the interval something may turn up."

And David had yielded though it went against the grain. He was taking it all very hard. He slept badly and could hardly be persuaded to eat. Lady Agatha was anxious about him. She confided to Pettigrew that she wished it was over. "Even if that poor girl—I can't think she did it, James, unless, of course, she was insane at the time. That's possible, I suppose. A fit of mania. Very dreadful. We ought to find out if there's any family taint—"

"The worst of it is," said Pettigrew, "that his haggard appearance tends to confirm the rumours—of course it's absurd—that he is the man in the case. You know how people talk." And then poor Lady Agatha had begun to cry and he had to comfort her as best he could.

The old lawyer was right. Though David himself was unaware of it many curious glances had been directed at him that day as he sat in the well of the court listening to the evidence of the witnesses for the prosecution, and there were not lacking whispers that when the case came to be tried before a jury at the Assizes there might be two prisoners in the dock.

The hearing was to be resumed in the morning. The magistrates had filed out through the arched doorway that led to their private room; the press men had hurried away to send off their stuff; while the crowd that had filled the public gallery clattered down the wooden staircase into the street. The prisoner had been removed from the dock. David got up and went to the door by which she had been taken out. It was guarded by a young policeman.

"You can't go out this way, sir."

"Rubbish!" he said irritably. "I want to see Miss Merle. You can't stop me. She's only on remand—"

Lamb came up. “Anything I can do for your lordship?”

“I want to see Miss Merle.”

Lamb led the way into the corridor, closing the door after him. His big red face was shining and he mopped it with his handkerchief. “Hot in there,” he complained, and then he looked at the younger man and went on with a slight change of manner. “You felt it too, I see. You’re all out.” For an instant he hesitated. “You’re Lord Haringdon, and I’m just a superintendent of police, but I’m older than you. May I speak to you as from man to man?”

“Of course.”

“Then I say don’t see her!” he said earnestly. “I ask you, am I the sort to hound a woman down for the fun of the thing? I don’t like this case any more than you would in my place, but I’ve got to do my duty. If you get mixed up in this more than you are already it will mean a peck of trouble for you and for her ladyship—”

David was surprised and touched. He had not expected so much fine feeling from the Superintendent. “You’re a good chap,” he said, “but I don’t care a damn what people may think. I’ve got to see her.”

“Very well.” Lamb led the way down the corridor and opened the door of the anteroom where Linda was waiting, with the wardress who had accompanied her from Aylesford, for the closed car that would convey them to the station. She rose as David entered, with a little gasping cry. The wardress, who looked good-natured, glanced quickly from one to the other and then walked over to the window where she stood apparently admiring the view of a blank wall.

David took the girl’s hands in his. They were very cold and trembling. “My dear—”

“You have been so kind from the very first,” she faltered. “Without you I believe I should die. They all think I killed Vi. I can see it in the way they look at me—as if I was—different. It’s so awful!”

"Linda—my darling." He drew her to him and she came unresisting. "It will be all right. You'll see," he said, trying to convince himself and failing lamentably, "don't lose hope—"

The wardress spoke without turning her head. "They've backed the car up to the entrance. We shall have to go in a minute."

"Thanks," said David. Then he bent his head and whispered in Linda's ear. "I love you. Kiss me. Quickly—"

Silently they clung together.

The wardress glanced at her wrist watch and went to the door and opened it. Lamb and a constable were waiting in the corridor. David gave Linda's hand one last firm pressure and stepped back a pace as the wardress came up to her and took her arm. Involuntarily he shut his eyes that he might not see her go. When he opened them he was alone. He waited a moment to recover himself, for he had been very deeply moved, and then made his way out of the building.

At the foot of the stairs a constable came up to him. "Beg pardon, my lord. I'd go out the side way if I were you. This door will let you out on a passage that leads through to the yard of the Crown if your car is garaged there."

"It is. But—"

"The crowd in the Square hasn't dispersed yet," the policeman explained, "and we don't want any trouble."

David stared at him blankly. "Do you mean that I'm unpopular? Good Lord! What am I supposed to have done? Oh, all right. The side door by all means."

When he reached Spinacres he had a bath and changed before seeking out Lady Agatha. The gong had sounded and they met in the dining-room with Parker hovering in the background. David was glad of it. He did not feel equal to discussing the day's happenings with anyone. Lady Agatha only ventured to ask one question.

"Is it over?"

"Not yet."

She looked across at him doubtfully. The heavily shaded lamp left his face in shadow. When, at last, Parker had brought in the coffee and gone downstairs she tried again.

"David—"

"I had to leave the Guildhall by a side door to avoid the attentions of the mob apparently. They seem to think—oh, hell! who cares!"

"David dear—"

"I see now what the Superintendent meant," he said. "I've been slow in the uptake, I suppose. The theory of the prosecution is that Linda and the other quarrelled over a man. I heard Lumley say it and never grasped that he meant me. It's—it's too silly!" He laughed mirthlessly. "Me!"

"If we only knew what really happened!" she sighed.

He flared up at once. His nerves were on edge, fretted by the intolerable suspense. "You do know! You've heard Linda's story!"

"Yes, yes," she said hurriedly. "I mean to the other—who killed her and why—"

He got up. "Don't let's talk about it any more. Come and play to me, Aunt Agatha. Forgive my bad manners. Soothe the savage breast."

"My dear boy, I don't mind. I understand—"

He was holding the door open for her. She looked up at him, her old eyes rather dim. They had been so happy together. And now—this.

"David, just one thing. I think I ought to prepare you. I had a letter from Diana Culver today. She says she is coming down tomorrow—"

His face was like a stone. "I won't have her here."

"Not here. She's been called as a witness for the prosecution."

"Diana? Why? What can she say?"

"I don't know. But she didn't like Linda. They didn't hit it off—"

"And so she's joined the pack," he said bitterly. "All right, Aunt Agatha. I'm forewarned."

Chapter XXVII
THE ELEVENTH HOUR

Diana Culver drove her new car down to Jessop's Bridge. She took a young man, one of her most recent admirers, with her. Elena Saigon was no longer available, for her father had come over from Italy and had taken her back with him after her husband's funeral. In any case she might not have cared to come. Diana had seen her off at Victoria, looking frail and lovely in her widow's weeds.

"Poor Michael," she sighed, "he was so fond of me," and dabbed at her eyes gingerly so as not to disturb her make-up. No one had been brutal enough to tell her all the truth about the dead man. If they had she would not have understood. His statement had been taken possession of by Colonel Bellingham. It had not been referred to at the inquest.

Diana was in high spirits. She had never been called as a witness in a murder case before, and she was avid of new sensations. She parked her car at the Crown. Her attendant swain was to try to gain admission to that part of the court allotted to the public and afterwards they were to lunch together.

"The really rather sweet policeman who served me with a what-is-it seemed to think my examination wouldn't take long," she said. "It'll be even more exciting at the real trial. I do hope I shan't be one of the witnesses they weed out."

They were crossing the market square to the Guildhall. The young man, who was known to his friends as Rags, glanced down at her doubtfully and made no remark. Could it really be true that Diana had been engaged to the new Lord Haringdon years ago, before she married old Culver? Haringdon was mixed up somehow in this case. Didn't she mind?

The crowd trying to get in was larger than ever, but one of the unemployed who had a good place in the queue offered it to the young man for a ten-shilling note.

"It was worth the money, old thing," he told Diana afterwards, "only to see you kiss the book."

She made a grimace. "Fancy bringing me all the way from Town just to ask me if I had noticed the scratches on that girl's hands! I had, of course. Hands are so important, I think." She glanced down at her own. They were having lunch in the dining-room of the Crown.

"Yours are lovely," he said rather perfunctorily. He was recalling the scene in the court room with a touch of discomfort. Diana, slim and girlish in the beige silk frock that barely reached to her knees, looking, in those drab surroundings, like a butterfly that has settled momentarily on a dustbin, and answering readily, perhaps a little too readily, those questions so suavely put by the counsel for the Crown.

"I don't know that you need have told them that the palms of her hands were so blistered," he said suddenly.

"Good heavens, Rags! Why ever not?"

"Well, you volunteered that. He hadn't asked you."

She laughed gaily, but her eyes were hard. "My dear Rags, you haven't fallen in love with the murderess, have you? I know heaps of men do. They get offers of marriage. Extraordinary."

She, too, was remembering. As she was leaving the witness box she had seen David across the court. She had not noticed him before. Their eyes had met but in his there had been no sign of recognition. So that was that. Her heart, perhaps, had never been involved, but her vanity could and did suffer a fresh wound. And Rags, who was too young to be tactful, did not change the subject.

"Shall we try to get in for the afternoon sitting? They'll finish with Haringdon today, I suppose. He sticks to it that he met the girl for the first time that night, and never knew the other at all, but Lumley seems to think he's lying."

"Of course he's lying, you infant!" said Diana impatiently. "He was Violet Hunter's lover first, and then he got tired of her and picked up her friend. That's obvious. Naturally he has to deny everything for her sake as well as his own."

"Rotten for him if you're right," was the young man's comment. "Poor devil! But had there been time for him to get into that sort of mess? He only came into the title a couple of months ago. He'll be cold shouldered after this, won't he? They're still very fussy and Victorian in these country places, I've heard."

Diana lit a cigarette. "Bring the bus round, Rags. We'll go back. I don't want to hear any more of that stuff today. It's only a trial run anyway. Those magistrates are stodgy. I want a real judge in red robes. You shall take me out to dinner and we'll dance afterwards." Going back she drove so recklessly that Rags felt impelled to remonstrate. "Hold hard, old thing."

She turned on him savagely. "Get out if you're afraid!" As they came up Whitehall the newsboys were crying the last editions of the evening papers. "Mystery of Strangled Girl! Linda Merle Committed for Trial!"

Diana dropped her admirer at his club. He was to call for her at her flat later. She had a bath and half an hour's facial massage.

"What will you wear, moddam?"

She chose one of the frocks she had bought when she was over in Paris with Elena Saigon. Why had Elena's husband committed suicide? Money worries. David was poor. "Fool!" she thought bitterly. She hated him now for he had humiliated her. She had let him see that she was willing to marry him, and he— She bit her lip hard. Men were extraordinary! What was there so fascinating about that girl whom she had watched that day, a pale mute figure sitting by her attendant wardress in the dock? "I hope they'll hang her!" she told herself.

"A little colour tonight? Moddam is tired," hinted the maid.

She examined her reflection in the mirror anxiously. Yes, that sagging under her chin was beginning to show. She must marry Rags before he noticed it. After all, she might do worse. It was a pity that his ears stuck out so and that he was such a boy, but it could not be helped. She heard his voice in the hall and winced. David had cut her that morning in the court. Oh, why hadn't she married him thirteen years ago when he had cared!

Her maid stood waiting with her wrap of gold brocade. "You needn't wait up, Mullins. I shall be late . . . Hallo, Rags darling!"

CHAPTER XXVIII
THE VOICE

DAVID WOULD NOT leave Spinacres.

"Don't you see that it would be better to go right away until the opening of the Assizes?" pleaded Lady Agatha. "Alone, if you prefer it, or I would come with you anywhere."

"Thanks, Aunt Agatha, but that would be throwing up the sponge. I can't do that. I'm still hoping to hear from Glide. He's a queer little beggar, and the Chief himself said his methods wouldn't bear much looking into, but we can't afford to be squeamish. If only he'd tell me what he's up to," said David restlessly. "I lie awake at night wondering—"

Lady Agatha looked at him anxiously but made no comment. It was obvious that he was sleeping badly. And people were talking. They were saying things even in the village where half the inhabitants were their own tenants. They had seemed to like David, but they had not had time to get to know him well. One could hardly blame them for their doubts and suspicions.

"Really," he said, "I would almost rather Bellingham screwed his courage up to the sticking point and arrested me. I believe he and Lamb are inclined to think that Linda and I did the job together—" He broke off as Parker came into the breakfast-room with the coffee and the morning post. There were several letters for Lady Agatha, only one for her nephew. His tired face brightened.

He had had one note, very brief and very vague, from Hermann Glide already, and he recognised the fine crabbed writing which suggested the divagations of a fly rescued from the ink pot. On the former occasion the postmark had been London; now, he noted, it was Jessop's Bridge. Eagerly he tore open the envelope and drew out a crumpled half sheet of paper.

"Meet me tonight at nine on the towing path past the mill. H. G."

He showed it to Lady Agatha, who raised her eyebrows. "Why can't he come here to see you? I don't think I should go."

David thought a moment. "Probably he knows that if he came here there would be talk. We're a centre of interest just now. His one chance of getting fresh information is not to appear to want it. But I wish he wasn't quite so terse."

She shook her grey head sadly. "I'm afraid it is that he has nothing to say. You must not be disappointed, David dear. Why should he succeed where you failed, you, with all your experience."

"I got on a false scent at the beginning," he said, "one never really recovers from a bad start. I believe Glide may do better. Don't try to sap my faith in him, Aunt Agatha. It's all I've got now."

David came to the place appointed some minutes before the hour. It was raining, as usual, and as there were no houses on that bank of the river and the mill had long been abandoned he met no one as he turned to the left from the bridge and walked along the path. A low railing painted white glimmered ghostly in the darkness. The Abbey clock was striking nine as a shadowy figure appeared beside him.

"Good evening, Lord Haringdon."

"I didn't hear you come up."

"I wear rubber-soled shoes," said Glide. "I hope you haven't been worrying."

David could almost have laughed at the inadequacy of this description of his state of mind, but he had not come there to enlarge upon his own condition and he let the understatement pass. "Have you made any progress?" he asked.

"A little," said Glide modestly. "I'm lodging with Miss Coleman."

"Well, she'd help you if she could, I suppose," said David, "she was absolutely devoted to the dead girl, oppressively so, in fact. That accounts for her violent prejudice against Linda. She's never forgiven her for taking Violet away."

"Yes," said Glide, "she's a woman of strong passions, remarkably strong. Very interesting. I like to hear her talk. She walks out to the cemetery every day with flowers for the grave. And she's never forgiven Miss Merle, as you say. A good hater. Quite refreshing in these half-hearted days. And, mind you, she's not unprincipled. On the contrary. She justifies every step she takes to herself."

"What do you mean, Glide? You don't think she's withheld something that would clear Linda?"

"I'm almost sure of it," said Glide calmly. "I believe she knows who actually murdered Violet Hunter. But she has persuaded herself that Linda Merle's influence was a bad one and that she is, in any case, morally guilty and deserving of punishment."

"As vindictive as that? I can hardly believe it, though of course she's shown herself hostile from the first. But why should she shield the murderer? I can't swallow that, Glide. Unless she's afraid. If it's Ebermann or one of his gang, they are pretty tough customers. I suppose it wouldn't be so difficult to terrorise a woman living as she does alone."

"She's got a queer look in her eyes sometimes," said Glide reflectively, "and I've noticed she keeps a light burning all night in her room. I think I'd better be getting back, Lord Haringdon. She likes me to be punctual for meals. As a landlady she's arbitrary but efficient. She tells me of it if I forget to wipe my feet on the mat, but the toast is always crisp. I know just how she must have messed around after that poor girl. Young people won't stand for it nowadays. They'd rather be neglected and have a little freedom."

"Well, get on with it, Glide, for God's sake. We haven't much time. Is there nothing I can do?" said David feverishly.

"There may be before long. I've got a plan. I won't tell you what it is because you wouldn't approve. I rely on you to back me up though. There isn't much time, as you say, and if it fails we're done."

"Must you be so mysterious?"

"Good night, sir. There's still a chance—"

"Oh, good night."

Glide turned back along the towing path. David waited to light a cigarette before he followed.

Hermann Glide crossed the bridge and walked up through the town to his lodgings.

"You're later than you said," remarked Annie Coleman as she opened the door.

He answered in a tone of apology. "I'm sorry. I simply couldn't tear myself away. I wish you'd let me have a latchkey. I could slip in then without bothering you to climb all those stairs from the basement."

"I wouldn't feel that my house was my own," she said. "Vi used to beg for one but I never gave in. 'If it's not too late for you to be out, my girl, it's not too late for me to sit up,' I told her."

"That reminds me," said Glide as he hung up his hat and his raincoat and prepared to follow her into the sitting-room. "I believe I've a message for you."

She turned up the gas. "If it's some of your spooks I don't hold with them. A parcel of rubbish."

The supper was laid on the table, bread and cheese and a salad. Glide, who had a weak digestion, seldom touched meat.

"It's a pity you feel that way," he said, drawing his chair up to the table. "A loving message from a dear one that's passed over. There's a deal of comfort in that to my mind."

He was watching her without seeming to do so and he noticed that her manner had changed. She was listening now with a trace of wistfulness, waiting, obviously, to hear more. He decided to let her wait, and after lingering for a minute at the door, she brought herself to ask the question he had expected.

"What was the message?"

"It was just before the medium woke from the trance state and it seemed to come through a new control, a girl's voice but very faint, hardly more than a whisper."

"Go on," said Annie thickly.

"It said 'Tell her I'm so happy and safe now! Tell her to come here. I want to speak to her. Thank her for the flowers.'"

Annie's heavy face brightened. "She said that? I took her some lilies today. Fourpence a bloom in the market but I beat the woman down to threepence. It's cruel the prices they ask. Something ought to be done about it. But—I don't know, Mr. Glide. I'm obliged to you, but I can't believe it's really Vi. I wish I could."

Glide ate his supper and went up to bed.

Meanwhile David had returned to Spinacres. He found Lady Agatha waiting up for him and he related the substance of his interview with Glide.

"He thinks that Miss Coleman knows who committed the murder and is shielding the criminal. I think he's wrong, but what can I do about it?" he said despairingly. "I shall have to let him carry on. There's so little time. I can't put a new man in charge of the inquiry at the eleventh hour. Glide would throw in his hand and it is just possible that he may have got hold of something."

"Surely no jury would convict Linda," said his aunt. "You have only to look at her."

David shook his head. "I'm afraid we can't bank on that. The circumstantial evidence against her is terribly strong. Sometimes—" He did not finish his sentence.

She laid her hand on his arm. "Sometimes—what, my dear?"

"Sometimes I feel that she can only be saved by a miracle—and—and miracles don't happen nowadays."

Chapter XXIX
TELL THE TRUTH

"I don't know," said the maid doubtfully. "Mrs. Bellingham and the Colonel are dining out. I think he's gone up to dress."

"It's rather urgent. Tell him it's Lord Haringdon. Here's my card—"

The maid, somewhat flustered, for she had not recognised him at first, showed David into the Chief Constable's study, a small book-lined room on the left of the hall, and left him. Bellingham, coming in, found him pacing restlessly to and fro.

"Nothing wrong, I hope," he said solicitously. He had taken a fancy to the new Lord Haringdon and was sorry for him. He knew that the Superintendent was not altogether sure of him and that sinister rumours concerning him were abroad, but he had resolutely refused to admit any doubt of his integrity. Apparently the liking was mutual for the young man gripped his hand hard and his expression was frankly appealing.

"I've come to ask you a favour, Colonel."

"Anything I can do. Could you look in again tomorrow? We're dining out—"

"Could you give that up? I want you to come with me now. Here, read this—"

The Colonel adjusted his eyeglasses.

"Please come tonight to Number Three, South Terrace, not later than eight. Bring reliable independent witness. Do not fail. H.G."

"Dear me! South Terrace. Tall old-fashioned houses, difficult to work in these servantless days. I have a friend living at Number Two. I fancy the house next door has been to let furnished for some time. Do you know the writer of this note, Lord Haringdon?"

"Yes. He's a private detective who was recommended to me by my Chief at the Yard—unofficially. I engaged him and he's been here about ten days now. This looks as if he'd got on to something at last."

Bellingham glanced at his drawn face but was careful not to show the pity he felt. "Well, well—I—personally, should be only too glad—"

"Then you will come with me?"

"Yes. The people with whom we were dining are very old friends. My wife can go alone. It is not a formal affair. Excuse me one moment—"

David heard him speaking to his wife and then at the telephone. When he returned he was wearing a thin overcoat over his dress clothes. "Twenty to eight. We'd better start. Have you any idea what your man requires of us?"

"Not the slightest, but he'd hinted that he was up to something of which I as an ex-member of the C.I.D. should be bound to disapprove."

Bellingham groaned, with a dismay that was not entirely feigned. "Sounds bad! And now you're dragging me into it. If it comes to Lamb's ears I shall be in the soup."

South Terrace was a row of high stuccoed houses at the top of the Castle hill. It was on the outskirts of the town and ill lit by one lamp at the corner of the street, which, at that hour, was quiet and deserted. David parked his car near the entrance to the Castle gardens, in the dense shadow of the overarching trees. Bellingham and he walked up the Terrace without exchanging a word. Many of the houses were unoccupied. Agents' boards with the legend "To be Sold" were attached to the area railings.

"Here we are," said Bellingham, pausing at the foot of the flight of steps that led up to the front door of Number Three. A dim light was visible through the fanlight and in the front window of the first floor. They went up the steps together and David rang the bell. The door was opened at once by a young woman whom he recognised as the typist he had seen in Hermann Glide's office in Southampton Row. She shut the door hurriedly while they waited in the passage.

"I was so afraid you were going to be late. No, please don't hang up your hats here. Will you just come into the back room while I explain—"

They followed her into a dingily furnished back drawing-room where a solitary candle in a bedroom candlestick was flaring in the draught.

"I'm going to blow this out in a minute," she said. "Mr. Glide wants you to wait here. The double doors into the next room are open a couple of inches. They are screened on the other side by curtains so that the fact that they are ajar will not be noticed. In any case there will be very little light. Mr. Glide hopes that you will listen very carefully, and begs that whatever happens you will not intervene. If either of you could take shorthand notes it might be a good thing."

"In the dark?" said David. "I'll try—"

"But you must be very quiet," she said anxiously.

"Look here," began Bellingham and broke off as the doorbell rang. "Hush!" she said. "Don't make a sound"—and she blew out the candle and left them. A moment later they heard the opening of the front door followed by a murmur of voices. Some one was being shown into the front room. The girl who had admitted them was speaking.

"I'll see if he can give you a sitting. He had not arranged for anything tonight. It's very exhausting, you know, and he's sat with a circle every evening since we came, but I'm sure he'll do what he can for a client recommended by Mr. Glide. Why didn't Mr. Glide come with you? There might have been more power if he'd been present. He has some mediumistic gifts himself—"

It was Annie Coleman who answered. "He had to go up to London on business, but anyway I'd rather come alone. Not that I believe in this sort of thing." Her voice sounded defiant.

"That does not matter," said the girl confidently, "it will not affect the phenomena. We have had some wonderful experiences when those present were hostile. He goes into a complete trance, you know, and has no recollection of what has occurred when he comes to. Do you wish me to stay or would you rather be alone—that is, if he feels able to see you?"

"I'd rather be alone," said the visitor.

The secretary appeared to hesitate. "It may be rather alarming if you have no experience of psychic manifestations. On the other hand, nothing may come through. One never can be sure."

"Do I get my money back if nothing happens?" inquired Annie.

"No, madam. That would hardly be fair, would it? The medium has given his time, and often the fatigue is almost as great. I'll go and tell him you are here. You won't mind sitting in the dark? Light dissipates the force—"

There was silence for some minutes, a silence broken abruptly by the scraping of a chair being drawn forward followed by a startled exclamation from Annie Coleman.

"Who's that?"

A deep voice answered her. Apparently the door from the passage had been opened and the medium had entered without making a sound. "You wish to hear from some one who has passed over? I am very tired tonight, but I will see if it is possible for me to go into a state of trance. Please remain where you are, and do not attempt to touch me or to wake me. That would be very dangerous. You understand?"

"Yes. But I don't know—I've half a mind not to go on with it," she said.

"As you will," said the deep voice indifferently. "My control has transmitted messages from friends beyond that have brought comfort to many. So I have been told. I am not conscious when he speaks through me. But you may go now if you wish, my sister. Only be quick, for I feel drowsy. He is there already on the threshold—"

David heard the quick catch of her breath as she said "I'll stay."

The medium had begun to breathe heavily and to groan like a man in a fit. David felt his companion moving uneasily and he laid a warning hand on his arm. He wondered how Annie Coleman was standing the strain upon her nerves. If this was all a trick it was a cruel one, he thought. The loud breathing had subsided. There was a long silence and then a stifled sigh and a rustling as of dead leaves stirring in the wind, and then, when that had ceased, a sound of music, of some one far away playing the violin. David recognised the air. It was the "Valse Triste" of Sibelius. Gradually it died away. There was a sob from Annie.

"Vi? Oh, my darling—"

The answer came—so faint that it was barely audible—but it came.

"Annie—"

"Darling, are you happy? Oh, speak!"

Annie, forgetting all her acidly expressed contempt for the nonsense about spooks, pleaded desperately.

There was another pause that seemed interminable before the whispering voice resumed.

"Annie, tell the truth. The whole truth. You must—"

The tenuous thread of sound snapped and after a moment of profound silence the heavy breathing began afresh. The medium moved in his chair and spoke in his normal deep voice. "Have I been gone long? I hope you were satisfied—"

His client made no answer. There was a sound of footsteps, the opening and closing of a door. Then, abruptly, while David and Bellingham still waited uncertainly, some one turned on the electric switch and the dingy room was flooded with light. Hermann Glide was standing on the threshold blinking at them.

"She's gone," he said, rubbing his hands together. "It's rather lucky, isn't it, that my secretary can play the fiddle. Quite effective, I thought. How did it strike you?" Bellingham looked red and angry.

"What the hell does all this mean? Where's the medium? If the fellow's fraudulent—and you seem to be saying that he is—I'll expose him—"

Glide grinned. "As you will—"

Bellingham started. "It was you? Haringdon, will you explain?"

David looked at him gravely. "It seems fairly clear. Mr. Glide thinks that Miss Coleman knows more concerning the mystery of Violet Hunter's end than she cared to reveal either at the inquest or before the magistrates. He has chosen this method of persuasion. He warned me we might disapprove—"

"I do very strongly," said Bellingham. "Miss Coleman was an excellent witness. It was through her that the police began their investigations, and she has been most helpful throughout. It is outrageous that such a heartless and cruel trick should have been played on the poor woman. If I had dreamed that anything of the sort was to be attempted I should have put a stop to it. It is too late now. To enlighten her would only inflict further pain. But I can at least demand that these unauthorised proceedings should end here and now. And I shall expect an apology, Lord Haringdon."

"I'm sorry you are so upset," said David. "I quite understand. I didn't like it myself. But I must remind you that a human life is at stake."

The Chief Constable, who was normally an easy-going person, was beginning to cool down. "But why should you imagine that she has not told us all she knows?"

This time it was Glide who answered. "If I'm right she'll go to the police station tomorrow. She'll have the night to think things over. I'm lodging with her but I'm supposed to be up in London and I shan't go back until tomorrow morning."

"You think she's shielding some one, that she may have been threatened even?" said Bellingham doubtfully.

"I may be wrong," said Glide, "but if she's going to speak at all it will be soon, while she's still under the influence of the voice she heard just now. Would you two gentlemen meet me somewhere tomorrow morning at eleven? If she hasn't amplified her previous evidence by then she never will."

"Very well," said Bellingham. "I shall be at the police station. I'll see you there if you like. There's to be no more of this hanky-panky meanwhile," he added sharply.

Glide grinned. "I thought I was pretty good."

Bellingham ignored the remark, but he was fuming again when he and David left the house. "That fellow of yours has no manners."

"I know," said David. "He's never known discipline. But he's a clever little devil. I only hope—" He broke off with a sigh.

Bellingham touched his arm. "My dear fellow," he said kindly, "I don't blame you for catching at straws."

Chapter XXX
THE MEANS—AND THE END

When David was shown into the Chief Constable's office the following morning he found the Superintendent there before him.

"Your chap hasn't shown up yet," said Bellingham. "Sit down, won't you, and try one of these cigarettes. You won't mind my going through my correspondence while we wait?"

David took the chair indicated and resigned himself to waiting. The Chief Constable sat at his desk dealing with a pile of letters while the big Superintendent stood by him, jabbing now and again at some passage in an opened letter with his forefinger and making comments in a husky undertone. The Abbey clock chimed the hour and the bells of St. Jude's ceased jangling. Eleven. David's heart sank. Glide had failed.

Bellingham looked up. "It seems—" he began, and broke off to say "Come in."

The constable who had knocked at the door opened it.

"A person of the name of Glide, sir—"

Glide wasted no time in civilities. His tie was crooked and he was out of breath. "She hasn't been here then?"

Lamb smiled with undisguised satisfaction. "She has not." Annie Coleman was his witness, and he resented the suggestion that he had failed to extract all the relevant information she had to give. "You can take it from me that she's told me all she knows—"

But Glide was not listening. "I'd like you to come back with me now," he said to Bellingham. "She expected me down from Town this morning, but I can't get into the house. I've been knocking and ringing. And the bottle of milk has been left on the doorstep and the blinds are not drawn. I'm afraid something has happened."

The Chief Constable frowned. "I hope not," he said, "for your sake. You know my opinion of last night's mummery. My car's in the yard. You'd better all come with me."

Linden Road, with its double row of semi-detached houses set in their little gardens, drowsed in the June sunshine. The woman next door, who was shaking her mats, watched the four men curiously as they came up the path.

"Miss Coleman's away, I think," she volunteered. "I generally hear her moving about but there hasn't been a sound this morning."

The Superintendent rang the bell. It could be heard pealing in the basement. "Is there any way in at the back?" asked Bellingham after a moment.

"Yes. The back gardens have gates opening on a cinder path that skirts the railway cutting," explained Glide, "but Miss Coleman kept hers locked. She preferred tradesmen to come to the front door."

"I don't quite see my way," said Bellingham uncertainly. "She has a perfect right to shut up her house and go away for a bit—"

"That's right," said Lamb, vigorous in support of his superior.

Glide sniffed delicately. "And to leave the gas turned on?"

Lamb started. "You don't smell gas? Now you mention it I do notice a whiff." He glanced up at the front of the house. "Wait here, will you? I expect I can get in through a window at the back. Don't strike a match, anyone—"

He hurried off. Bellingham looked worried. David, aware of a growing excitement, glanced at Glide, but the little man's wizened face revealed nothing of what he was feeling. Bellingham was standing watch in hand. "Five minutes. Ah, here he comes—"

Lamb opened the door to them and leaned against it, wiping his forehead with his handkerchief. "Excuse me," he muttered. "I feel rather sick. The whole house reeked of gas. But I've turned it off at the meter and opened the windows at the back. It'll clear off soon—"

"Miss Coleman?" said the Chief Constable.

"You'd better come in, sir, and see for yourself. The air's not so bad now—"

He led the way down to the basement kitchen. "There you are!" he said bitterly. "That's what comes of interfering and frightening helpless women out of their wits." He jerked at the blind cord with a violence that brought the roller down. "Put a cushion in the oven, laid herself down, and turned on the gas. I haven't moved her. No use. I felt her hand. She's been dead for hours."

"Terrible!" said Bellingham. He was profoundly shocked.

David was silent, but he had turned white to the lips. Of the four men Glide was the only one who showed no emotion. He stood looking contemplatively at the huddled figure on the floor. "Yes," he said gently. "I wonder—" He turned away, his quick brown eyes searching the kitchen for something he hoped to find. "Ah!" He pounced on some scrawled and blotted sheets of paper, torn from an exercise book, that lay on the dresser with a penny bottle of ink and a pen. "Splendid!" he purred.

Bellingham glared at him. "Really! Have you no sense of decency?"

"I beg your pardon. Perhaps I was rather carried away. You'd better take charge of this, sir. It's important."

"What?" The Chief Constable adjusted his glasses and took the scribbled sheets. "Good Lord!" he muttered. He spread the paper on the carefully scrubbed kitchen table and the others came and read with him.

She says tell the truth. Perhaps it is best. Anyway I am very tired, and I want to go to my darling. I killed Vi's body to save her soul. When she came to me that Saturday evening she told me she was taking a post in London that some man had offered her, the man I had seen with her once at the café, a bad man, I am sure. She would not listen though I begged her to come home to me. She only laughed. She said she meant to enjoy herself while she was young. That man had told her that her beauty was an asset. I knew what the end would be. The next day I could not rest. She had told me she was going to the cottage for the last time. "I'm letting Linda down," she said. "She's more right to be angry than you have." I thought I'd go to the cottage and try to persuade her. I walked. I'm a good walker. They had left when I got there. It had begun to rain. As I stood by the gate I saw Vi coming back along the road. She was too full of herself to wonder at seeing me there. The other had asked her to get help for the dog they found run over, but when she had gone a little way she discovered that she had left her ring at the cottage. The string on which she wore it had broken and she had laid it on one side meaning to put it in her purse and then she had forgotten it. She had the key so there was no need to go back to Linda Merle. "I'll just get it," she said, "and then hurry along back to her." I went into the cottage with her, and then I tried again to persuade her. I begged and prayed. No use. So I did it, and afterwards I kissed her, and I dug a grave. It was past three in the morning when I got home. Afterwards it came to me that it was all through that Linda persuading her to leave me. The moral responsibility for Vi's death was hers. I shall always think so. And it seemed a good plan to go to her lodgings while she was out and put the ring among her things.

That's all, I think. I've done what you asked, Vi dear. I hope you'll be pleased—

The blotted manuscript ended with some meaningless scratches. The Superintendent spoke first. "A delusion, of course," he said loudly. "That séance business last night turned her brain. At least—what do you think, sir?"

Bellingham shook his head. "It needs confirmation, I'm afraid."

"It's true," said Glide quietly.

They all looked at him, David eagerly, the two officials with some reserve.

"It may be," said Bellingham, "but you must know that whenever a murder is committed the police get people giving themselves up for the crime who have nothing to do with it. It's a form of mania."

"Quite," said Glide, "but here there was a motive, and a very strong one, the motive of jealousy. Unusual, I admit, but one does come across these grasping natures that cannot bear to share those they love with any other. But you want material proofs. Will you come upstairs?"

He led the way up to the dead woman's bedroom. It was very neat, in spite of the fact that it was overfull of furniture and ornaments.

"She was the sort of person," said Glide, "who never throws anything away. A good manager, and very economical. She cooked well too, and if she gave me margarine and charged me for butter—and I fancy she did—I am sure she was able to justify herself to herself. I've been studying her very carefully, you see."

He opened the old-fashioned mahogany wardrobe whose mirror had so often reflected Annie's broad red face and thickset clumsy figure and took out a brown stuff skirt that was hanging behind other garments. The Superintendent took it from him and carried it over to the window.

"It's torn, a small triangular piece of the stuff clean gone," he announced. "And there's a smear of green paint on the side."

"I have the torn fragment," said Glide. "She caught it on a barbed wire coming back that night. She was physically and mentally exhausted after her terrible experience and it's a wonder she got home when she did. When I first came to lodge here I professed to be very fond of long rambles across country and she told me that she had similar tastes when she was younger and described several walks I could take. I saw that she had a good working knowledge of all the byways and field paths about Jessop's Bridge and I got an ordnance map and worked out the route she might have followed. The bit of stuff on the barbed wire was a lucky find. You'll see that it fits."

"That's all very well," said Lamb, "but—I don't want to be offensive—we've only got your word for it that you found it where you say, and as to the smear of paint lots of people use that shade of green about a house. However, we can consider this later. I've got to get the doctor and the ambulance. It's a clear case of suicide, that's one comfort. But there'll have to be an inquest, naturally."

Bellingham took the hint of his subordinate.

"I'll drive back to the station and send a man to relieve you here. Then you can rejoin us and we can talk this over," he said.

An hour later they met again in his room. David was anxious. Though he personally was convinced that Glide was right he could not blame the officials for their attitude of reserve. He guessed that they had rung up the Yard to make some inquiries about Glide and that what they had heard had not been very reassuring.

"Speaking for myself," said Bellingham, "I should be only too pleased if we could drop the case against Linda Merle. I've never been entirely satisfied. But I think that the Grand Jury must be given the opportunity to throw it out."

"Can't she be released immediately?" said David.

"I'm afraid not. The evidence of the torn skirt is purely circumstantial."

"There is Miss Coleman's own written confession of guilt—"

"It needs confirmation. Her mind may have given way. We know the ordeal she underwent last night, Lord Haringdon. Mr. Glide is a trifle too ingenious for my taste. There is such a thing as suggestion. Take a weak brain—"

"I should not call Annie Coleman weak," said David. "Warped is the word."

"That séance," growled Bellingham. "It reminds me of that Italian fellow, what's his name, Machiavelli."

But Glide only smiled. "You do me too much honour. I'm not as subtle as that. But I see your point and I'm not at all offended. I'm not always truthful. But in this case the truth suits me all right. You want corroboration. I'll tell you something. It will show you the sort of woman Annie Coleman was. Ruthless, terrible. The sort that sticks at nothing to gain her ends."

"Carry on," said Bellingham. In spite of his disapproval he had to admit the little man's queer fascination. There were many things to be done, but they sat there listening, literally, in the Superintendent's case, open-mouthed.

"Two years ago Annie Coleman's young protégée became engaged. The man was a veterinary surgeon recently established in the town. He had an excellent connection and was very popular, and it seemed altogether a very suitable arrangement. But Miss Coleman, who had devoted her own life to looking after her old mother until the latter's death, saw no reason why Violet Hunter should not follow her example and remain with her friend. Oddly enough, considering poor Violet's extraordinary good looks, a lover had not entered into Annie's calculations. She disapproved of Tom Lovell and forbade Violet to bring him to the house. The girl was frightened and unhappy but she refused to give him up.

"Annie changed her tactics and withdrew her opposition. Lovell was allowed to spend his Sunday evenings with them and Annie so far unbent as to cook savoury little suppers, while she and Violet sometimes had tea with him, after business hours, at his surgery. The only cloud on the horizon now was the fact that though he was doing so well at Jessop's Bridge the place did not seem to suit him. He developed gastric trouble and the doctor's medicine seemed to do him no good. When he died, after a few hours' illness, the doctor diagnosed a duodenal ulcer and gave a certificate accordingly. I heard all this from Lovell's landlady. She was much attached to him and willing to talk to me about him. She showed me his photograph and a lock of hair she had cut off as a souvenir. I told her I had a jeweller friend who would mount it for her in a brooch for a trifling sum and she let me have it. So far I had no evidence of foul play. But if a canary has been left in a room with a cat and the bird disappears we make a certain deduction founded on our knowledge of pussy's weakness—"

"Get on with it, man," said Bellingham impatiently.

"You know that in cases of arsenical poisoning by means of small repeated doses, the nails, the skin, the hair are all impregnated with the poison. I had the hair analysed. Arsenic. Annie Coleman had access to the drugs in Lovell's surgery. The lovers often left her there to boil the kettle for tea on the gas ring while they went for a stroll. As for the motive—she meant to keep Violet by hook or by crook. An obsession. She called it love. You know the French proverb: *Il y a toujours l'un qui aime et l'autre qui se laisse aimer*. To the girl the older woman was merely some one who had been kind but who was inclined to fuss too much; to the older woman the girl represented everything that made her life worth living."

The Chief Constable looked at his Superintendent.

"This must be followed up. We'll have to get an order from the Home Office and have Lovell exhumed." He turned to David. "We won't keep you longer. Though I can't congratulate your Mr.—er—Glide—on his methods, he certainly has delivered the goods. I must say I never had the least suspicion. We've been in the wrong all through. But I'm glad. Thanks to your efforts Miss Merle's release must follow before long. She has been fortunate in her friends."

Hermann Glide had slipped out of the Constable's room without waiting for formal leavetakings. He had set the machine, the huge, cumbrous, but terribly efficient machine of the law, in motion. The wheels were beginning to revolve and this time instead of closing they would open the prison doors for the girl on whom he had looked down, from the public gallery, as she sat in the dock. Once her terrified eyes had met his. She had stared at him blindly, without seeing him. She was, and would remain, ignorant of his very existence. Yet he told himself that he had saved her life just as much as if she had been drowning and he had jumped into the water and brought her to land.

He went back to Town the same afternoon. The following day he received his employer's cheque for his services.

"Well earned," he told his secretary. "You'll get a bit of it for helping me with the séance."

"Oh, thank you, Mr. Glide. You were splendid, I thought. You gave me the creeps."

"Did I? Did I, Miss Briggs?" He rubbed his bony little hands together. "Well, as a student of human nature I must say I've enjoyed the case. I wiped that Superintendent's eye. Neat, very neat. I'm proud of myself. And why shouldn't I be? I'm on the side of the angels."

"Of course," said the secretary.

He chuckled. "Miss Briggs, you're invaluable. And now we must tackle all these arrears of correspondence."

Chapter XXXI
THE LAST

The inquest on Annie Coleman was opened and adjourned for a week. In the interval the body of Lovell was exhumed and a post-mortem established the fact that he had swallowed a fatal dose of arsenic shortly before his death.

"No need to drag that up," the Chief Constable told Lamb, after consulting the authorities at the Home Office and the Yard.

"She's gone to her account, anyway. Her written confession that she killed Violet Hunter ought to be enough."

It was duly read out by the coroner when the inquest was resumed and created an enormous sensation. Hermann Glide was called and told the jury that he had been lodging with the deceased. He had noticed that she was depressed. He was away one night on business. Returning the next morning he was unable to gain admittance and as he fancied he noticed a smell of gas he went for the police. The Superintendent described the finding of the body and the written statement which they had just heard. The jury were not long in considering their verdict. "*Felo de se*—and they hoped immediate steps would be taken to release the prisoner whose innocence had now been proved."

Two days later the Assizes opened and the bill of indictment Rex v. Linda Merle was duly indorsed "No true Bill" and the prisoner was discharged.

The picture papers printed snapshots of her driving in a car with a rather hard-featured old lady by her side. "Miss Merle, with Lady Agatha Chant, who, from the first, was convinced of her innocence. Inset, a portrait of Lord Haringdon, who, until he succeeded his uncle a few months ago, was a detective in the Criminal Investigation Department at Scotland Yard. Lord Haringdon and Miss Merle are to be married shortly."

They were married, as soon as might be, by special licence, in the tiny village church just outside the park gates. Lady Agatha and Mr. Pettigrew were the only witnesses. It was early in September when they came back from Cornwall and lunched with the old lawyer at the Trocadero. They were both in high spirits. Pettigrew, watching Linda, thought he would hardly have known her for the same girl whom he had seen sitting, white-faced and with hunted eyes, in the prisoner's dock.

David spoke to him of their plans for the future. "We don't mean to live at Spinacres. It would have been a struggle to make ends meet anyway, and we want to get away from the associations. I'm going to sell the place and start fresh in British Columbia. I hope Aunt Agatha won't mind too much. Spinacres means a lot to her. But we hope to persuade her to come with us."

Mr. Pettigrew sipped his Burgundy and put down his glass. He had turned rather red. "She won't do that," he said. "She would be leaving Spinacres in any case. The fact is she has done me the great honour—that is—in short—I have ventured to make a proposal which I now realise I should have made years ago, and we are going to be married—"

"Oh, I am glad!" cried Linda, "Lady Agatha is a darling."

Pettigrew smiled at her. "She's very fond of you. Perhaps I may bring her out to see you both when you're settled in your new home overseas. Meanwhile—" He looked at his watch. "I've booked two stalls for the matinee at His Majesty's."

It had been arranged that he should take Linda out while David paid a visit to his old friend Trask in his Battersea flat.

He was expected and Green, the ex-convict who was Trask's devoted manservant, welcomed him with a broad smile. Trask, as usual, was on his sofa by the window that overlooked the planes whose leaves were already changing colour and beginning to fall. To him, too, David spoke of his plans, and the older man approved.

"You'd be reminded at every turn of things that are best forgotten if you stayed on at Spinacres. I hear Black Ridge is for sale too, but Mrs. Saigon's trustees will have a job to get rid of it. That business was hushed up but there were whispers and I hear the place has got a bad name since it was closed down so hurriedly."

David looked at him. "Would the authorities have arrested Mr. X if they found him?"

"I suppose so," said Trask slowly, "if Saigon wasn't lying he murdered that little chap you met on the road. But—the man was a homicidal maniac. They couldn't do more than shut him up in an asylum. If the authorities ascertained that that had been done by his family it might be best to let it go at that and save a lot of people, rather important and highly placed, pain and shame."

"I see," said David, "then do you know who Mr. X is?"

Trask indicated his press cuttings albums. "Studying the papers as I do I notice who drops out of public life. Unexplained disappearances are not so infrequent as you might think. I put two and two together. It amuses me, lying here. But I may be wrong so I'll name no names. By the way, I'm thinking of entering into partnership with Hermann Glide. He's a funny little freak but he's got brains and initiative. He'd do the running about while I lay here and thought things out. I've been able to help him more than once with scraps of information from my store. He's coming to see me this evening but I shall take another day or two to decide."

David hesitated. "I owe him a lot. It's not for me to speak against him. But I don't know that you'd get on. He's not over-particular."

"So I have gathered," said Trask. "Must you be going now?"—for David had risen. He looked up rather wistfully. "You'll come again before you leave England?"

"Of course, and bring Linda. She wants to know you—" David gripped his old friend's hand hard.

"You'll be up and about again one of these days," he said rather huskily.

"Never," said Trask, "but I'm all right here. I watch the world go by—"

When Glide arrived David had been gone some time. The curtains had been drawn and Trask, who felt the chill of the autumn evenings, had put a match to the fire when Green had wheeled his sofa close to it.

"A former client of yours was here a while ago," said Trask presently. "Lord Haringdon."

Glide smiled. "Ah, yes." His smile broadened and became a laugh. "That case! But for me what would have happened to that pretty young girl?" He jerked his head sideways in a horribly expressive pantomime. "That, or twenty years of getting up at six from a plank bed and scrubbing her cell. I saved her. It took some doing and it was a big risk. Mind you, Trask, I wouldn't have taken such a risk if I hadn't been absolutely certain of her innocence."

Trask looked puzzled. "I don't quite understand."

Glide glanced over his shoulder to make sure that the door was closed. "I don't mind telling you," he said. "I can trust you. It must go no further."

Trask was aware of a slight acceleration of his heart's action. What was he about to hear? Glide edged his chair nearer to the fender and held out his bony little hands to the blaze. "You know about the faked séance?" he began.

"Yes."

"When I went for the police the next morning I led them to think that I had only just been to her house and had failed to get in. As a matter of fact, I was extremely anxious about the effect of the spirit voice's communication on her and I went after her that same night at about two o'clock. I got in easily enough for I had got a wax impression of the front door key and had one made when I first went to lodge there. The place was reeking of gas then, and she was in the kitchen where she was found the next day and quite dead. I turned off the gas and opened the windows but I was careful not to touch her. There was no need. She was obviously past help. I was upset, Trask, very much upset, because I had failed."

"What do you mean?"

Glide looked at him. "She had gone beyond the reach of human justice, leaving the innocent to suffer for the guilty. The truth! She hadn't told it, and her lips were closed for ever."

"But the confession—"

"There was no confession. Not a line, not a word! For a while I despaired. Then I sat down in that kitchen, by the light of a guttering candle, and I wrote it for her."

"Good Lord!" said Trask.

"I knew more or less what must have happened. I knew what her line of reasoning would be. I'd heard her talk. It was a relief to her to discuss the case with a perfect stranger like myself and she hadn't been able to hide her jealous hatred of Miss Merle. When I had done I turned on the gas again, shut the windows, and left the house. The birds were just beginning to twitter in the eaves."

"You've got a nerve!" said Trask. "Does Lord Haringdon know?"

The little man shook his head regretfully. "I could not tell him. He would have been as shocked as you are. A nice young fellow but hampered by his training. The official touch. Narrow, very narrow. No. You can take it from me that if I hadn't had the handling of this case at the crucial moment Annie Coleman would be alive today, while Linda Merle would have gone to join her other two victims."

"You may be right," conceded Trask, and, remembering that his friend's happiness had been at stake, he made no further comment.

Glide had produced his precious lump of wax and was rolling it between his palms to soften it. He glanced up now with his impish grin. "The end justifies the means. That's my motto. About that partnership we talked of? Shall we call it off? I'm so used to working alone. Do you mind?"

"Not at all!" said Trask heartily. He was greatly relieved. "I have a few scruples left and I might cramp your style."

"That's what I was thinking," said Glide placidly.

THE END

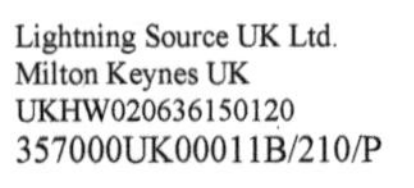
Lightning Source UK Ltd.
Milton Keynes UK
UKHW020636150120
357000UK00011B/210/P

9 781912 574919